To Barb—
this is my second
book – let me
know what you
think ...

TaNellie

A Novel

RICHMOND
LAFAYETTE
HOLTON

outskirtspress
DENVER, COLORADO

Outskirts Press, Inc.
http://www.outskirtspress.com

Paperback ISBN: 978-1-4787-1435-4
Hardback ISBN: 978-1-4787-1331-9

Library of Congress Control Number: 2013906252

Outskirts Press and the "OP" logo are trademarks belonging to Outskirts Press, Inc.

PRINTED IN THE UNITED STATES OF AMERICA

Dedication:

Tanya F. Black, my cousin,
whose light ceased shining on April 28, 2010

Acknowledgments:

Willard Jenkins, Joe Mosbrooke, Burt Kay, Maurice Christopher, Abdullah Quran, Dolores Spence, Bianca Quran, Ellen Woodruff, Patti F. Gibson, Ariyan Y. Holton, Kelly F. Dietrich, Fredd Bradley, Corvette Hales, Abdul Sunni Ghani, Sandra Smith, Nate B. Jones, Sandra and Greg Fletcher, Eric K. Holton, Edward Parker, Anna B. Merriman, Elba G. Santiago, and the talented team at Outskirts Press.

Prologue

Visually, TaNellie was a sight to behold, possessing the classic lines of a stallion in every sense of the word. Tall, handsome, and immaculately groomed, his chestnut coloring and graceful bearing were well noted. He bore a unique carriage both inimitable and formidable at the same time. TaNellie was blessed with a rhythmic gait accentuated by long powerful strides denoting an Arabian lineage spanning a thousand years. When in public, his lean musculature twitched nervously under the hot afternoon sun, exposing an innate high-spiritedness unique to his stable. TaNellie was a throwback to days gone by when champion thoroughbreds christened the Kentucky Derby on that first Saturday back in May of 1875.

TaNellie's track was light years from Churchill Downs and the Rolex Hunter Jumper Classics, not to mention ritzy polo clubs where fashionably attired prim and proper ladies dined in designer hats and white silk polka-dot dresses. Affluent club members wore laced gloves with pinkies extended, while sipping tasty mint juleps and vodka martinis…toasting to health, wealth, and happiness. It all seemed so innocuous when glancing through eyes that looked without seeing and ears that listened but did not hear. In this pristine setting, indifference was welcomed, because it masked both reality and the dregs in which café society often dwelled. Only when an astute observer—one who leaves no stone unturned—intuitively peeked underneath meticulously appointed linen-covered tables and finds adulterous fingers wantonly exploring opened legs like hungry spiders did the truth finally reveal itself.

At a random table situated in the center of a busy polo club dining room sat three acquaintances. "Marta, my dear...it's been far too long since we've seen you. Bradford and I would love to have you stop by to continue our sinful...." The woman hesitated momentarily... "I mean—our delightful conversation—do let us know when you have some time."

After those curious words, the woman looked into her husband's eyes, then glanced admiringly, as if possessing X-ray vision, at the linen napkin resting comfortably upon her lap. Finally...she took one long lustful look into Marta's seductive eyes, then continued pleasuring her own pink sweetness until satiated. When finished, she wiped her palm across the napkin still positioned on her lap. Then without a word she pressed her fingertip against Marta's beautiful lips. The unknown becomes obvious when you learn to read between the lines. It's a useful skill when refined— one which differentiates salaciousness from the obscene.

TaNellie's home wasn't nearly as picturesque or complicated as Kentucky's bluegrass country with its fabled horse farms distinguished by expansive white wooden fencing dissecting the landscape. A scenic place, to be sure...where graceful equines grazed and romped intermittently like elementary school children during recess. TaNellie's turf was in the heart of Cleveland's gold coast, where he was comfortable as the proverbial rabbit in the briar patch from tales spun long ago by Negro slaves. It was a four-block citadel—an ecosystem unto itself, propelled by a mishmash of constantly haggling souls. Blaring music and the scent of BBQ ribs served as a backdrop to distant sirens, honking horns, scurrilous language, fistfights, fender benders, and a occasional gunshot, all unfolding harmoniously like a big-budget movie soundtrack. This small glimpse into everyday life in the fast lane operated year round, enabled by overcrowded bars whose neon signs served as beacons—mesmerizing desiring patrons while enticing the timid with veiled promises of seduction.

Enticingly clad women were willing partners for a walk on the wild side, strolling the thoroughfares, sidewalks, corners, and dark alleyways. Tricks often received more than they bargained for—in the form of robbers, drag queens, con artists, boosters hawking hot merchandise, and the ever-present scourge of venereal diseases. Johns...as the tricks were often called...risked all on forbidden pleasures. Flophouses offered brief respites, supplying cheap rooms for a few moments' thrill. Landlords raked in thousands, thanks to sheer volume. Moonlighting off-duty police officers maintained the peace in many of these establishments. Squad cars harassed and disrupted the pimps' lucrative skin trade at every turn. They scattered streetwalkers like birds when patrolling assigned patches, a term used by rollers (cops) when referring to an area of responsibility. Shady vice detectives carved out their own little niches—enjoying the best of both worlds by allowing play for pay and pay to play...resulting in kickbacks from johns and prostitutes alike. The fast life... it's a bastion of opportunity and haunt for the corrupt, where law and order be damned.

(1) Nem di gelt...

On the east side of town, in a dimly lit back room of an abandoned brick building, a bright fluorescent light looks down upon a long rectangular table. Animated shadows move incognito amid dense cigar and cigarette smoke, punctuated by boisterous laughter and loud voices whose gut wrenching tones pleaded with the Almighty to "HIT DICE!"

TaNellie's manicured nails lifted the dice off the green felt-covered slate table. He gingerly caressed the bones between his nimble fingertips while blowing warm breath onto them. In this rough-and-tumble world, he had won some and lost some, but was unsure of his exact statistics. Past performances play an intricate role when selecting the cream of the crop within any profession. And so it was with TaNellie, who expected to win on each and every pitch of the dice. He was the best, a major-league player among gentlemen of leisure, who considered himself Babe Ruth, Josh Gibson, and Iceberg Slim all rolled into one.

When the timing felt right, TaNellie gracefully flipped the dice over the mandatory spread rope, snapping his fingertips loudly when they bounced against the table's eight-inch-high curved green wall. Upon impact, the dice spun vigorously before eventually coming to a halt. "SEVEN! A WINNER!" yelled the stickman in a melodic tone—quickly retrieving the dice with a 30" hooked rattan stick he called a whip. TaNellie was no fool and didn't want to press his luck by continuing to play, and decided to leave the game. He signaled his intentions by tossing a crisp hundred-dollar bill in the stickman's direction for services rendered. Before the C note settled onto the well of the table, TaNellie pulled a bankroll from his pocket large enough to choke a horse. He removed the thick purple rubber band, compliments of Fisher Foods' produce department, and fanned his bills like a deck of cards, inserting the newer denominations in order. His winnings tallied just over $2500 -- *Chump change*, he thought to himself. *I'll be a million-aire when all is said and done.* After refolding his cash, he secured the rubber band, making certain it lay flat all around. On the commodities exchange, gold remained steady at $32 an ounce. TaNellie glanced into an imaginary mirror and cocked his red fez to the side--ace deuce, as the gamblers would say. He liked wearing a fez; it disarmed those who looked down on coloreds. TaNellie felt like royalty from a faraway enchanted land.

"HEY, TEE...AIN'T YOU GONNA GIVE ME A CHANCE TO WIN MY MONEY BACK?" yelled a penny ante hustler from Detroit, a midget with grandiose schemes. His wide eyes eagerly awaited a response.

Without breaking stride, TaNellie angled his head downward, answering, "Damn, Short Stack...you sound like a little bitch! Quit your bellyaching! It ain't your money, it's mine! I done told your ass once...you'd better get some white hoes before them black wenches start pimpin' you!" TaNellie was a master of the spoken language—a wordsmith—who slammed his point home by adding insult to injury upon the little man. "Then your short ass really will be broke!" The joint was packed to the rafters with assorted ne'er-do-wells, including Big Tom Martin, Perry Ford, Gorgeous George, Richard Drake, Greg Todd, White Al, Irish O'Brien, Raymond Paul, Hessi Carr along with premier booster, Track, and a host of other fast-life night owls. They erupted with thunderous laughter and applause after TaNellie's rant. It was a reaction usually reserved for popular foul-mouthed comedians like Pigmeat Markham, Jackie "Moms" Mabley, Redd Foxx, and the great Henny Youngman, king of the one- liners, who espoused *nem di gelt*--which is Yiddish, and means "get the money."

The summer of 1954 may have been hot, but the Cleveland Indians were on fire and destined to win the American League pennant race with the best record in baseball. Cleveland, Ohio was at the center of the sports universe and proudly proclaimed to America that it was "the best location in the nation." Excited fans tuned radios to station WERE and listened to legendary announcer Jimmy Dudley along with Ed Edwards as they painted colorful images of game action. Those fortunate enough to own TVs watched Ken Coleman and Jim Britt call the game action on Channel 8...WXEL TV, giving fans the opportunity to witness exciting plays on black and white television. These were happy times, and every neighborhood celebrated each victory with pride as prosperity flowed from Public Square to Shaker Square... Lakewood to Beachwood...West 25th Street to University Circle's Hessler Street and from Bay Village to the Village of Bratenahl and everywhere else in greater Cleveland. Team caps and jerseys were the uniforms of the day. Tribe manager Al Lopez, along with pitcher Bob Feller, spearheaded the unbeatable Indians. Two former Negro League players, Larry Doby and Al Smith, contributed mightily to the team's success. A World Series win would be the Indians' second championship in the last six years, and Clevelanders bought into their team's potential--hook, line, and sinker. It sparked a season to remember in the hearts of Tribe fans everywhere.

(2) Café Tia Juana...

L eaving Mattie Matt's new spot was an exercise in futility. TaNellie's problem was basic; he just knew too many people. Everyone wanted to touch him, talk with him, or be in his presence. Some shook his hand with presidential reverence, while others believed his persona could somehow be shared by osmosis. To speak with him was tantamount to having an audience with heads of state. TaNellie was sidetracked by a pesky chili pimp... that's a wanna-be hustler looking for a meal ticket. His name was Front-man, he was sporting a weatherbeaten stingy- brimmed hat he bought at J. Miller's, and wearing a three-carat fake diamond pinkie ring.

"Hey, TaNellie...I got this white wench I can let you have if the price is right."

"Sounds good, my man! Have her stop by, and make sure she's got $2500...I don't school broads...or pimps...for free!" Even the *squares* gravitated toward him like sailors to Lorelei's mythical song.

"Mr. TaNellie, may I have your autograph please?"

After a thirty-minute diversion, TaNellie reached the metal reinforced exit door. Moose, a muscular dark-skinned fellow, was recently home from Korea. His muscles bulged in a tight USMC olive drab tee-shirt as he peered into a viewing slot, making sure the coast was clear. The former Marine was armed to the teeth with a sawed-off shotgun, a Colt .45 automatic tucked into his belt, and a Ka-Bar killing knife strapped to one leg.

"Everything's cool, TaNellie," observed the man.

"Okay, Cat! See you when I see you!" The gambler slipped the henchman a fifty-dollar bill, a security investment against future perils, if you will.

Before exiting, TaNellie pulled back the slide on his silver-plated pearl-handled .32 automatic, making certain it was locked, loaded, and ready to go. Although he was alone, the nattily dressed gambler stepped stylishly as he walked to his car, exhibiting the gusto of a mummer in a Philadelphia parade. TaNellie knew pimping was a full time job. In the fast life, image is everything, and making money is based on perceptions. He arrived at his car and quickly opened the door. After inhaling the new car aroma, he slid behind the wheel and started its powerful engine... "Vvrooommm." The sound was music to his ears and fed his ego like blood nourishes vampires. The 1954 white Cadillac convertible had massive chrome bumpers, hooded headlights, and fishtail lights featuring a hidden gas tank. Numerous chrome accessories added class to an already beautiful automobile. Tee often bragged, "I pick cars to match my stable...either white as snow or pink like pussy. When you're pimping the way I do... *pink gold* is money in the bank!" TaNellie Lafitte Purifoy didn't trust the government--or people, for that matter, opting to place his cash and jewelry into bank safety deposit boxes.

Once settled in comfortably, TaNellie placed his red fez beside him and raised the volume on the radio. Billie Holiday was singing..."I fell in love with you the first time I looked into... them there eyes!" He checked his gold watch. It was 1:30 in the morning and bars were still open. With a little musical enticement from Billie, he decided to check out the scene at Café Tia Juana. It was a beautiful world-class musical venue with a scenic south-of-the-border theme. It was located at the corner of East 105th Street and Massie Avenue. A large colorfully lit neon sign shaped like a Mexican sombrero rested just above the entrance. The popular jazz club was owned by policy banker Arthur "Little Brother" Drake, and was light years ahead of its time. It featured the very finest acts in the world: Nat King Cole, Pearl Bailey, Billy Eckstein, Miles Davis, LaVerne Baker, Anita O'Day, and Carmen McRae, had all played the room at one time or another. With four full- service bars under the same roof, and a spectacular revolving stage, the Tia Juana--as most called the show bar--was a sight to behold, nestled amid residential homes whose manicured lawns, pink flamingos, and miniature black-faced jockeys combined to make the Glenville neighborhood an eclectic masterpiece. The area first gained national prominence as home to Jerry Siegel and Joe Schuster, creators of Superman, both having attended Glen-ville high school a few years earlier.

TaNellie's thoughts climbed aboard a time machine, whisking him back into the past. It began with his latest Caddy, to his very first Coupe de Ville, almost six years ago. It was when the twenty-one year old began the tradition of paying cash for his cars. His reasoning was simple...something he learned years ago from a Jewish friend of the family. Ishmael Silverman hammered home the concept to an impressionable youngster: "It's always better to earn interest than pay interest." Silverman dabbled in all sorts of things and was a successful businessman, stock trader, and real estate broker. Rumors suggested Ishmael had a roving eye...but he was always a perfect gentleman around Tee and his mother. He leased Bessie Mae the space for her very first beauty shop.

Whenever TaNellie traded in his cars, the mileage was usually less than two thousand. In an undisclosed scheme, the dealer sold Tee's used cars as demo models to prospective buyers. TaNellie received a $150 kickback for his share. As a good will gesture, Tee instructed his girls to service the sales contact right in the deal-ership's men's room. This sordid little detail explained why the welcome mat was always extended to TaNellie. He was the only player in Cleveland--the only Negro, for that matter--who purchased cars directly from the new car showroom. It afforded him bragging rights and unequaled admiration among his peers. Most of his associates were second- or third-tier title holders whose cars were purchased through middle men. Most reputable dealers considered ill-gotten gains as dirty money and frowned upon doing business, fearing poor public relations. For astute young businessmen like Aubrey Charles Eastman, the dealership's oversight was the opportunity of a lifetime. He owned Ace Motors, a used car lot on the northeast corner of East 71st Street and Euclid Avenue. Aubrey--or Ace, as he was known to his clients-- was an enterprising Jewish fellow who purchased luxury cars by the dozens. He catered to gangsters, racketeers, and hustlers who emptied his inventory regularly and craved more. His costly services were based on his personal economic tenet: "If you can find it cheaper anywhere else...please be my guest."

TaNellie drove his cars sparingly. He loved checking on his female traps, by actually walking in their very footsteps along the busy stroll. For Tee, the magical bright lights and flashing neon signs never lost their allure. They were an intricate part of his world. He enjoyed the sounds, the smells, and especially the people with whom he rubbed shoulders. The grittiness of the city streets has touched him deeply ever since he was a kid working in his mom's salon. There was a quality of intrigue and adventure behind every shadowy door and alleyway, which stimulated and excited him. The whole bustling scene made him come alive. Prior to his evening activities TaNellie regularly took afternoon walks. They soothed his spirits like a warm bath, allowing him to focus like a laser on the job at hand. Other than pockets filled with cash and prestige among peers, the best perk of all was chatting with old friends. They kept him steadfastly grounded no matter which way the wind blew. He was anchored to the neighborhood's pulse: the people.

His favorite place to stop in was Cotton's Top Barber Shop. Old Ezekiel Cotton was eighty years old and an excellent barber. Zeke's been cutting folks' hair since he was twelve or thirteen. He began his career using a pair of those vintage Brown & Sharpe hair clippers. They had to be manipulated and guided by squeezing motions controlled by the barber's hands. The old Macon, Georgia peach was also a great listener who soaked up information like a vacuum. He knew everything about everyone and never gossiped or divulged a single word shared in confidence.

"Hey, Mr. TaNellie, I'm so happy you stopped in! You know I hit on that number you gave me last week. I played fifty cents straight on 410. I won two hundred and fifty bucks. I really do appreciate the tip, Mr. TaNellie! Like my great-grandbaby would say...'Ta Ta!' It was right on time, too, Mr. TaNellie...it gave me the chance to pay some long-overdue bills." The old man glanced toward his feet. "I even bought myself a brand new pair of $19.99 ankle-high Florsheim's comforts...best shoes money can buy!"

TaNellie scoped out the new captoe kicks. "Zeke, you got those babies shining like a brand-new silver dollar! They look good, old-timer...I'd like to get a pair myself one day!"

"Thanks, Mr. TaNellie. You know I'd deem it a real treat if you'd stop by for a haircut and shave every now and again--on the house, of course!"

"Thanks, Ezekiel...that's mighty kind of you, sir. I accept your offer... I'll see you when I see you!"

TaNellie visited Scatterbrain at his BBQ joint... aptly named Scatter's. He made sure he stopped by before business got a little too hectic. As usual, the charcoal pit was smoking up a storm, riding the breezes like a modern-day Paul Revere spreading the word about Scatter's throughout the enclave. Scatterbrain, whom everyone just called Scatter, made some of the best ribs in town. "TaNellie… you 'bout ready for somethin' to eat?" asked the former numbers runner. "Friday is always a long night!"

"Naww, Scatter…I don't feel like pork…I've got a taste for a thick, juicy well-done porterhouse. Can you fix me up?"

"Sho can, Tee! I ain't just twiddlin' my thumbs around here, ya know!"

"Don't you dare run out of those ribs! Not until my wenches get some…they love 'em! Scatter, you remember Ana, don't you?"

"Sho do!"

"I'll have her stop by and pick up some vittles for the girls." TaNellie handed Scatterbrain a fifty-dollar bill. "Man, let me pay you for everything now, and get it outta the way! Set them wenches up with a few slabs, fries, coleslaw…the whole shebang…and give 'em some sodas, too." While Scatter prepared for the busy night ahead, they continued shooting the breeze for another twenty minutes. "See you when I see you, Scatter."

Old Scatterbrain used to be a big shot back in the day. He ran his own policy bank but lost everything gambling. It was all because of a hunch. The old man risked all he'd worked for on a bullshit tip. His whole world vanished with one roll of the dice… "Snake eyes…a loser!" Had it not been for Sarah, his lady, who was savvy enough to stash away sizable amounts of cash during the good years, Scatter's old ass would be in a terrible bind now. He wouldn't have a pot to piss in or a window to throw it out. In the life, nothing beats having a good woman in your corner. If she can separate the bullshit from the reality…she is worth her weight in diamonds. Many a hustler has bitten the dust because they thought they knew it all. TaNellie constantly informed his girls, "Even General Motors has a suggestion box! If you've got a better way of doing things, let me know!"

TaNellie had some time on his hands and continued moving

down the block, visiting his friends. Each day he wisely cemented personal relationships by spending a few minutes with local businessmen--store owners like Seymour the florist, Tom and Randy at the market, Bostonian Shoes, Jack's Poultry, A.B.'s candy store, and Dave over at Vienna Distributing, were the life and breath of the tightly knit group of friends. Tee was admired by almost everyone, for whatever reason. His daytime persona revealed a caring person who was always ready to help others. TaNellie's thoughts had finally brought him full circle...it was time to return to the present.

Tee turned down the volume on the car stereo and drove to the jazz club on East 105th Street. Just a week earlier Tee, Ana, and Justine had been invited to the Café Tia Juana as guests of the legendary jazz singer Billie Holiday. She never failed to get in touch with him when she was in town. Billie made sure he had a complimentary bottle of Piper-Heidsieck champagne and a table right up front. TaNellie felt entitled and enjoyed being in the spotlight alongside his white wenches. To the public, TaNellie's exploits were as noteworthy as those of any other mainstream celebrity of the day. Musical entertainers, baseball players, prizefighters, career politicians, and the general public enjoyed mingling with the charismatic hustler. Never considered a hanger-on, TaNellie always carried his own weight, a quality that endeared him among *causes célèbres*. They were intrigued by his fierce independence and carefree lifestyle. He was proud of what he was and didn't make excuses...he was a gentleman of leisure. Tee parked his hog right in front of the Tia Juana and lowered the convertible top before sauntering inside the club. The unique night spot featured multi-colored leather booths that encompassed the entire venue. Before 2:30 a.m., late-night regulars took full advantage of *last call*...just prior to closing the doors.

On the night Billie Holiday was in town, the capacity crowd's anticipation grew, as the house speakers sputtered and crackled with earsplitting static. Folks seated in folding chairs nearer the center of the club reacted to the noise with puckered faces, as if fingernails were scraping against chalkboards. Last-minute tinkering by the club's handyman soon squelched the problem, and the set started right on schedule.

The evening's entertainment was ready to proceed. After introducing himself, a comic known simply as "Be Funny" from Scottsdale, Arizona warmed up the capacity crowd. With microphone in hand, the huge man immediately began to poke fun at those seated near the stage. "Hey, my brother...is that your wife seated next to you?" His question was quickly accompanied by large rolling eyes.

The man lovingly placed his arm around his woman. "She most certainly is!"

"Well, she needs to do something 'bout the hair underneath them arms. It looks like she got Buckwheat in a headlock!"

The husband was not happy, but the raucous audience howled with approval, which prompted Be Funny to dish out even more insults. "Pardon me, miss--who does your hair?" The woman blushed. Be Funny answered, "NOBODY!" Guests were crying in the aisles...trying their best to contain themselves.

Be Funny set his sights on TaNellie and his ladies. "Sir, what do you do for a living? Wait a second...good-looking Negro accompanied by not one, but two gorgeous white women? Never mind, sir...I know what you do! Since you doubled down on the white chicks, it's only fair to assume you're a...gambling man! What's your name, sir?"

Tee responded loud and clear. "TaNellie!"

"Well, Mr....TaNellie...a birdie told me your gambling habit has been getting a bit out of hand lately. He say...you spending lots of cash and time away from the crib. I'm also told one of your women called the gambling spot the other night checking on your ass." Be Funny put his hand on his hip and walked around the stage switching. Then he pursed his lips, mimicking a female's voice. " 'Hey, Joe...let me speak to TaNellie... T.A.N.E.L.L.I.E.?' You were excited and out of breath when you reached the phone. 'HELLO!' 'Tee, when are you coming home?' 'Don't bug me, woman...I'm winning at craps!' 'Winning?' she asked. 'Yeah, wench... WINNING! I've got a stack of quarters as long as my dick!' 'Well, Tee...you'd better pick up that seventy-five cents and bring your ass home!'"

The Tia Juana practically caved from uproarious laughter. Ta-Nellie smiled and snatched the mic, saying, "Be Funny...are you going to take the word of these two wenches about my dick? Why don't you speak to someone you trust, like your bitch! She'll set you straight about some TaNellie. Just last night she told me she loved me and how grateful she was to have me in her life. 'TaNellie...if it weren't for you... I wouldn't be getting any DICK!'" Once again the joint went crazy.

Be Funny was not in a laughing mood, and angrily took back his mic. "Okay, TaNellie... enough already. What the hell kind of name is that, anyway?" The comic raised his hands and silenced the crowd while he spoke directly to Tee. "Well, Mr. Tallahassee... Throckmorton...or whatever you call yourself, take my advice. Don't quit your night job. And by the way...let me tell the jokes if you don't mind, please, sir! If it weren't for you, my old lady wouldn't be getting any dick...NEGRO, PLEASE!"

It was show time and Jimmy Saunders, the house piano player/band director, introduced the headliner to the audience. "CLEVELAND, OHIO! Please put your palms together and give a nice warm round of applause to the one...the only...MISS BILLIE HOLIDAY!" The walls reverberated with excitement. When it reached a crescendo, the world-renowned singer walked confidently onto the stage, wearing her trademark white gardenia contrasting with her dark hair. She looked exquisite in a shimmering silver designer gown. Billie politely acknowledged the band director and gave the audience a curt bow once reaching center stage. The songstress took a minute to assimilate with the revolving stage and once comfortable, she began to sing.

Her velvet voice eased inside the chrome microphone, trying it on for size, just before oozing seductively past the speakers then out among the patrons. Soon they were under her hypnotic spell. *"My man don't love me...he treats me...ohhh so mean! My man he don't love me...he treats me awful mean. He's the lowest man...that I've ever seen!"* TaNellie quickly made his presence felt.

"Billie, when you get tired of him, I'm sure I can find a spot for you!"

Billie quieted the band. "Pardon my French, but I've been down that bullshit road before! It might sound good to your snow Janes, but you gotta do better to impress this crow Jane!" She was cracking wise on his stable and her not so distant past. The crowd gave their approval and Billie asked the band to resume. She continued singing, gazing directly into TaNellie's eyes. *"Treat me right, baby...and I'll stay home every day. Just treat me right, baby...and I'll stay home night and day. But you're so mean to me, baby...I know you're gonna drive me away! Love is just like a faucet...it turns off and on. Love is like a faucet...it turns off and on. Sometimes when you think it's on, baby... it has turned off and gone!"*

TaNellie patted his feet to the music while shaking his head from side to side. He raised his champagne flute and toasted the singer, and his girls followed suit. "BILLIE...Billie...Billie...don't you be so mean." The singer knew TaNellie well enough to realize he just wanted to relax...a little down time, so to speak. She'd been around hundreds of pimps and hustlers before, and skillfully pitted her sensuous lyrics against TaNellie's saucy rhetoric.

By show's end, everyone had been thoroughly entertained and was putty in Billie's masterful hands. She closed the set with "God bless the child," but not before thanking the members of the band. "Let's give a well-deserved round of applause to the band, featuring...Jimmy Saunders at the piano, Ray Ferris on the drums, Ernie Krivda on the tenor sax...with Kenny Davis on trumpet and last but not least...Ike Isaacs on bass! Thanks, guys!"

Billie dedicated her last song to the ladies in attendance. "Them that's got shall have...them that's not shall lose...so the Bible says...and it still is news."

When Billie finished, the standing ovation shook the building to its foundation. The pimp took a sip of champagne and tilted forward, informing his girls. "It was a privilege seeing Lady Day in person!" His blank eyes revealed an inner callousness...a harshness he usually suppressed. With his index finger pointing just inches from their faces, he laid down the law. "I want you two white wenches to understand one thing. Out of my whole stable, I picked you to share this evening with me. Tomorrow is Sunday, a work day. I don't want to hear any more bullshit about Billie Holiday or the Café Tia Juana once we leave this joint! Not another goddamned word!" He loved the singer's music, but this was business--and besides, listening to his personal record collection would tide him over just fine, at least until he was able to see Billie in person again. This evening belonged to the singer, however. Despite her tumultuous life, the voice of Eleanor Fagan shared top billing and world prominence with her alter ego, the great Billie Holiday. Billie's universal musical appeal regularly raked in more cash during a year than TaNellie could shake a stick at. His goal was to make a million dollars during his career. As far as Tee knew, he would be the first Cleveland pimp to accomplish such a feat. A word to the wise often suffices.

(3) Mattie Matt...

Matthew (Mattie Matt) Matthews was an oldschool racketeer who often boasted he was so nice they named him twice. He cut his teeth in the New York underworld scene while running numbers for a black woman from French Martinique. Her name was Madame Stephanie (Queenie) St. Clair, a big-time policy banker. The organization's under-boss was Ellsworth Raymond "Bumpy" Johnson, a career criminal. During the Great Depression, they were among a handful of Negro gangs who fought the notorious Dutch Shultz's mob for control of Harlem's numbers racket. One of Mattie's most noticeable features was his bowlegs, which were never talked about in his presence. Friends joked that if his legs were straightened, he'd be a giant. He was very good-natured concerning most things, and smiled easily. But there was an ugly side to this multi-layered man who, when provoked, could turn on a dime, displaying unforgiving and unrelenting fits of fury. He once beat a man into submission with a lead pipe over a five-dollar debt. Mattie went about his business in a very careful and methodical manner, never taking unnecessary chances--only calculated risks. Even when eating a meal, his bites were thoughtfully measured, as though he expected the unexpected. Mattie would tell anyone who'd listen, "I makes my own luck! Besides," he'd explain, "my daddy told me to always keep 'em guessing. Where I'm from, money makes right—when you got jack, I is rich takes you a helluva lot further in life than...I am poor."

His philosophy, at first blush, appeared to be true, especially if successes are based wholly on new cars and the inexhaustible flow of ready cash. In the life...what you see isn't necessarily what you get. Mattie Matt continued, "I always appear to be what I expect to be. The scriptures say it best: 'As a man thinketh in his heart... so is he.'"

Currently, Mattie was semi-retired and living in New York City. Some twenty-five years earlier he'd made up his mind to retire in Ohio after a friend suggested, "If you're ever in Cleveland... look me up...just ask anybody in Little Italy how to get in touch with me, and they'll put you wise." It was just a casual comment, but Mattie filed it into his memory bank along with other tidbits to be revisited later. During those early days his friend, Frank Leo, was an enforcer with the Charles "Lucky" Luciano crime family. He and Mattie had met by chance and had been friends ever since. Frank was 5'9" with chiseled features and a solid build. His jet-black hair was combed to the rear with a straight razor edge lining his ears and neck. He reminded some people of 1930s matinee idol George Raft. Frank was positive the actor had patterned his own style directly after him. The gangster loved his custom-made suits and always sported a white carnation in his lapel. This prompted his cohorts to nickname him "Frankie Flowers," a moniker he readily embraced...and wore with pride.

Frankie Flowers was an okay guy with a well-deserved reputation for being a good friend or worst nightmare. Frank and Mattie bumped into one another while searching for a deadbeat who owed their respective mob bosses money. On the day they met, Frank approached Mattie after seeing him hanging about the Bowery neighborhood, and decided to cut into him. "Hey, buddy...I'm trying to find this friend of mine...have you seen him?"

Frank showed Mattie a small photograph of the guy he was looking for. Mattie glimpsed the picture, scratching his head. "He looks real familiar--what's his name?"

"That's none of your business, buddy...I just asked if you've seen him?"

"Yeah...I seen him all right." With that, Mattie reached in his pocket and pulled out the very same picture, showing it to Frankie. "Like I said, mister, I seen him...I just don't know where he is!"

They both laughed. "That's really fucked up! This cocksucker owes some people I know money." Frankie felt bad about cracking wise. "I'm sorry for hassling you just now, friend. What's your name, anyway?"

The two shook hands. "I'm Matthew Matthews...so nice they named me twice...but my friends just call me Mattie Matt."

"Then Mattie Matt it is. I'm Frank Leo...everybody calls me Frankie Flowers! You already know why I'm carrying this photo... what's your excuse?" The dapper enforcer's eyes narrowed as he sized up Mattie, awaiting a response.

"That same fellow owes my boss some money too, and I'm trying to collect."

"Mattie! You've got to be shitting me. Say it ain't so!"

"Naww, I ain't kidding...I don't play around when it comes to money."

"Well, that makes two of us."

All the pair really knew about the man in the picture was that he came from Louisiana—a Creole who loved gambling but was down on his luck. He owed Bumpy Johnson and Lucky Luciano a ton of markers, or IOUs. It seemed a natural enough progression for Mattie and Frankie to put their minds together and find this guy. It would save them both time and energy. They agreed that whoever found the mark first would immediately inform the other by leaving word at Blossom Restaurant, a split-level greasy spoon on Bowery Street where the man had last been seen.

During the early years of this unlikely collaboration, respect was the common denominator. Trust would take much longer to develop, because it had to be earned. No one has ever made instant old friends. It's a bond that can be substantiated only by deeds tempered with time. Frank was born in Palermo, Sicily. His parents moved to Ohio when he was just a baby. Mattie's home was Mason, Tennessee...a small town near Memphis. Aside from the obvious color differences, the two men shared similar backgrounds, both having lost parents at an early age. Those circumstances, coupled with other variables, found the orphaned boys attending school less and less, eventually dropping out entirely to work odd jobs. In spite of their lots in life, they learned to fend for themselves. The two became very enterprising souls while living among the lowest levels of society. To raise money they often gathered soda pop bottles wherever they found them. Each spent hours scavenging the city's dumps where they lived, scouring open fields, rummaging alleys, combing parks, ransacking restaurant back lots and corner stores, and grubbing around other remote places harboring glass cash. Once the bottles were rinsed and returned to the bottling companies, they received a two cents deposit per bottle. This was tedious labor and one had to be mindful of leaving booty unattended. Many a day they found themselves chasing glass bottle thieves, to no avail. To thwart theft, most deposit bottle collectors worked in pairs. Although they lived in different cities and never happened upon each other, their quest for survival was similar and eventually led them to New York City.

In the fall it was commonplace to see groups of indigent men with shovels, boarding freight trains in groups and tossing scoopfuls of coal from railroad cars onto the grading below to be gathered later for use in furnaces during the winter. Hundreds of pounds of discarded paper and tin cans, once sorted by special recycling centers, offered welcome relief for enterprising cash-strapped vagrants. Public schools jumped into the act by sponsoring newspaper and tax stamp drives, raising money for red feather agencies and other charitable organizations. While playing impromptu games of chance, both Mattie and Frankie learned to deal from the bottoms of decks. They deceived unsuspecting players with the skill and expertise of card sharps. Eventually they became adept in the intricacies concerning most sporting games. During those days, deceptive skills notwithstanding, folks did what was necessary to earn a living, with very few exceptions. Mattie shared his thoughts on the subject. "It's a poor frog who can't find success in his own pond." Mattie's sayings were memories borrowed from his parents and other Negro elders from his hometown of Mason.

Frankie and Mattie were simultaneously drawn into the rackets because it offered quick money and an opportunity to control their own destinies. Although they took different paths to success, initially every newcomer starts out the same way: at the bottom rung. Both performed menial tasks for individual gangsters, like running errands, washing cars, or serving as lookouts. The jobs weren't glamorous, but were easy enough to perform without being hassled. After whetting their appetites, it was only natural to yearn for more money. Despite their mutual lack of formal educations, they both developed into streetwise, ambitious young fellows who wanted desperately to make something of themselves. In their new roles, neither was afraid to sully his hands, which quickly got them noticed within their organizations. The boys took full advantage of their opportunities, ultimately moving up the underworld hierarchy. This happened concurrently and the youngsters soon became men, racketeers, who could not have been more different. When a twist of fate intervened...Mattie Matt and Frankie Flowers were intrinsically linked.

The team worked tirelessly in the months ahead, tracking skips and collecting record amounts of cash from defaulted loans and gambling debts. The bosses were quite pleased, and increased their responsibilities and pay substantially. One day, out of the clear blue sky, something unexpected happened. They found the proverbial needle in the haystack: The Creole. It was Mattie Matt who spotted him, living under the assumed name of Jack Sprat. Matthews quickly telephoned Blossom Restaurant and alerted his partner. "Frankie, our boy's in Room 218 at the Harvard Hotel--it's a dive on Delancey Street in the Bowery."

"*Minghia!* Good work, Mattie—I'll see ya there in thirty minutes—don't let that cocksucker get away!"

After hanging up the pay phone, Frankie sat back down at the counter and quickly finished what was left of his steak, hash browns, and onions. He grabbed a hanky from his rear pocket and wiped the tasty juices from around his thin lips. "Darla...tell Gene I said his blue plate special was just like *mama mia* [my mother] used to make!" The unpretentious waitress smiled, stacking his soiled dishes atop a large heaping tray with one hand and securing the dollar bill in the other. "Keep the seventy-five cents' change, Darla!" he said, while slipping into his suit jacket. "See ya tomorrow around lunch time, toots--kiss baby Monica for me!"

Darla appreciated Frank's tips, which always came in handy, helping to keep her supplied with cans of PET evaporated milk, clean cloth diapers and safety pins for the baby. The new mother's prospects for the future were bleak, to say the least. It was a sure bet that talent scouts wouldn't be dining at Blossom Restaurant anytime soon, making it highly unlikely Darla would ever win a beauty contest and become a movie star—especially with her lackluster curly brown hair and sorrowful eyes. Their puffy circles underneath made her look at least ten years older. But in spite of her appearance, she had a very special talent deep within, something you couldn't quite put your finger on, but knew existed. When it came to men, however, except for their names, she always fell head over heels for the same flighty Daffy Dan types.

It was a phenomenon that occurred all too often. Recently the father of Monica, Darla's baby, packed his bags and left them high and dry, saddled with two months' back rent. They lived in a so-called furnished flat, with a bug- infested Murphy bed, worn-out davenport, wobbly-legged table, and two chairs. Included in their rental was a shared urine-scented restroom just down the hall. It was stocked with a thick tattered-paged Sears catalog, which doubled as a library and toilet paper. Darla wasn't aware of it at the time, but being abandoned by her boyfriend was a blessing in disguise. Of course it didn't keep her from pining over losing him.

After her sadness waned, she turned her attention toward a more pleasant thought: Frank Leo. He was the one guy who never made a pass—yet was always concerned about her and Monica's well-being. He was their guardian angel without wings. She recalled his comments after he first noticed her pregnancy. "What's the skinny, toots...you having a baby?"

"Yeah, Frank," she answered while wiping up coffee spills from off the counter. "I'm due in three months."

"Wow...only a prick would do that! Get it, toots...'PRICK'!"

"Sure, Frank, I got it. First from my jerk boyfriend...and now you! A real good-looking, smooth-talking nice guy. Yes sir, Frankie boy, unlike my baby's daddy, you know exactly how to treat a lady." She rolled her eyes. "I can't wait to see what you come up with next!"

Darla was not amused and Frank Leo tried his best to make amends. "I'm so sorry, toots, it was just a terrible joke!" For once in his life he wished he'd kept his big mouth shut. The last thing Frank wanted was to hurt her feelings. With eyes nearing the brink of tears she continued gathering dishes, just grateful for a job...even this one. At Blossom Restaurant Darla faced many undue pressures from which sleep offered little respite. The young woman felt lost amid indiscriminate patrons and reprobates whose endless foul mouthed chatter never ceased. Those in Darla's circle struggled to exist--but not Frankie Flowers; he was immune to life's hardships. It was as though he was charmed and held the world by a magical string that somehow carried him well above the fray and far from the doldrums and economic woes of the Depression.

Frankie left the restaurant... crossing the busy thoroughfare to buy a freshly cut carnation from Signora di Domenico. She was an amiable flower vendor who always insisted on pinning a boutonniére directly onto his lapel for good luck. When it was perfectly situated, just like clockwork she'd give him a couple of playful pats to his cheek, saying, "Frankie, you such a nice-a boy. Go and find you self-a good wife, then go home and make-a the baby. Before it's-a too late...okay!"

The woman had maintained a small flower stand across from Blossom Restaurant for twenty years, and never missed a single day. Signora di Domenico was Frankie's personal florist, but also the closest thing he had to a mother since his own passed away years ago. While sidestepping traffic, he trotted back across the street to catch up to Mattie. He glanced back over his shoulder and smiled, seeing Signora di Domenico kiss the sawbuck ($10 bill) he'd just given her before stuffing it into her bosom. *What a grand old dame,* he thought to himself.

When he arrived at the hotel, Mattie was waiting outside the building, having just glanced at his Timex after spotting Frankie. "I saw him go in forty minutes ago and he hasn't come out!"

Together they walked inside the seedy hotel and through a dimly lit vestibule, past a lackadaisical desk clerk, then up a flight of stairs. They gingerly avoided a wino sprawled out cold on the second floor landing, clutching an empty bottle of muscatel like a security blanket. Finding the room was easy, so with gats drawn, they burst inside without hesitation. They knocked the door off its hinges and never minded the commotion they caused, which was more normal than not. The occupant instinctively sprang from his bed still dressed, heading straight for an open window, attempting to climb out onto the fire escape. Just before he made it through, Mattie grabbed his ankle with one hand while desperately trying to grasp the other to pull him back into the room. In the midst of the melee, he kicked Matthews hard to his lip, bloodying it with the heel of his shoe.

"Why you asshole sombitch!" With his adrenaline pumping, Mattie went postal, pulling the man back into the room, limb by limb, like a game of tug-of-war. "You done did it now, man!" warned a pissed-off Mattie. He quickly slipped into a pair of brass knuckles, then put the man in a headlock. He pummeled the Creole's face while an incensed Frankie Flowers kicked the mark repeatedly in the groin with abandon. Their actions caused the deadbeat to fall onto the floor and cover up. They were experts at breaking bones, and continued punching and stomping the hapless victim...stopping just short of beating him to death.

Being on the lam exacted its toll on the mark. He was about thirty years old -- 6'3" with an extremely slim frame. He hadn't shaven or taken a bath since God knows when, and reeked of wine, pee, and Lucky Strike cigarettes. Unfortunately, this was a time of reckoning for him—a day he'd expected but was ill-prepared for. After literally having the shit beaten out of him, the Creole lay in a heap on the dust-laden floor. He was ordered in no uncertain terms to pay up or die. How he managed to maintain his vision through a plum-sized purple slit of an eye defied belief. His jaw and nose were broken in several places, and were bleeding profusely. Blood even trickled from his ear as he lay on the dusty floor, cradling his family jewels with a bruised hand. It was the only way to protect against another onslaught from brogues and brass knuckles. Those two impromptu tools utilized by most enforcers were effectively demonstrated by the pair of intruders.

Between intermittent breaths accentuated by hopelessness, the man pled for his life. While struggling to speak, his garbled words were just mumbo-jumbo to the deadly duo. "Please...no more...I'll pay what I owe...just don't shoot me!"

Frankie threw up his hands in disgust. "You've been bustin' our balls for thirty minutes already!" He glanced down at his scuffed-up shoes and gave the man another swift kick to the balls for GP...general principle. "Mattie, do you believe this cocksucker! He's fucked up my brand- new wingtip spectators [two-toned shoes]. Why, I ought to...." Frankie hesitated, pointing his finger in the man's face. "Look, you Creole fuck! Don't you mess with me, cocksucker!" Frankie regained his composure and quickly switched strategies to a more congenial approach. Until now, the only thing he'd accomplished was getting angry. "You owe forty G's, for crying out loud... where's a guy like you gonna get that kind of jack?"

The man again attempted to speak, but his undecipherable words continued to betray his thoughts. "I...I hit today...n...no shit...I HIT!" Once the words reached the ears of the two confederates, it sounded more like an anesthetized patient speaking to his dentist...blah blah blah blah...yet another opportunity wasted.

In a last-ditch effort to save his life, the man reached inside his pocket and retrieved the policy slips, extending them at arm's length to give the enforcers a closer look. "I...I...had a hunch about 218...it's my room number. I've been playing it for a while, but yesterday I felt really lucky and plunked down $50 straight at two different banks...it came out! I won 50 grand!"

Once they saw the policy slips, the dimly lit room filled with thoughts of avarice. The gambler's number had come, but was it a case of too little too late. "We got orders to cap your ass, money or no money!" They aimed their pieces directly at his temple. The nervous Creole was quickly running out of options. His wide-eyed glances alternated between the two men, searching for a glimmer of reason or hope...anything. With a lump in his throat, he forced himself to swallow, but nothing happened. His mouth was dry as cotton.

"Please!" he pleaded, having somewhat regained his voice. His words weren't succinct, but did make sense. "I can't take it anymore. Let's make a deal? There are only two things left to do. You can let me go. Or you guys can kill me and turn over the 50 G's to your bosses. If you give them the money, I'm betting my life they'll never trust either of you again. So why not keep the goddamned money, and nobody's the wiser! Where's your pride, for Pete's sake? Stealing is an art--it's what racketeers do for a living... this is your legacy!" He handed over the policy slips. "Take the fucking scratch. I don't want it! I'm giving it to the both of you, free and clear...I swear to God! Just let me live, and I'll move to the West Coast. You'll never have to worry about ever seeing my ugly face again." The men looked at each other without saying a word... seconds later, they holstered their weapons.

Now they were faced with yet another dilemma—either they kill this guy outright, and hope to leave without being noticed, or drive to a bus station and send him on his merry way. New York's Port Authority Bus Terminal was completely out of the question. After weighing the odds, they decided to drive 200 miles to Baltimore and put him on the first thing smoking to Los Angeles. After giving the man just enough jack to get by, Frankie Flowers looked him dead in the eye and reiterated his position. He jabbed him in the chest with his finger. "If I ever see your cocksucker face again--and I do mean ever, you blue-ball cocksucker fuck!--I'm gonna blow it the hell away, CAPISCI!"

"Sure...I understand...I'll never come back...I swear...thank you...thank you!" They drove the three and a half hours to Baltimore, stopping only once along the way for sunglasses to hide the man's damaged eye, and some bandages for his wounds. When they arrived in Maryland they circled the bus station a few times looking for a parking space. Once inside, Frankie sat beside the man while Mattie bought a one-way ticket to Los Angeles. When the announcer called for the bus to board, Frankie escorted the mark right onto the coach. He placed both palms on the Creole's shoulders and slammed him down hard onto the seat.

In a low voice Frankie Flowers whispered, "Okay you cocksucker fuck...remember what I told you today."

"I will," replied the Creole.

Meanwhile, Mattie picked up the car and drove it back to the terminal. When the bus departed, the two friends were following close behind. After an hour or so, Mattie and Frankie turned around and headed back to New York. Their plan had worked like a charm...the man left town without so much as a look-see. They were positive he'd never return. "That cocksucker would sooner double-cross the Devil incarnate than show his face around here again!"

In the gangster parlance of the day there's just one simple rule... "You pays your money... and you takes your chances!" This was a bet the two friends had faded with their lives. After splitting the winnings, the two men informed their bosses that the mark had been permanently eliminated after being unable to pay his debt. They confirmed his body was burned beyond recognition and stashed somewhere on the outskirts of town. The truth of the matter was the friends buried a dead dog they'd found along the roadside.

Numbers betting slips are negotiable, and when turned into the proper policy bank, the bearer receives payment on demand, no questions asked. Both Mattie and Frankie utilized a trusted associate to redeem the policy slips--for a small fee, of course. The new pals had experienced their first trial by fire: a rite of passage, so to speak...a positive step in a budding friendship. Neither man spent a dime of the money, deciding to sit on the winnings, no matter how long it took for suspicions to allay. Patience is a virtue... even among gangsters.

(4) Déjà vu . . .

In the spring of '54, Mattie Matthews finally put pedal to the metal, leaving New York City behind in his rearview mirror. He drove toward Cleveland, Ohio to embrace his destiny. He'd made his decision to retire from the life and pursue a dream he'd courted since the Depression. Mattie had always wanted to be his own man, since starting his illicit career. Being referred to as the chief cook and bottle washer, big enchilada, the man in charge or boss...were titles his uneducated father respected, but never enjoyed.

Once in town, Mattie rented a room at a boarding house on Tuscora Avenue. It was owned by Miss Emma Cindy Stewart, a widow of six years. She was in her mid-seventies, a pleasant sort, who was feisty enough to mix it up with the big dogs. Miss Emma didn't need to interview prospective tenants...just sizing them up for a few minutes was all the time she required. The pair hit it off immediately.

"Well, Mr. Matthews...so nice they named you twice. Here's my rules: rent is due by noon on the first of each week. I serve supper in the dining room at 6:30 sharp, Monday through Friday. Bed linens are changed and washed every Wednesday--that's once a week, son, come rain or shine. If you forget, then shame on you. For safety reasons, cooking and smoking aren't allowed in my house. I'd hate to go to bed one night and wake up in Heaven...I'll get there soon enough. And last but not least, young man—absolutely no consorting in my rooms—I run a clean and honest establishment. Now…if that's all right with you, Mr. Matthews… pay me one week's rent in advance and I'll give you the key."

Mattie paid cash for the whole month and Miss Emma wrote out a receipt, giving it to him along with a room key.

His diggings were rather stark, but spotless. Floral-patterned wallpaper, dark-brown baseboards, and a small radiator were the same in every room. A wide windowsill held a leafy green plant framed by sheer white curtains with a beige shade pulled down halfway, to cut glare. A double bed facing the east window was carefully made…complete with hospital corners. Two comfortable-looking pillows spanned a modest wooden headboard, and a thick patchwork quilt was neatly folded into thirds at the foot of the bed. A brass lamp rested on starched ivory-colored needlework atop the nightstand. The chest of drawers, with a perfectly centered chipped white enamel metal pitcher filled with fresh water, provided abundant storage space. It juxtaposed a small narrow closet. Behind the entry door was an oval mirror and small sign: "God bless our home." A neatly penciled in afterthought reminded roomers: "No smoking or cooking allowed." Mattie quickly folded his clothing. After putting it away, he was ready. He had forgotten just how the smells of home cooking soothed the mind, body, and spirit…he couldn't wait to dig in.

The newest house member joined his fellow tenants in the dining room, making sure he arrived at exactly 6:30. Everyone was already seated. Miss Emma was laden with plates, but gave a quick nod to Mattie, directing him to his chair. There was an obvious pecking order in seating arrangements, based solely on tenure. First up was Mr. Blair, an insurance man, who specialized in industrial or burial insurance protection for poor people. His policies sold for pennies per week and covered families, but had no real cash value. Blair always wore a suit to dinner and was a little heavy-handed with the Old Spice cologne. Miss Emma placed his

dinner before him, having already made certain his food was separated and not touching...an idiosyncrasy of his. Second in line
was Miss Lurline Smith, a light-skinned woman whose faint mus-
tache was bleached regularly. She taught fourth grade at Miles
Standish elementary school. Mattie smiled after observing her
daily dinner ritual for the first time. No matter what was served,
Miss Smith's brows arched and her eyes sparkled. She acted like a
kid on Christmas day, excitedly rubbing her hands together. Miss
Joy Hensen was next: she had already glanced admiringly at Mattie a couple of times, catching him unawares. Mr. Roebuck was
fourth--a resident for just two months. He sat patiently, armed
with a fork in one hand and knife in the other, waiting for grace
while holding his position like a soldier. He was happy to be moving up in the pecking order by shedding his *new tenant* label. Mr.
Matthews hadn't eaten ham hocks and great northern beans with
cornbread since his mother passed, and was positive the landla-
dy's efforts wouldn't disappoint. Once everyone was served, Miss
Emma took her customary chair at the head of the table, blessing
the meal, which always, ended with, "In Jesus' name, amen!" Mr.
Roebuck wasted little time in pouncing on his meal like a starving
alley cat.

Mattie finally caught Joy Hensen staring at him during dinner...but averted his eyes and continued eating. A short time later,
he glanced up from the table and she was still looking his way.
This time he returned her interest with a pleasant smile. Joy re-
ciprocated, and her warm eyes invited him up to her place. Mattie
quickly responded with a twinkle in his own eyes, happily accept-
ing the invitation.

After supper, everyone gradually retired to their rooms.
Mattie went directly to the restroom where he lollygagged for
a while, spending time on his nose hairs and thick moustache.
Before leaving, he rinsed and dried his hands. Mattie slowed as

he approached Joy's room and placed his ear right against her door, and knocked softly. It opened quickly and he slipped inside unnoticed...running smack into Joy's waiting lips. She had planned this encounter during dinner, and a loose, scented, sheer gown revealed her intentions. Before he could say Jackie Robinson... she had yanked off his sport jacket and shirt—carefully unzipped his pants and pulled them down around the ankles as he stood there erect. He freed himself by kicking off the pants one leg at a time. With his trousers gone, he resembled an exclamation point standing bowlegged in the center of her room. His mammoth member throbbed like a beating heart. He felt silly after realizing he still had on his shoes and socks. Joy grabbed hold of Mattie, quickly pulling him onto her bed... almost knocking over the lamp in the process.

"Shhhh..." she giggled. "It's now or never!" The final taboo imposed by Miss Emma was about to be broken. They kissed lustfully and began moving even closer...for the kill. Mattie cocked his hammer for the long haul and knew Joy would cometh with the dawn. When her ecstasy peaked, she let go with a shrill scream... he had hit the spot. "Ohhhhhh! she shouted, wrapping her arms around Mattie's waist and squeezing tightly. "I must confess," she sighed, "I've never ever had it this good...not even close!" He'd heard others express the same sentiment and had even said it himself on a few occasions. He wondered why couples never fully relished those feelings. To him it was a no-brainer...surely one would want to savor a once in a lifetime experience for at least a couple of hours.

Mattie chuckled to himself, because he anticipated just what was about to happen next. Joy was wearing a sly rapturous smile after their ten-minute intermission. She sidled closer and delicately stroked his Johnson with her hand. "Can we do it again?" She hoped lightning would strike twice...it did. After an hour or so of lovemaking, it was déjà vu all over again. "Wow," she murmured, "I can't remember having felt like this in my entire life!" Joy slipped her tongue inside his open mouth, moving it along his front teeth just behind the lip. "Matthew, you really outdid yourself this time, man." They soon drifted off to sleep. Hours later they were gently awakened by warm sun rays.

Mattie dressed hurriedly, then raced to his room, none the worse for wear. "That was some good booty there, boy!"

Miss Emma was soon doting over Mattie like a long-lost son. He enjoyed every minute of her company and always looked forward to spending quality time around the dinner table with the other roomers. Miss Emma's down-home wisdom, humor, and culinary skills made his rent seem paltry by comparison. He learned to appreciate everything about the boarding house--especially his quaint little room with its comfortable bed, fluffy feathered pillows, and the smooth feel of freshly laundered white sheets. He enjoyed being awakened by his very own solar alarm clock whose face happily shone through the east window regularly. Joy and Mattie's trysts became more and more frequent. Their synergy was high-voltage, and each encounter increased in sexual intensity and emotional content. It's a fair assumption to say they were falling in love with one another.

Since violating Miss Emma's no-consorting rule, Mattie found it rather disconcerting whenever he looked into her winsome eyes. He couldn't help feeling like a bald-faced prevaricator. One afternoon, while he was helping Miss Emma put away some groceries, she inquired, "Mr. Matthews... how are you and Miss Hensen doing?"

"Uhhh...nice, I guess...she's a fine upstanding God-fearing young woman...the salt of the earth. I'm mighty privileged to know her. Why do you ask, Miss Emma?"

"I declare, son...don't mind me...I was just wondering out

loud. Kinda like wake a body up in the middle of the night loud! Or scaring the bejesus out of a person during a sound sleep LOUD!"

That was the first and last time she ever mentioned her two roomers in the same breath. Mattie felt relieved by Miss Emma's admission, and in the future tried to minimize Joy's histrionics by gently covering her mouth with his hand whenever she became a little too excited. He began to think maybe he was the best partner she'd ever had...he certainly knew Joy was at the top of his list.

After an exhaustive search, Mattie found himself a great-looking four-bedroom Tudor in Shaker Heights. It was the same Ludlow neighborhood in which actor Paul Newman had once lived. *If only my momma and daddy could see me now.* The house was just a stone's throw from Cleveland, making it an ideal location for his latest pursuit. Not surprisingly, bank financing was a breeze, and the sale went through without a hitch after he used Frank Leo as a lifelong reference. Mattie always said, "It's not what you know in life, but who you know!"

A few months later, Mattie gave Miss Emma his notice and tipped her for an additional month. No matter what, she always made certain her tenants received home-cooked meals right on schedule. She laundered their linens even when feeling tired or sickly, come rain or shine, just like she promised. Mattie cut her lawn whenever needed, and looked in on her regularly. Emma Cindy Stewart's presence in his life made him feel needed. From now on, he would forever think of her as Mother Emma. Mattie gathered his belongings and left the boarding house, which had been his initial foray into Cleveland hospitality. He made sure both Mother Emma and Joy Hensen had his new phone number.

Mattie's new lodgings had been decorated by one of the premier designing firms in town. The company had been personally recommended by Frank Leo. Their work exceeded Mattie's expectations, and he expressed his genuine gratitude to both Frankie and the design team. Spending a king's ransom on the furnishings and design concept had been well worth the cost. *If only his momma and daddy could see him now.* He soon settled in comfortably, and eventually asked Joy Hensen to accompany him. Push had finally come to shove, and it was time for him to concentrate fully on his dream and the business at hand.

(5) Murray Hill...

A t precisely 3:00 p.m., and as instructed, Mattie dialed Sweetbriar 5-4212 on Thursday afternoon. The special phone number was used only to confirm business arrangements with Frankie Flowers. Someone picked up the phone on the first ring, but said nothing. "Wrong number," whispered Mattie before hanging up. His words were a prearranged code and corroborated his meeting with Frankie Flowers on a preauthorized time and date. The two men hadn't seen each other in years, and looked forward to getting together. The scheduled meeting arrived quickly and Mattie had left no stone unturned preparing his business proposal. Little Italy's annual Feast of the Assumption was in full swing, and the enclave was inundated with Italian flags, dignitaries, and thousands of Catholic faithful. This annual celebration commemorated the death of the Virgin Mary and her assumption to Heaven, where she sat on the throne beside God. Today was perfect for a meeting, what with all the comings and goings on in the neighborhood. Mattie was confident he'd be approved once he pitched his concept. He knew Frankie was leaning his way, but still had to be sold on the project. After all, it was business--those involved in the decision-making process had to be sure that Mattie's idea, and his plan for implementation, were viable.

Meanwhile, at Municipal Stadium, in downtown Cleveland, the tribe was leading the New York Yankees, in spite of Mickey Mantle's 22nd and 23rd homers of the year, off pitchers, Early Wynn and Ray Narleski. As far as Mattie was concerned, the tribe's winning ways were an omen, validating his decision to move to Cleveland. All his adult life he had patiently bided his time, saving every penny he earned until his ducks were all in a row. He was completely consumed by his dream, and knew life was about to change for the better. First on the agenda was the right location, which was already a done deal. It was a secluded area easily accessible from every part of town. Secondly, he wanted to identify Midwestern high rollers. This would be left up to Frankie Flowers, who knew everyone. Mattie also needed advice from fellow gamblers. Since they were experts in the field, who was better-qualified to identify what was expected when selecting venues to risk their own money? Mattie presented copies of architectural renderings to bring his concepts to life. As a student of the game, he sought approval from the powers that be. It was the most important reason for the meeting. Requesting permission to operate in another territory was protocol, and smart business too. No self-respecting gentleman would dare wed a daughter without first seeking the father's permission. Matthews' research confirmed that diversity was a key element in a successful venture. His concept was based solely on a New York club known as the Town Casino. Mattie knew high rollers followed big money, and it didn't matter what color or creed the patrons were as long as the money was substantial legal tender. His club would be the kind of venue affording gamblers an opportunity to vie against the savviest players in the world. Among true professionals, this was an opportunity...a challenge impossible to overlook.

Mattie was never one to put on airs, "no such-ee-much," as his late mother might have said. He drove to the meeting in Mother Emma's 1949 Ford, leaving his new Lincoln Premier hidden safely away in the garage. He found the nondescript social club on Mayfield Road at Murray Hill Avenue, hidden in plain sight between a pizzeria and cigar smoke shop. Once inside, he was treated cordially. Just prior to the customary search, he voluntarily turned over his weapon, a demonstration of respect for Frank Leo. After being thoroughly searched, Mattie was escorted into a large smoke-filled wood-paneled meeting room.

Italian-American pride was palpable, based in part on the many framed photos of entertainers, movie stars, baseball players, and prize fighters of the day. Frank Sinatra, Old Blue Eyes, was prominently featured on a wall of fame alongside autographed pictures of Frankie Lane, who once worked the night shift at Parker Appliance in Cleveland. Other photographs included Louie Prima and Keely Smith, undefeated heavyweight champion Rocky Marciano, Jake LaMotta, Enrico Caruso, and Mario Lanza, the former Philadelphia truck driver whose singing and acting transformed him into an overnight sensation...all graced the meeting room. Mattie remembered losing a bundle the night Carmen Basilio's picture was taken. The fighter's battered face beamed with joy after a tough win over World Champion Sugar Ray Robinson. On a separate wall, secluded from the others, was a tribute to Italian partisans who fought during World War II. Mattie was intrigued by a black and white photo taken in April of 1945. Fascist dictator Benito Mussolini and members of his Blackshirt party, including his girlfriend, were killed and displayed to crowds after being strung up by the ankles. Their bodies were desecrated, spat upon, and shown the utmost disrespect. This photo was displayed between the American and Italian flags...proof of the pride and patriotism shared between both countries.

Mattie's face lit up with joy upon seeing his old buddy Frankie Flowers. They had gone through some tough times in The Big Apple. Frank Leo was dapper as ever, his movie star good looks still intact. A full head of silver hair was kept neatly in place by Wildroot cream oil hair dressing.

Frank opened his arms wide. *"Minghia!* If it ain't my old

goombah—Mattie Matt—*Benvenuto* [welcome], my friend, long time no see! How the hell you doing?"

"Frank Leo...you ain't changed a bit, not one single bit...you still look just the same...UGLY as a sombitch!"

The Sicilian feigned a couple of jabs to Mattie's midsection. "That goes double for you... ya bowlegged cocksucker!"

They laughed as vigorously as they shook hands, just like brothers. Even among racketeers, friendships are commonplace... just as long as they don't interfere with business.

Frank introduced his associates. "Mattie, these are a few of my not so wise guys. Chuck Rundo, Bocky Boo, and Joey Cerito. You'd better watch 'em, because they'll do anything for a buck! Fellas, this is Matthew 'Mattie Matt' Matthews...so nice they named him twice!" They all took seats around a beautiful vintage mahogany table. Mattie was given thirty minutes to present his case. "Gentlemen...I would like to personally thank each of you for allowing me this opportunity to share a concept I've developed for the Midwest market. As you men already know, thanks to Bugsy Siegel, Las Vegas is king of the gambling empire and always will be. But there's still an awful lot of jack to be made right in this area. I might be getting along in years, but my ideas are fresh and Cleveland is ripe for the plucking. My idea is just what the doctor ordered. It'll help keep this town vibrant for years to come, with opportunities and flowing in jack. Just think...even regular folks will have the chance to visit a real casino, right here in their own back yard. I'll do it up really special with honest games, slots, tables, everything! Since people won't have to catch a plane to Vegas, it'll leave more profits for us."

Mattie was on a roll; even those in attendance added ideas of their own. When his allotted time was over, drinks were poured all around. Then the bullshit really hit the fan. After forty-five minutes of bull pucky, Mattie and Frankie decided to spill the beans of being real enforcers. Frank's crew moved their chairs in closer to hear two gangsters tell it like it was during the Depression.

"Mattie...do you remember the day Signora di Domenico missed work! It was the first time I wasn't wearing my trademark carnation. I was naked as a jaybird. *Minghia!* I loved the old broad, but I was so pissed I could've whacked her ass! Not wearing my carnation fucked up my whole day!"

Mattie agreed. "Yeah, I'll never forget that day...it was a Tuesday. We was searching for a deadbeat when we passed by a couple of guys dressed in grey suits, standing right in front of Canal Street Station. They never even noticed me...but gave Frankie boy here the stinkeye, checking him out with a fine-toothed comb. One of them made a slow pass toward his coat pocket...but stopped when his pal whispered something."

"*Minghia*, Mattie...that's right. After giving me the once-over, this cocksucker turns to his buddy and says, 'It ain't him...he's not wearing a carnation!' Now mind you...I didn't hear him say it...I just read the cocksucker's lips!"

Mattie picked up the story from there. "Yeah, so we keep walking...deciding right then and there to take some kinda action... but what? After about a block, we stop and I hand my coat and hat to Frankie boy to hold—so's not to tip off the goons. Then...I circle around and head back down the block and across the alley. The two men was standing in the exact same spot. You could tell they was packing heat, 'cause they acted kinda cocky, if you know what I mean. I goes over and cuts into 'em—polite like."

Mattie continued the story. "Excuse me, boss, is y'all looking for Mr. Frankie Flowers?"

"Yeah, spade...what's it to ya!" said the bigger of the two.

"It don't mean nothing to me, boss...I was just wondering. If y'all is lookin' for him...I can put you wise for a sawbuck!"

"Well...have you seen him or not?" said the big guy.

"Sure have, boss... he's up the street in PJ's Restaurant." Mattie pointed toward the general vicinity. "Just past the alley."

The man thumbed through his cash until he found a five-spot, and handed it to Mattie. "Here's a fin, spade."

"But boss...the tip cost a sawbuck."

"That's the best I can do, nigger...take it or leave it. Now why don't you pick the cotton from your eyes and show us the way?"

"No sir...ree...boss--I hates gettin' involved in white folks' business."

"You won't be involved, spade...just walk ahead of us and nod when you get to PJ's. It'll be the easiest money you ever made...no muss...no fuss."

Mattie hesitated for a few seconds, patiently tucking the five-dollar bill into his empty wallet. "Hurry up, spade, we ain't got all day--it's gettin' dark out—kinda like you—only different!"

The bigger man looked over at his partner and smirked as Mattie began walking toward the restaurant. "Say, spade, how we gonna recognize him?"

Mattie kept moving, answering on the fly without missing a beat. "That's easy, boss...he'll be the one wearing a dark-blue box-back coat with straight-leg trousers and a white carnation in his left lapel."

The natural sights and sounds of New York after dark are impressive, to say the least, and permeate every corner of its urbane landscape. Thankfully, there was still about one hour's worth of daylight left on what was a warm and pleasant summer day. The cool shadow of the Third Avenue elevated line overpass grew longer and longer as the sun inched westward. The assassins wore grey fedoras pulled low over their heads, with the brims turned down in front. They were without expression and followed closely behind the bowlegged Negro, being careful not to allow anyone else in between. Mattie noticed them in a window reflection, nonchalantly slipping into gloves and putting their hands inside their coats' custom-made pockets. It was an old gangster trick, used for concealing weapons both large and small. This was a sure sign they were armed and dangerous.

After passing the alley, Mattie neared the restaurant. As instructed, he paused momentarily, and slowly nodded his head in the direction of PJ's. Now emboldened, the men were clearly focused on the job at hand: to knock off Frankie Flowers. The reason didn't matter; it was just business. They walked in deadly earnest now, anticipating an indulgence more gratifying to them than making love with the glamorous 1930s movie star Carole Lombard. These killers were tops in their field. Experience had taught them to take nothing for granted, so waiting nearby was a plain-looking black sedan with a full tank of gas. The car was souped up, fitted with out-of-state tags, and all ready to go at a moment's notice. After today's hit, the two men would be standing pat, in the money, with gun molls swooning all over them. Without warning, two shots rang out in rapid succession. "POW...POW!" Both gunmen crumpled to the ground before they knew what hit them, their partially opened eyes stilled forever. Two unused handguns remained dormant...held by gloved lifeless hands. Each man was shot once in the back of the head at such close range that powder burns singed the hair. Blood spurted from pea-sized intrusions, forcing crimson remnants of life onto the sidewalk and forming into one massive dark-red pool. Mattie quickly snatched up his hat and coat from where Frank tossed them and headed in the opposite direction. Frankie disappeared back into the alley... making his way to Blossom Restaurant just in time for dinner. "Hiya, toots!"

The memories of yesteryear soon faded and were quickly replaced by the jovial religious commemorative celebration now going on outside, but Frankie Flowers refused to let go. "Those fucking cocksuckers never knew what hit 'em. That damn Mattie is the smartest spook I know. He pulled the old switcher-rooni on those bastards and hooked 'em in with that Stepin Fetchit routine of his...he was masterful. This bowlegged bastard in front of me had the balls to charge those cocksuckers five dollars for a front row seat to their own funerals. Mattie, I take back what I just said...you are the smartest man I know! You ought to run for president, you cocksucker, you!"

Everyone laughed at the implausibility of such a thing ever occurring. The incident in New York served as a wakeup call for Frank "Frankie Flowers" Leo, who hadn't worn a carnation since, and never again saw Signora di Domenico. She had saved his life, and was definitely his lucky charm. Within a few weeks, he too packed his bags and returned to his hometown, but not before impregnating Darla, the waitress at Blossom Restaurant, while on honeymoon in Reno. In Cleveland, Frankie found himself a nice little place with a white picket fence. He permanently settled in Little Italy with its paved red-brick streets. The house was in a family-oriented neighborhood, an ideal location to share with Darla, Monica, and his new baby. For almost fifteen years Frankie regularly sent monthly Western Union money-grams to Darla Carpenter, who never left New York. Eventually he lost contact when Darla changed jobs and moved. He asked a couple of friends to keep an eye out for her, but to this day...not a word. Staying married wasn't in the cards for Frank, who never divorced Darla... or returned to New York. *Well, that's life,* he thought to himself.

After greasing the necessary palms, Mattie was given the okay to open his after-hours spot. He was relieved, and all that remained now was to spread the word to all comers about his high-stakes gambling emporium. Frank promised Mattie he'd steer personal acquaintances his way--those who enjoyed a game with no limits. This was a real coup, allowing Mattie to concentrate on business without being muscled by rival organizations or the law. Everything was taken care of by Frankie Flowers. There was a caveat: each party was responsible for abiding by the rules as agreed upon. Before leaving, Mattie extended warm handshakes to Frankie's crew, thanking them for a wonderful afternoon. He saved his buddy's hand for last. "Nice seeing you again, you old grease ball!"

"That goes double from me, you black cocksucker!"

The two hugged one final time before Frank walked Mattie to his car. It was getting late, and based on a recent killing of a Negro folk singer just passing through the neighborhood, Little Italy was not where Mattie wanted to be after dark, regardless of his friendship with Frank Leo.

As they moved amid the celebrants, Frankie's neck craned whenever they passed a parked car, wondering if it were Mattie's. When they finally stopped at the borrowed Ford, Mattie unlocked the door, got inside the car, and rolled down the window. He started up the car just in time to hear Jimmy Dudley say: "Strike three called! The Indians win it!"

"Go tribe," said Frankie-boy, a lifelong fan since childhood.

Old Sol vanished below the horizon and was replaced by night air, flashing traffic signals, street lamps, and colorful neon lighting. The Feast of the Assumption crowd had grown since Mattie's arrival. Frankie-boy appeared stoic, but was biting his tongue to keep from laughing. "*Minghia*...Mattie, where'd this heap come from—and don't bust my balls? I know this ain't your wreck!" They both laughed simultaneously as Mattie stubbornly forced the standard shift into first gear, resulting in a strained grinding noise. "See...I knew it, ya cocksucker!"

Mattie smiled once more, then turned on the headlights and eased off the clutch as the car jerked forward before slowly rolling down Mayfield Road. Mattie dodged a couple of inebriated pedestrians while riding past packed outdoor restaurants with red-checked cloth-covered tables, bedecked with tasty-looking pasta dishes, baskets of assorted Italian bread, and more than ample supplies of red wine. Cigar smoke wafted from tobacco shops while pizza makers tossed floured dough high into the air with the greatest of ease. Eventually Mattie made a left turn onto Euclid Avenue, heading west toward East 55th Street.

With the old days still fresh in his mind, he commented aloud, "Frankie's one smart dago and he really knows his shit...always has. We're gonna make a lot of money together."

Frankie Flowers turned to his crew. "Mattie's a stand-up guy... if he were Sicilian, he'd be a made man by now. He's a good soldier, especially when you need someone covering your ass. Believe you me, Mattie's one smart spook, and he never jokes around when it comes to money. We're gonna make a ton of dough!"

(6) May 20, 1928...

On a quiet morning, three vehicles following dangerously close to each other interrupted pre-dawn serenity with loud sirens and howling tires, as they negotiated the twists and turns along Liberty Boulevard. Headlights pierced the darkness, changing direction at the whim of an ever- winding road. The speeding cars, just inches apart, roared upwards of 60 mph and were serendipitously spared accidents.

The focus in this race against time was an impatient fetus who'd decided to make his debut. It lay poised on the precipice of a world full of opportunity. The car's driver, a distinguished-looking gentleman in his early fifties, was sweating profusely in his soaked white shirt and loosened striped tie. He adjusted the rearview mirror, affording himself a better look at his pregnant passenger. Centrifugal forces had her pinned against the car's locked rear door.

"Hold on, baby...we're almost there," said the man while clicking the turn signal to the down position. The cars slowed drastically before exiting at East Boulevard and onto Parkwood Drive just minutes from their destination. Glenville Hospital was Jewish, and staffed in part by a sparse sprinkling of Negro doctors and nurses.

The vehicles came to a screeching halt in front of the emergency room entrance, barely avoiding one another. Five ruddy-complexioned police officers jumped from their cars and ran over to the 1928 Chevrolet sedan just as the driver unlocked his doors.

After assessing the situation, Sergeant Dale Murphy took charge. "We'll take it from here, Councilman!" He and his men carefully placed the pregnant colored woman onto a stretcher, then by-passed the waiting room, heading directly for the maternity ward on the second floor.

Councilman Thomas W. Fleming, a Republican, was the first-ever Negro elected to Cleveland's city council. While standing alongside the car, he reached into his pocket and pulled out a white handkerchief, embroidered with navy blue initials: TWF. "Ooooh weeeh! What a ride!" he chortled, wiping his brow until the hanky dripped with perspiration. After requesting assistance, his female constituent, who lived in the infamous Roaring Third District of Cleveland, had finally made it to the hospital. Thanks to Councilman Fleming, who was able to call in a favor owed him by a District Police Commander, who bypassed red tape and officially ordered the two-vehicle escort. It was Fleming who now owed the District Commander a favor. It was just the price of doing business.

(7) Bessie...

The young woman's name was Bessie Mae Purifoy. She was a migrant from New Orleans, Louisiana, having arrived in Cleveland almost eight months ago. For reasons of her own, she wanted her child born in a hospital with Negro doctors. This was her second pregnancy in two years. Her first occurred while living in the family shotgun house she shared with siblings. The home was located on Simpson Street in the heart of the lower Ninth Ward. It was bounded on the east by a busy railroad crossing. After being brought to term, her fraternal twins were stillborn. Their undetermined deaths were so unexpected that the babies hadn't been baptized or given birth names. They were buried as baby boy and baby girl Purifoy. A despondent Bessie Mae promised herself she would rather die than face such another heartbreaking loss. Exactly eighteen months after their deaths, on a day filled with angst, a name was revealed to Bessie during a dream. She slipped from underneath the covers, careful not to awaken her common-law husband. Bessie sank to her knees and clasped her hands together.

"This dream is a sign from the Almighty," she whispered, "another opportunity!" Bessie lay back down and snuggled into the arms of Frederick Douglass Purifoy, the man she loved. "Slim," as Bessie called him, and she loved each other deeply although they weren't officially married in the eyes of the state. The couple kissed passionately and began to make love. In the morning they awakened still in each other's embrace. Bessie placed her palms on the sides of Slim's face. "No matter what happens, Slim...know in your heart I love you and always will."

He kissed her forehead, whispering, "I love you too, Bessie... for just as long as we live!"

In a matter of days, a hopeful Bessie Mae gathered a few belongings and said goodbye to her brothers and sisters. They were lined up just outside the house from youngest to oldest. She embraced each of them separately with such passion that they seemed to meld together as one.

"I'm really gonna miss you, Charlie. When I get settled...you be sure and write me." Her eyes had already begun to water as she wrapped her arms around Lilly Ann. "I love you so much, sister. I'll be thinking of you every day, I promise." Nanny was a year older than Bessie Mae. "I love you big sister." Bessie Mae was fighting back the tears by the time she reached her oldest brother. "Georgie...you're the man of the house, and It's up to you to take care of the young ones. I love you so much!"

A large red bus was right on schedule and stopped in front of their shotgun house and opened its door. It was all Bessie could do to tear herself away from Georgie. Using both hands, she handed her carpet bag to the friendly, rosy-cheeked driver. He tagged and tossed the bag into the luggage compartment, handing her a perforated yellow claim check. The Trailways bus was heading for Nashville, where Bessie Mae would catch the L&N train. Bessie Mae boarded the coach, bypassing the "whites only" seating and finding an empty seat toward the back of the bus. She blew kisses to the family from her window and touched her heart upon seeing a tearful Georgie standing alongside the parched dirt road. As the bus began to move, the children tried to keep up. They walked faster and faster, while simultaneously waving goodbye. As the bus shifted gears and gained momentum, the children broke ranks and began running as fast as they could. Soon they were obscured by billowing clouds of dust. When the Purifoy children faded from view, Bessie's heart and soul were forever linked by blood, along with loving memories that could be revisited whenever she felt the need.

Upon leaving the bus in Tennessee, Bessie walked into Nashville's Union Station Railroad Terminal, fully prepared to move forward with her life. After asking directions from a porter, young Miss Purifoy waited her turn in line, then went over to the ticket agent spreading cash and assorted change onto the counter. She requested passage wherever her meager funds could take her. Bessie was heading north, and not a minute too soon.

She arrived in Cleveland, Ohio during September on an unusually hot afternoon. Not surprisingly, the near record-breaking temperature wasn't quite what she expected, to say the least. The humidity was similar to New Orleans, and she assumed the warm waters of the lake were the cause. Since her destination was randomly selected and predicated on funds, she didn't fret--how could she question providence? Bessie was about to become a Clevelander, but was certainly aware that New Orleans would forever be her home.

She was a congenial likable young woman in her twenty-second year of life. Her intelligence, wit and easygoing manner endeared her to most people. Bessie wasn't smart in the traditional sense, even though she had completed her graduation requirements at Gailor Industrial School when she was only sixteen. Calling her smart overlooked two important qualities she had possessed since birth: overachievement and determination.

Hours of traveling and listening to small talk from gossipy fellow passengers had taken a toll on her; finally the journey was mercifully nearing its end. Bessie felt relieved when the stodgy Pullman coach rattled into Terminal Tower station in downtown Cleveland. She'd had her fill of the hot sweltering segregated car with its crying babies and children playing tag along the restricting aisles. After arriving inside the terminal, she followed those small silhouetted pointing fingers all the way to baggage claim. She gave her perforated ticket stub to a short stocky redcap who, after a few minutes of searching, returned with her large bag.

"Here you go, miss," he said, while tipping his hat and welcoming her to Cleveland. "I hope ya'll enjoy your stay."

Bessie smiled, wondering how many times a day he uttered his prepared greeting. She thanked the porter by giving him a ten-cent tip. It was a bit excessive, to be sure, considering two Hershey bars could be had for the same price. She reckoned he deserved it. Bessie made certain her appearance was in order by adjusting her clothing prior to leaving baggage claim. Special notice was paid to those hidden safety pins securing her hem. Once she felt complete, she took in a long deep breath of fresh air and grabbed hold of the bulky carpet bag. After a brief walk she joined the surge of people walking up the inclined narrow concourse. Gradually the granite floor widened and leveled off after passing by Higbee's Department Store. Just to her left was a bank of polished brass/glass entry doors. The bright sun mesmerized onlookers like the great Houdini's magic act. After stepping outside into the afternoon air, Bessie allowed herself to be jostled by the passing crowd in exchange for a moment of basking in the invigorating sun.

It was 4:00 p.m., the beginning of rush hour on a gorgeous Friday afternoon. Cleveland Electric Railway cars were as thick as thieves and lined Public Square. The yellow transit cars with maroon detailing patiently waited an opportunity to travel the gleaming sun-drenched rails. The long winding tentacles of ties and tracks touched each corner of the city. Conductors unloaded passengers before boarding the new, with the precision of marching soldiers. They accepted fares, made change, punched transfers, and even alerted riders to closing doors with a toot of their whistles. Taxicabs and automobiles circled the square, passing the Old Stone Church and Soldiers & Sailors Monument like carousel rides in a never-ending procession.

Poor Bessie Mae must have inquired of at least thirty colored passersby where she could find a room to let. A young lady about her own age referred her to the Phillis Wheatley Association (PWA). She explained the center was for Negro women and specialized in housing assistance, employment, and other services for young girls. Cleveland lawyer Jane Edna Hunter founded the organization and named it after a famous Negro poetess. Most people she'd spoken with during her first few hours in Cleveland were quite friendly...especially those from the south. After jotting down directions to the PWA, she decided to buy a weekly colored newspaper. It was the *Cleveland Call and Post*...she hoped it would aid in her search for a full-time situation, or "employment," as it was called in the north. The newspaper was full of articles pertaining to coloreds living in America. Politics, sports, entertainment, and news from across the nation was good copy...and interesting reading. This week's *Call Post*, as the paper was called, included the Negro League World Series highlights. Buck O'Neil of the Kansas City Monarchs and Buck Leonard of the Homestead Grays in silver gelatin black-and-white prints graced the front page, whose headlines screamed: "MONARCHS SWEEP GRAYS IN FOUR."

Bessie wasn't tired, but seemed to be feeling the residual effects of being cramped up during the long train ride. She was completely unaware of a healthy fetus growing inside her. Bessie Mae decided to stretch her legs and began walking the six miles to PWA. Being a country girl, she enjoyed being in the fresh air and hoped to take in some of the sights on this sun-kissed day. She started her journey on Public Square, working her way eastward via Euclid Avenue. The streets were packed with people, each scurrying about like ants with their own agendas, hopes, and aspirations. While strolling along the avenue, Bessie imagined shopping in every store, spending lavishly at the May Company and Bailey's just past Ontario Street. She was flabbergasted by the Hippodrome Theater's vastness, which extended between Euclid and Prospect Avenues near East Ninth Street. They featured a retrospective of the late silver screen icon Rudolph Valentino... *How exciting!* she thought. Bessie couldn't help pressing her nose against the windows of high-end stores...department stores like Taylor's, Halle Brothers, and Sterling Linder Davis routinely displayed the latest styles from New York, Paris, and Rome.

Walking through the theatre district at East 14th Street was amazing with its flashing marquees, during daylight no less. Nickelodeons featured plays and movies she'd never even heard of before. She took time to glance at each of the publicity stills of coming attractions and was awestruck. Cleveland's millionaire's row reminded her of what Camelot must have been like. She marveled while passing the grandiose mansions whose touring cars were parked in circular drives--carriages awaiting the beck and call of imagined royalty prompted thoughts of England's kings and queens. Uniformed Negro chauffeurs clad in brass-buttoned tunics, jodhpurs laced to the knee, khaki puttees, and contrasting dark brown spit-shined shoes busied themselves polishing Rolls Royce, Packard, and LaSalle automobiles. For a lucky few, she thought, "Life is just a bowl of cherries"--words made famous by lyricist Lew Brown, from a song of the same name.

As she continued her jaunt eastward, the tinsel and skyscrapers became more distant with every step. Bessie's comfort level, however, rose as she nodded and smiled whenever she saw a person of color. It was occurring more and more often. The neatly trimmed manicured lawns and well-maintained city blocks downtown began to fade and soon were replaced by tall weedy fields strewn with broken glass. With directions still in hand she continued walking eastward, regularly checking her notations. Bessie thought about all she had seen today, and calm swept her entire body. She felt very special, like a beautiful princess in a fairy tale. *Life is such a blessing, full of wonderment that nourishes my soul like water and sunshine.* The future was unfolding before her eyes. She felt encouraged...positive that her decision to travel north had been the correct one.

After a while the glitz and glitter had all but disappeared, and Bessie's steps began to take their toll. The tight shoes caused her feet to swell and she paused momentarily along the way to alleviate their discomfort. She sat the carpet bag on the sidewalk and rested her left hand against a sturdy tree for support. It wasn't easy, but she managed to free one shoe while continuing to maintain her balance. Bessie wiggled her grateful toes and massaged her foot from front to back, then top to bottom. She repeated the process several times. "Gracious sakes alive...this feels so good!"

Suddenly the young woman felt a crushing body blow that caused her to black out. She somersaulted high into the air like a Raggedy Ann doll. Bessie Mae had been blindsided from behind and was falling rapidly toward the ground. An awkward landing caused her to smash headfirst onto an unforgiving concrete sidewalk. After a while she regained consciousness but felt warm blood running across her eye and alongside her face. A small group of women accompanied by a couple of runny-nosed children looked down at her. Their curious faces seemed relieved that she was still alive. As the gathering grew larger, it spread apart as a gentleman maneuvered his way toward the front.

The light-brown-skinned Negro wore a nicely tailored business suit and quickly made a beeline toward Bessie. He knelt beside her and placed his handkerchief on a very nasty gash. He pressed firmly to stop the bleeding. Still dizzy, Bessie Mae focused in on the letters...TWF. She had never seen a colored man--or any man, for that matter--with initials sewn directly into his hanky. In a clearly educated voice and a northern accent, he asked, "What happened, miss?"

She tried hard to make sense of the question, but was still dazed. "I...I don't know...I can't remember. Where's my bag? Someone's taken my bag!" Bessie caught a glimpse of her own blood on the handkerchief and started to panic. "All my things were inside!" Her voice was rapidly elevating.

"Calm down...I'm Councilman Tom Fleming...I want to help you, so please...easy does it, young lady. Tell me your name?"

Bessie struggled to sit up, using her hands for assistance. Her palms ached all over and were terribly bruised. "Stay put, miss... please...I insist." With his blood-soaked hanky still pressed against her head, he continued, "You've got a nasty wound there, young miss...it's just above your brow. Your hands probably saved you from losing an eye--they helped to break your fall. Tell me exactly what happened."

From somewhere within the still-expanding crowd came the robust voice of a woman. "Beg pardon...excuse me...excuse me... beg pardon!" As she meandered forward, the assemblage displaced like water. The elderly woman's stout body ambled from side to side, her gait steady and sure. When she was face to face with the well-dressed man, she didn't mince words. "I seent da whole thang, Councilman Flemin'...dem two young mens knocked dat lady high in da air like uh burlap sack full uh spuds. Den she tumbled down to the ground and banged her head on da concrete. She was powerful hurt! Den dey took off runnin' down yonda," she pointed toward Central Avenue, "like uh bat outta hell, wid dat lady's carpet bag in tow. I told ya I seent da whole thang!"

Councilman Fleming always treated his constituents with the utmost respect. "May I have your name, mother?"

"My name is Lucille Green, and I'm ninety-three years old... folks 'round here jus' call me Big Momma." The councilman wrote down her pertinent information for future reference. Later he would make sure his police contacts received a copy of her account. He hoped it would help in their investigation.

Tom Fleming took hold of the lady's hand and shook it gently. "Thanks so much for your assistance, Big Momma...you're a credit to the neighborhood and to the Negro race." The elderly woman stood a little taller while beaming her satisfaction. A few of the neighborhood boys helped Bessie Mae to her feet and escorted her to Councilman Fleming's automobile. Once she was situated, he started his car and drove to the doctor's office a few blocks away. Twenty stitches later, Bessie's wound was closed; soon she would be on the mend.

"Doctor Champion, you're an artist...great job! Please send the bill to my office, and my secretary will cut you a check."

Councilman Fleming extended his elbow to Bessie and they walked through the door. They went down the brick steps and along the sidewalk to his Chevy. The Phillis Wheatley Association was a stone's throw from the doctor's office on East 44th and Cedar Avenue. When they arrived, Bessie was officially registered by an intake specialist...the process lasted about an hour. She was now a resident of the Phillis Wheatley Association.

Doctor Champion had given Bessie medication to ease the pain. Her head wound still throbbed but the pain had greatly dissipated. She was feeling much better...even her dizziness had subsided. "Thanks, Councilman Fleming, for all of your help...I really appreciate what you did."

"Think nothing of it, Bessie Mae; it was all in a day's work. Here's my business card, Miss Purifoy--if you ever need any help, don't hesitate to call me."

Mr. Fleming shook her hand and left. Bessie Mae's faculties

were almost back to normal. She realized what happened today was child's play compared to some events she'd witnessed back in New Orleans. Today's occurrences served only to make her more determined than ever to accomplish her goals. Nothing was going to stop her...especially not a couple of nappy-headed, thieving, snatch and grab hooligans! She may have been young...but she learned long ago that obstacles weren't barriers--they were guideposts.

Ella Becton, an employee of PWA, escorted Bessie Mae to a more than adequate room similar to a college dorm. Two twin beds, two dressers, a desk with two chairs and a large window overlooking Cedar Avenue...it was perfect. She shared the space with another newcomer, Gloria Jean Williams, from Xenia, a small town in southern Ohio. She arrived a few hours before Bessie, making her senior roommate. Gloria Jean was a talkative extrovert and always got right to the point. She wasn't shy in the least.

"Bessie...I thought you said it took over twelve hours to get to Cleveland?"

Bessie was puzzled by the question. "I sure did, give or take a few minutes either way. Why do you ask?" responded Bessie.

"I know you were banged up pretty good today. But I'm wondering why your hair looks none the worse for wear. Other than some dirt from your fall, it looks like it was just done...who fixes it for you?"

Bessie used her bandaged palm to test the bounce. "I had the opportunity to fix it up a little while at Doctor Champion's office. After all that's happened to me today, I'm sure my hair looks terrible. But truthfully speaking, I do it myself."

"Girl, don't you play with me! It looks like you just left the beauty shop. Let me ask you a question, Bessie Mae...how much to do mine?"

"I'll tell you what, Gloria...."

The woman stopped her in mid-sentence. "Just call me Gjay... like the rest of my friends."

"Well, Gjay, let me do it first and we'll figure out a fair price later!"

"Sounds good to me, girl--when can you get started?"

"I'll have to replace some things that were stolen."

"Girl...not to worry, we can solve that problem in the morning. I saw a real nice beauty supply store...it's close. Girl, my hair can't wait another minute; it needs help now. Hell, I need help!"

With her spirit rejuvenated, Bessie Mae looked forward to visiting the beauty supply store and getting her life back on track in spite of all that happened today.

Bessie Mae thought about her home town. There were some in New Orleans who still practiced the old ways of their African ancestors. She trusted her recent difficulties would soon be resolved. She never told Slim, but a few days before moving to Cleveland, Bessie Mae had been warned of a hex on her family. Cleopatra Wisdom, a highly esteemed practitioner of spiritual remedies, warned Bessie of the spell. According to the fifty-year-old Wisdom, someone wanted Bessie's whole family eliminated without mercy.

"Bessie Mae...I believe this curse includes any future offspring. That surely would explain why your twins were stillborn." Miss Cleo, as Cleopatra was known professionally, encouraged Bessie to leave Louisiana as soon as possible. "Honey, you need to put down some new roots, a place with a change of seasons. With you safely somewhere else, it'll give me time to conjure a stronger counter spell. Bessie Mae Purifoy...I need to lift the curse as soon as possible. We're up against a wicked and powerful foe. Someone has forgotten the true dictates of real voodoo, opting instead for an evil path. It's imperative you follow my directions exactly. In our universe, good magic always trumps the power of evil spells.

You must do whatever I ask in a forthright manner without hesitation or any misgivings.

"Now, Bessie, this is important...wherever you decide to move, send me a penny postcard signed Bessie B. Goode, and I'll understand. Bessie Mae, you'd better shake some of them cobwebs from your head, because this ain't a game, and we're in extreme danger. This is a matter of life and death for us both. Are you willing to stay the course so we can defeat whatever we're up against?"

Bessie Mae answered without batting an eyelash, "I can, and we will! Miss Cleo, you've never steered me wrong before. I may be weary, but let me assure you...I'm not about to falter now, because my family's whole future is at stake!"

"Well, you've certainly got the right attitude, so let's get this show on the road."

(8) Complications...

Meanwhile, back at Glenville Hospital, Sergeant Murphy led the way. Bessie Mae was rushed to the second-floor maternity ward without a minute to spare. Titus Champion, a colored physician, along with midwife Arnetta Houston patiently awaited Bessie Mae's arrival. Once the officers rolled her into maternity, she was immediately placed on a metal-framed bed with rubberized white sheeting. The baby was due any moment. Doctor Champion decided not to sedate, opting instead to let nature take its course. The attendees wanted to ease any discomfort by having her try the latest experimental breathing exercises. When a tiny foot appeared between Bessie's legs, all bets were off.

The midwife sprang into action. "It's a breech birth." she whispered, trying not to cause undue alarm or stress to the patient. Doctor Champion grabbed a pair of forceps from the instruments tray to help with the delivery. The experienced midwife cautioned him, "Doctor Champion...with all due respect, let's not turn to these just yet. Why not let her contractions and gravity aid in the baby's delivery? I've handled more breech births than I care to remember...I know exactly what I'm doing. So put those forceps away for now. We don't even have time to alert hospital staff." The midwife had a plan. "Bring Sergeant Murphy and his officers in here right now!"

"Why?"

"Doctor this child's life is in peril, and it's depending upon decisive action. Please hurry and don't dally...time's wasting!"

Reluctantly the doctor left the delivery room and hurried to get the officers. Arnettta used this time wisely by soothing Bessie and explaining what to do.

"Bessie Mae, the baby needs our help. The best thing you can do now is try to relax. Everything's gonna be just fine." The midwife spoke in a calm and reassuring manner. "Trust me, honey... I've done this many times before, and you're in capable hands. You're having a breech birth, Bessie. It simply means the baby is coming out feet first instead of leading with its head."

Bessie had been using every epithet she could imagine to describe the baby's father. She quieted down only after listening to Arnetta. Bessie realized if the baby were to survive, she'd have to follow the midwife's instructions. She surely didn't want a repeat of what had happened to her twins.

"Miss Purifoy, there's always complications associated with full-term breech births. Sometimes things can-- and will go awry. Problems from loss of oxygen, brain damage, or possibly even hip displacement are only a few of the concerns. I need you to concentrate fully on the job at hand."

At that very moment, Doctor Champion burst through the swinging doors along with Sergeant Murphy and his men. They quickly gathered around the midwife and gave her their undivided attention. After explaining the situation, Arnetta informed each officer of his precise role.

"Gentlemen, we're going to carefully lift the patient off the bed and rotate her in such a manner that will allow her to face downward. I want her on hands and knees, gentlemen. This child is going to enter the world in the same manner as with mammals in the wilds ...on all fours!

"Our main concerns are: (1) Hold her steady and (2) Keep her relaxed. Now let's be alert and try not to make any unexpected or sudden moves. We'll function like a highly synchronized machine. Our group actions will be independent, simultaneous, and well-coordinated. We'll maintain discipline during the entire process of performing our tasks. The goal is to deliver a healthy baby without causing any undue harm!"

The midwife gently guided each officer by his arm, making sure he was positioned perfectly. "I want you and you up front. You'll both be controlling Bessie's back and shoulders. Understood?" They nodded in the affirmative. "You two officers will secure her thighs and buttocks, making sure her legs stay apart and don't squeeze the baby. Sergeant Murphy, I want you to be my rover...you'll fill in wherever needed. Doctor Champion and I will manually manuever Bessie's torso."

It was time to get started. Nervousness and second-guessing were not options. Everyone was to follow the midwife's instructions to the letter. "Now, gentlemen--on the count of three we will lift...turn over...rotate...and place the patient on her hands and knees. ONE...TWO...THREE...!" Bessie Mae clenched her teeth, trying her best to fully cooperate. The patient's moans were muffled but under control. Under the circumstances she was doing remarkably well. Officer Callahan sneezed suddenly as everyone froze in place...like a game of *Simple Simon Says*. "Easy does it, gentlemen...steady—just a little further and she'll be in position. Slowly...easy does it... okay...put her knees in place... slowly...slowly...and now the hands. Sergeant Murphy, give them some help over there...perfect... perfect...GREAT! We're all set... thanks, gentlemen! You were all great. Officer Callahan, you'd better take some Vitamins for that cough," joked the midwife. There was a collective sigh of relief in the delivery room.

Sergeant Murphy asked, "May we observe, Miss Houston?"

"What do you say, Doctor Champion?"

"I don't see why not...we couldn't have gotten this far without them."

The doctor passed out surgical masks to the officers. "Now, gentlemen...please give us a little elbow room so we can deliver this baby!" With surgical masks in place, the officers resembled cartoon characters with wide balloon-sized eyes.

Councilman Fleming was detained on the first floor, supplying clerical staff with Bessie's personal information. As soon as he finished, he made a mad dash to the maternity ward, arriving shortly after delivery. "Councilman Fleming, the mother is doing just fine, and so is the baby. It's a healthy baby boy. He weighs seven pounds, three ounces, and has all his fingers and toes. The baby's being cleaned up as we speak. If you hurry, you can view the newborn in the nursery ward before he goes for testing."

The councilman had endured a long morning and was finally able to relax. All was well with mother and son. Soon baby boy Purifoy was facing center stage at the viewing window. The newborn's eyes were shut and his wrinkled skin was wrapped in a soft light blue blanket. For those who labored during the breech birth...it was now time to observe their handiwork. A new life had just come into the world. The five tough burly officers may have helped save the day. But after seeing the baby for the first time, they proved to be softies. They wore their hats backwards while pressing their faces against the viewing window. The veteran crime fighters were proud as peacocks and made unusual gurgling noises accompanied by funny expressions. Their antics were directed toward a beautiful baby boy. May 20th would hold a special place in the hearts of the doting men in blue.

Pursuant to hospital rules, Bessie was confined to a wheelchair and was rolled into the nursery by an attendant. She slipped in unnoticed and was placed between the officers. They were still busy expressing themselves with funny faces and gurgling sounds. "Gooo gooo gaah gaah!" "Whad a coootey pie." "Widdy widdle babesby!"

Bessie was reminded of the antics of Keystone Kops from the silent movies era. She was extremely grateful to each of the men and didn't hesitate in letting them know. The happy mother of the baby boy listened as Sergeant Dale Murphy spoke for the men. "We're so happy to have been of service, Miss Purifoy."

"Today I consider each of you honorary fathers to my son."

The men were pleased. "Thank you for giving us the opportunity to help with the delivery. May God bless and keep you both forever in his arms! Now, miss...if you don't need us anymore...we'll be on our way." The officers took a last look at the baby, then loudly laughed along the quiet hallways to the dismay of staff and clinicians.

Councilman Fleming was pleased at the outcome. He stood behind Bessie's chair gently rubbing her back. "It's a brand-new healthy baby boy!"

"Yes he is, Councilman, a healthy boy."

"Have you decided what to call him, Bessie Mae?"

She smiled before responding. Her pride was evident even seated in the wheelchair. "His name is TaNellie!" she said proudly.

"TaNellie--what an interesting name...I don't think I've ever heard it before. Two questions, Bessie...how'd you come up with his name, and what does it mean?"

She paused a few seconds. "I didn't come up with it, Councilman. One night it actually came to me in a dream. I'm not really sure about the meaning. I'd like to think of it as another chance... maybe an opportunity! That's it, Councilman Fleming...TaNellie simply means another opportunity at life!"

Bessie was finally a mother, a privilege she'd sought a long time. Unfortunately for Bessie, the Phillis Wheatley Association had no accommodations for babies. It was a rule she had known about since coming to the PWA. Bessie Mae would have thirty days to make other arrangements or be asked to leave. She knew things would work out.

As soon as she was able, Bessie Mae went to the corner store for a *Call Post* newspaper. She desperately wanted to continue her search for employment. While leafing through the weekly paper, an article caught her eye. In New Orleans there had been a tragic accident. A drunken driver plowed past flashing red warning lights and a lowered railroad crossing gate at the Simpson Street crossing. He was oblivious to the lights and bells and smashed headlong into an oil tanker car at a high rate of speed. Railroad cars in the slow caravan derailed...precariously stacking atop each other like dominoes. They caused a spectacular pyre, showering burning fuel and twisted metal wreckage onto pedestrians and homes alike. Dozens of people were killed or injured in the lower Ninth Ward. The blazing inferno lasted days before authorities were able to put it out. When the smoke cleared, twenty-two people were dead. The deceased were all listed alphabetically in the paper. Bessie carefully guided her finger along the names, then crumpled to the ground. Her entire family was listed among the deceased. Bessie Mae was inconsolable. A concerned store owner hurried outside and was helpless as she sat on the ground...cradling her head in the palms of her hands. He enlisted the help of a young boy to run to the PWA for help.

When Bessie reached her room, she couldn't believe what had transpired. She read the article twice more, but events remained constant. She wondered why her name appeared among the dead. It was obviously a mistake made in reporting. Perhaps it might benefit her in the long run. She pondered what to do. Quite naturally, the horrific news saddened her. But she was still frightened and wondered if the hex might have been responsible for what happened. It seemed like only yesterday that she had said goodbye to her family. According to the newspaper, the accident occurred on May 20, 1928...the day of her son's birth.

Bessie's immediate reaction was to inform the authorities. Her heart was heavy and she mourned for all the souls lost in the tragedy. Surely nobody deserved such a fate. Her siblings ranged in ages from ten years old to twenty-five-year-old Georgie. Bessie decided not to go back to New Orleans. She hadn't talked with Miss Cleo since the day she left town. Bessie hoped her friend was working harder than ever to make headway and lift the spell before more people died. Her mind was flooded with so many thoughts. She remembered losing her parents...it was their final wish for the children to inherit the home. Silas and Elizabeth Goode, (pronounced Gŭd) died after a machine malfunctioned at the cotton gin where they worked. Fortunately, insurance payments were up to date and they were able to use the funds to pay off the home. The remaining money provided a funeral for their parents.

In the years following Bessie Mae's move to Cleveland she severed her ties connecting her to Louisiana, including Slim, the love of her life. He was a Creole's son and they adored one another. She missed him and wondered if he would ever get to see his son. She hoped her siblings were in a better place. All she had now were memories of what once was. Bessie was positive that nothing remained of the home, and felt she shouldn't return. She hoped after seeing her name listed as deceased...it would deter those persons who cast the evil spell. Bessie cried for weeks after the tragedy and wondered if she'd ever know why. She'd tried to run from the curse to no avail. The evildoers were winning, for the time being. Bessie continued blaming herself, although she knew in her heart this was a time to be strong and fight the spell.

(9) Marta de LaCosta...

By current standards, Marta de LaCosta was arguably one of the most beautiful women in the world. Every attribute society esteems was possessed by the lovely woman. Confidentially, she secretly loathed having one brown and one grey eye. She was an enchantress whose exotic good looks were either envied or admired. She held no office or title, and was neither royalty nor privileged, yet she caused doors to open as if by magic. She was from Barcelona and was recognizable as Hollywood's most revered stars. Marta was heir to the world and frequented only the most extravagant parties. Even aristocracy took notice when in her presence. She was thought to be a blueblood of the highest order and was often treated like royalty. Marta was steadfastly grounded, but did agree her looks were a blessing.

Pike's Peak Polo Club, just outside Louisville, was a favorite haunt when passing time, especially during the month of May. Marta was seated at her customary table sharing drinks and conversation with Bradford and Simone Michaels. During a lull in repartee, Bradford's wife reached across the table, stunning Marta. She placed her fingertip onto the young woman's lips. Astonishment inhibited Marta from questioning Simone's motives. Almost immediately she excused herself from the table and headed over to the bar. Feeling quite uncomfortable with what had happened, she took a seat.

"Miss de LaCosta, the usual?"

"Please, Charles." She slowly sipped the dirty Cajun martini, savoring its duality of hot spices and cool liquid. She smiled at Charles. "This was delicious as the preceding three." Marta removed the jalapeño olives and rapidly finished off the cocktail. Then, ritualistically, she tossed each olive into her mouth one by one, enjoying every morsel. Marta was no prude...and was well aware that the Michaels had been hitting on her for quite some time--months, in fact. The husband and wife team were in the tobacco industry and filthy rich...with minds to match.

The concerned bartender cautiously inquired, "Are you all right, Miss de LaCosta?"

"I'm fine, Charles...nothing I can't handle...another for the road, please."

The experienced barman quickly obliged, using only half the spirits. He placed the drink on a napkin and slid it toward her. "The last martini's on me, Miss de LaCosta...please enjoy!"

She tipped him handsomely and asked for her car to be brought around. As she stood up, she glanced over her left shoulder at the Michaels and gave them a cursory wave with a half-assed smile. Marta never liked being taken advantage of by anyone without her permission. She felt Simone's actions were vulgar and highly insulting. "Who does she think she is?" Simone's ill-timed slight would have to be avenged. The looming question was...how?

Marta reminisced about her childhood in Barcelona. She was without brothers or sisters, and fought constantly just to be respected. There was one little boy in particular--Raul was his name. He was tougher, older, bigger, stronger, and teased her without mercy. Raul purposely sought her out on a daily basis, always yelling "TUERTO, TUERTO, TUERTO!" It meant "cross-eyed," but was more hurtful than just saying Marta's eyes were different colors. After months of relentless bullying, her mind was made up: "ENOUGH!"

After school, Marta took a shortcut hoping to avoid the boy. El bosques cut ten minutes from her walk home. Halfway into the thicket she happened upon someone lying beneath an elm, using libros--or books--for a pillow. She tiptoed nearer...it was Raul, on his back and soundly sleeping. He must have skipped school because she hadn't been confronted by him all day. She started to flee then noticed some dead branches on the ground. Quietly she cleared them aside with her foot while keeping an eye out for Raul, who continued napping. She looked them over and picked a dagger-shaped limb with a long sharp point. Shrewdly she rotated her body 360 degrees, scanning the entire woods. They were alone. Marta tested the pointed edge by jabbing it into her palm, drawing blood. She was positive it would put out his eye. Marta formulated a plan and was ready to implement it. The young girl boldly approached her nemesis with one thought in mind. A few steps more and she would be in position. Marta straddled the unsuspecting boy. With lips tightly pursed she clutched the wooden dagger in both hands, raising it as high as she could. And without hesitation she simultaneously fell to her knees as she plunged her arms downward toward the target. The sharp point sank deep, nearly six inches, making a scrunching sound as it bore through the surface layer. Trembling, Marta let go of the wooden dagger. She had missed on purpose. Unsettled dirt landed on Raul's face waking him. For a few terror-filled moments he stared directly into Marta's menacing grey and brown eyes. Lying amongst loose sticks, debris, and leaves, Raul quickly scooted backwards, using his heels to gain traction. He was crying and hollering uncontrollably. Finally pushing Marta aside, he scrambled to his feet, grabbing his books in the process. Thankful just to be alive, Raul took off running as fast as he could, tripping several times. He kept looking back, expecting a demonic girl wielding a huge gleaming knife. Raul didn't tell his parents or school officials about the incident. During the next few weeks, and without prodding, Raul matured into a very well-behaved little boy. He was a model student who never bullied Marta--or anyone else, for that matter.

(10) Derby Day...

In Derby City, this week was the busiest time of year. All eyes are poised on Louisville for the 80th running of the world famous Kentucky Derby. According to the local Chamber of Commerce, millions of dollars were funneled into the city each May.

Marta was totally prepared for Derby Day, having already purchased the perfect hat. She found it by accident in Barcelona and couldn't wait to show it off. For the past few weeks Simone Michaels had left numerous messages, but Marta had yet to return any of her calls. Since the Pike's Peak Polo Club incident, Marta had busied herself with other interests. Logic suggested that she has moved on. With the Derby just a few days away, Marta opted for a quiet dinner at the Polo Club. She drove up to the entrance just behind a white Rolls Royce Silver Cloud. A small crowd had gathered around the car. Two men exited as onlookers took photos with Brownie cameras held steady. All the hoopla was over a very special guest: Joe Louis, Heavyweight Champion of the World. He loved the Derby and was a frequent visitor to the city even in the off season. Segregation was alive and well in Kentucky, but Pike's Peak Board of Directors granted Joe honorary membership status, and he was always welcomed. Members loved hearing his stories and enjoyed rubbing elbows with the Brown Bomber. Marta met the champ while at a film festival in Monte Carlo two years ago. He was a modest man—rather shy—but posed for pictures at the drop of a hat and never denied a request for an autograph.

She invited the honorary members to join her table. Once comfortably situated, Marta glanced around the room and noticed Simone sitting alone... intently staring in her direction. The young woman nodded her head while continuing her conversation with Louis and his guest.

"Joe, I haven't seen you since Monte Carlo. It was really a pleasure meeting you...I trust you had a pleasant stay."

Joe sipped his club soda with lime. "Monte Carlo is a beautiful place, and I left lots of cash for the casinos to remember me by! It was well worth it, though...I had a wonderful time."

"Do you remember meeting me?" she asked modestly.

"How could I forget? My wife's name is Marva, and yours is Marta, right?"

"Yes it is, Joe!"

"Word association...it's how I remembered. I must admit I never thought I'd see you again, but I do remember. Let me introduce my golfing partner. We just call him Tee because he plays golf like nobody's business."

The two shook hands. "It's nice to meet you, Tee."

"It's a pleasure meeting you as well, Marta."

The threesome enjoyed dinner while talking up a storm. Simone continued her vigil... champing at the bit to be included. She was prepared to do anything to meet Joe Louis.

Joe, who earned his living exploiting the weaknesses of opponents, commented, "Marta... do you know the woman who keeps looking over here? She may be a boxing fan, but I don't think she's interested in me."

Marta glanced up from the rim of her martini. "Her name is Simone...a very rich woman who thinks there is nothing she can't buy."

Tee informed Joe that he was leaving for the restroom. He didn't dare use the facilities in the club, choosing instead the outhouse used by Negro employees. It was located some forty yards behind the club. The still night was black as pitch and the crescent moon was the only illumination. Twenty minutes later, after checking on Joe's car and driver, Tee was again seated at the dining table.

"Marta, what's the skinny on the lady who keeps staring over here?" he asked. Marta checked her surroundings before speaking. "Keep this under your hats, gentlemen, but I think she needs to be brought down a peg or two. Her husband is loaded and she thinks it gives her certain rights!"

Joe left the table for the outhouse. Tee used the opportunity to walk over to Simone and introduced himself. The golfer returned after a brief interlude while Simone inexplicably rushed from the club. "What on earth did you say to her? Marta said jokingly.

"Nothing much...I just mentioned Joe was on his way to the Rolls Royce and would be waiting in the back seat."

"Oooohh...what a devilish thing to do...I'm impressed!"

"I already told Squirt, Joe's driver, to expect company. He's the spitting image of Louis... maybe even a little bigger."

"Tee...you're such an imp!"

A few minutes later Joe returned to settle his bill. Both men walked Marta to her car, which was parked directly behind the Rolls. The pristine white Silver Cloud glowed beneath the silvery moon's reflection. As they approached, slurping sounds intermingled with chirping crickets in the night air. With the windows lowered halfway, an inquisitive Marta looked inside. An aroused Simone glanced up but continued ingesting the milky white load as the glistening black cock pulsated. Simone ceased for a moment, swallowing hard, before catching her breath.

"No, Marta, your eyes aren't playing tricks, and you needn't be envious. I am definitely getting it on with Joe Louis!"

The young woman smiled. "Envious? Not at all, Simone--what

you choose to do with your own lips is of little concern to me. I do think you might be barking up the wrong tree, however. You do have quite a mouthful!"

Marta pulled her escorts into view. "This is Joe Louis," she said, rather blasé. "You're giving felatio to his chauffeur, SQUIRT. I'm sure by now you know just how he got his name! Before I leave, Simone...I'd like to give you a bit of friendly advice. For a very wealthy woman... you're way too common!"

Marta chuckled aloud while getting into her car. She rolled down the window and asked, "Tee...what exactly did you say to get her into the back seat of the Rolls?"

"It was as easy as pie. I said Joe needed to release some sexual tension. I also told her it was either going to be you or her...whoever won the race to the car!"

The door to the Rolls slammed shut with authority. Simone quickly walked to her car with one shoe off and the other on, spitting the thick residuals of her chance encounter onto the ground along the way. The three friends laughed like crazy.

"If she ever mentions what happened here tonight, I'm sure Squirt's name will be replaced with Joe Louis'!" Marta started her engine. "Joe...Tee...what a pleasure dining with you two this evening--and thanks for a memorable day! It was fantastic, and I hope to see you both on Derby Day."

"We'd love seeing you too, Marta," affirmed a smiling Joe Louis.

She turned her attention to Tee, inadvertently touching his hand as it rested on her door."I look forward to seeing you on Saturday!"

As Marta drove off, Tee acknowledged the obvious. "She's fine as a motherfucker!"

It rained Friday, but Saturday was made to order for Derby Day. The sun smiled upon Churchill Hill Downs, and on the record-breaking 100,000 racing fans attending from around the world. The mile and a quarter track was fast and the winning horse would rake in $102,000 in cash...the largest purse in Kentucky Derby history. Joe Louis was busy posing for pictures with song and dance man Bob Hope, and Arthur Godfrey, the old redhead, while movie star Irene Dunn perused her program trying to pick the winning horse. Joe also posed for pictures with everyday folks, making their day as well as his. "Wow! Thanks, Champ!"

Joe excused himself, waving goodbye to the fans while he and Tee went to the paddock area to tout horses. The 1954 Derby fielded seventeen horses...all three-year-olds. Marta spotted her friends through binoculars while seated in the clubhouse. She rushed to the ground level to be with Joe and Tee. Marta continued thumbing through the pages of her program.

"Well, gentlemen--who do you like in the featured race?"

"Ladies first!" Insisted Tee.

Marta pointed to the number **2C** horse from Crevolin stables. "I like Determine...he reminds me of myself...petite yet tough!"

"Aww, Marta, it's a chalk horse--besides, he's way too small to win anything."

"What's a chalk horse?" she asked.

"Anytime you place a bet at the track based on the chalkboard. The odds go down or up proportionally on the amount of money bet in the pool. The chalkboard has nothing to do with the colt's actual performances or his record."

Joe agreed with Tee. "He's giving it to you straight, Marta. Not to mention the fact that you picked a grey horse. They haven't won a race since the Derby began in 1875! Determine will be lucky to just finish this race."

"Ay, Dios Mio! [Oh my God!] I don't believe you two are assuming a horse can't win because of color! You two should be ashamed of yourselves."

Tee added, "Marta, I'm just telling you like it is. As a gambler, I don't mind taking chances--and I'll prove it to you! Marta, If your horse finishes in the money, I'll double your winnings!"

Marta accepted his offer. "I'll take that bet, Tee! What do I put up in return?"

"How about dinner at the Polo Club...loser pays!"

She extended her hand, making it official.

"That's a bet, young lady," confirmed Tee. "Joe--you heard it, didn't you?"

Joe simply smiled and nodded his head...yes.

After carefully going over racing forms and tout sheets, the men decided their best chance at winning was Corelation; he was the handicapper's favorite.

"You'll be sorry!" joked Marta.

"Ooooh, I'm shaking like a leaf in a summer breeze!" replied Tee.

With the time-honored musical selection "My Old Kentucky Home" playing in the background, a smartly dressed bugler, wearing a black riding cap, red blouse with brass buttons, jodhpurs, and spit-shined boots took his position at the track's entrance. He carried an extended mouth pipe bugle and stood at the ready. The Run for the Roses would follow his ten-second staccato rendition of "Call to the Post." Afterward the clanging of the bell signaled... THEY'RE OFF!

Record-breaking crowds created thousands of overflow fans. They soon found themselves walking through a long underground tunnel to access the Churchill Downs infield. Gatherings of this sort attract human predators, and the Derby was no exception. The massive slow-moving caravan proved easy pickings for teams of pickpockets from every persuasion. For those whose livelihoods depended upon nefarious pursuits, racetrack patrons represented the mother lode. Adroit artists worked the swells like salty fishermen sailing the open seas, netting wallets and other valuables. Working in teams of three, their first order of business was to identify a mark. Next was the all- important shill, or diversion. The initial steps were followed before the cop, or sting... where the valuables were actually taken. Finally there was the drop, or dump-off. It was the last step in the process, when the booty was whisked away by person or persons unknown. Unwitting victims were tapped quickly, and the culprits slithered away into anonymity. Undercover law enforcement managed some arrests, but it was like closing the barn door after the horse was already gone. The main concern with this type of crime was that the victim didn't realize his/her property was missing until it was needed. By then, there was nothing left to do except file a lost or stolen property report with the police.

Once the light at the end of the tunnel was near—those who managed to make it through the underpass unscathed were greeted by warm sunshine, obstreperous chatter, and conveniently located, adequately equipped parimutuel betting stations. Gambling at the track was unique because the public was playing among themselves. The track revenues were earned directly from each bet placed. The vast infield resembled a picnic smorgasbord of people, with blankets strewn everywhere. Only a small percentage of those in the infield would ever catch an actual glimpse of the race. Their only real connection to Derby action came from an elaborate public address system. "FIVE MINUTES TO POST... PLEASE PLACE YOUR BETS...FIVE MINUTES!"

As excitement built, the new friends were able to find great trackside viewing along the rail near the finish line. Joe Louis' celebrity status had all but disappeared when the thoroughbreds took center stage. Marta was overly excited after spotting her mount. "There's my horse... go get 'em, Determine!"

Tee glanced her way and was amused by her naivete. He

continued observing the remainder of the field through binoculars. "TWO MINUTES TO POST...PLEASE PLACE YOUR BETS... TWO MINUTES...DON'T GET SHUT OUT!"

Soon a hush blanketed the crowd. Handlers led the final horse into the starting gate. A few seconds elapsed before every three-year-old was on line. The start bell rang and the padded doors flung open. One hundred two thousand racing fans roared as one...with a collective thunderous avalanche of approval. Seventeen thoroughbreds rumbled toward the rails, narrowly avoiding a mishap when Timely Tip and Determine clipped hooves.

Track announcer Bryan Field's call commenced: "GOING UP FOR THE LEAD IT'S HASTY ROAD...TIMELY TIP...AND CORELATION! AS THEY PASS THE GRANDSTAND FOR THE FIRST TIME!"

"Come on, Determine...go...go!"

"Settle in, Corelation...this is gonna be a piece of cake!"

"Knock 'em out...Corelation!"

"INTO THE CLUB HOUSE TURN IT'S...HASTY ROAD, TIMELY TIP, AND ADMIRAL PORTER!"

The Champ peered through his binoculars, not uttering a sound...just rhyhmically snapping the thumb and middle finger on his left hand to the musical beat of horses hooves. "IN THE BACK STRETCH IT'S...HASTY ROAD FIRST...CORELATION IS SECOND BUT TIRING...WHILE DETERMINE IS MOVING INTO THIRD PLACE!"

"C'mon, Determine...you can do it, grey!" Marta was clutching her hat and holding the rail, rooting her horse on. "Let's go, baby...you can do it!" Joe and Tee's horse was in fourth place and fading fast. "Give him the crop, jock...whip it...c'mon Corelation!"

"AROUND THE FAR TURN THEY COME...HEADING FOR THE HOME STRETCH...IT'S HASTY ROAD, CORELATION, WITH DETERMINE COMING UP FAST ON THE OUT-

SIDE...IT'S HASTY ROAD AND DETERMINE! CORELATION IS BEING PRESSED HARD, BUT IS A BEATEN HORSE. DETERMINE'S AHEAD BY A NOSE...HASTY ROAD SECOND. DETERMINE IS PULLING AWAY...AT THE FINISH...IT'S DETERMINE BY A LENGTH AND A HALF WITH JOCKEY RAY YORK ABOARD... HASTY ROAD IS SECOND...AND GOYAMO THIRD!"

Winning fans cheered and losers jeered...tearing up tickets and tossing them onto the ground. Once the race results were official, Joe and Tee tore their own tickets into a million pieces. Marta jumped for joy, holding her winning ticket high in the air for all to see. Determine paid $10.60 to win...netting her over a thousand dollars. Her friends were disappointed with Corelation finishing out of the money, but were extremely happy for Marta. They walked her to the cashier's window as she beamed her satisfaction.

"Oh my God...I can't believe it...I won...I really won!"

Tee added, "You certainly did...here...this belongs to you!" Tee handed Marta ten crisp hundred dollar bills, payment for their side bet.

Marta hugged them both, saying, "Dinner's absolutely positively on me!"

Racing continued at Churchill Downs. The threesome decided to leave and prepare for dinner in Pike's Peak Polo Club at seven o'clock. Marta was staying in the home of friends who were currently vacationing in Europe. The Waverlys' mansion was located thirty minutes from Louisville in a secluded area with beautifully landscaped greens and a charming pond. It was ideally suited for those who loved being surrounded by nature. Marta perused the owner's automobile collection. She chose a silver 1954 Aston Martin to drive during her six--week stay. The car seated two comfortably, and she enjoyed soaring like an eagle when zipping along open roads. When in the company of Joe and Tee, Marta felt as if her two friends had spun a silken web where she couldn't be harmed. There she was free to be what she had always hoped... to be herself. She often thought her beauty was a curse, and was uneasy with many she met. Take the Michaels, for instance. When they first met, she was treated like a daughter. Then...slowly she noticed a change in both of them. They began coloring conversations with sexual innuendo. Things were so bad that she didn't want to be alone with them, for fear of what they might be capable of doing.

A few months ago the Michaels invited Marta to dinner. It was nothing special...just a simple affair she decided to attend alone. The catered spread was impressive and matched the subsequent conversations. After supper they retired to the living room and Simone made drinks. Out of the corner of Marta's eye she fortuitously noticed Simone slip a white substance into one of the cocktails. After returning to the living room Simone handed Bradford his Pinot Grigio...then offered the martini to Marta. Simone sat next to her guest in the bergère armchair. The light conversation continued where it had left off. A skeptical Marta glimpsed a small window of opportunity and switched her drink with Simone's, which was on the cocktail table. Within minutes of sipping her martini, the hostess became very promiscuous. Shortly thereafter she flailed off her clothes and sexually assaulted her own husband right in front of Marta. You needn't be a brain surgeon to realize Marta was the one who should have lost her inhibitions.

"I can tell you two lovebirds want to be alone--so I'll just excuse myself, if you don't mind!"

Marta quickly left the premises, leaving the couple to their own devices. Marta hadn't visited since, and never invited them to the Waverlys' mansion. The couple's behavior seemed to occur more and more often...and appeared to be a joint venture.

It was almost seven o'clock and Joe Louis was getting somewhat impatient. "Hurry up, Tee...I don't want to be late for dinner."

"Almost ready, Joe!" Tee took one last look into the mirror. "All set...let's go!"

The two men hurried outside the Negro boarding house and jumped into the back seat of the Rolls. Squirt got them to the club at precisely seven o'clock. Once inside, they immediately spotted Marta sitting at her table. She smiled broadly, beckoning them over. They stood politely while shaking her hand and waiting for an invitation to be seated.

"Please have a seat, fellas. Remember, dinner is on Tee... or should I say me!" Tee smiled as they took their seats directly across from Marta. "Gentlemen, I've already taken the liberty of ordering your favorite drinks...they should be here any second. I've also asked the chef to prepare three filet mignons...just the way we like them!"

"Sounds good, Marta...I'm ravenous," remarked Tee.

When the drinks arrived, Marta offered a toast in Spanish. "*La ganadora se lo lleva todo!*"

They clinked glasses and sipped away. "Just what did you say, Marta?" asked Joe.

Surprisingly, Tee decided to answer his friend's question. "Well Joe--if my high school memory serves me correctly...Marta's doing a little bragging. *The winner takes all!*"

"*Claro que si!* Absolutely correct! I'm impressed, Tee."

"Thanks, Marta...but I'd rather be bragging about me!"

"Sorry, Tee--I guess it's better to be lucky when taking chances. I hope this dinner will help ease the pain of losing money to a person who knows very little about thoroughbred horses."

"Ohhh, Marta--you really know how to rub it in...*muy bien!*

Just then, supper arrived. Linen napkins easily found their

way onto laps or under chins with quickness. "Miss de LaCosta...medium; Mr. Louis...well done; and yours, sir, is also well done. If there is anything you require, I await your beck and call...enjoy!"

The sumptuous meal loosened belts and conversation. In no time at all the three were talking about the exciting Derby. "Did you see my horse almost fall at the very start...I'm amazed the jockey was able to stay astride."

"Yeah...it would have changed the whole complexion of the race...I'm happy for you, Marta."

"Me too," added Tee. "I like winning, but not at the expense of seeing anyone hurt."

They talked about everything under the sun, and nothing was out of bounds. "Joe!" asked Marta. "What was your toughest fight?"

Joe didn't have to think long about the question. "It was Billy Conn...at the Polo Grounds in June of '41. He had won almost every round...but the thirteenth round was mine. I set the Pittsburgh Kid up with a right and was able to catch him with a hard left hook...knocking him out!"

"You must have been quite relieved."

"I was very happy...later when we were in front of the press, Billy asked me. 'Why couldn't you let me hold the title for a year or so?' I told him, 'You had the title for twelve rounds and couldn't hold on to it!'" He smiled. "Yeah, Marta, that was a tough bout!"

"It was a good night for me too," smiled Tee. "I won big that day!"

Marta's table faced the club entrance, enabling her to see Simone and Bradford Michaels being seated. They both acknowledged Marta and her friends with a nod. The waiter came over and informed Miss de LaCosta that the next round was compliments of the Michaels. Marta smiled to herself, thinking, *I'd better make sure nothing gets slipped into our drinks. I surely don't want to be involved in an orgy.* The friends toasted the couple from afar.

The conversation among the three ran the gamut: solving the world's perplexities while managing to tell a few jokes in the process. Marta enjoyed their company so much that she invited the two gentlemen to the Waverlys' for a nightcap. They would be leaving for Detroit on Sunday and wanted to get an early start. Since Marta was alone and had ample space, she suggested they remain in the mansion and leave the next morning. Joe, Tee, and Squirt were given guest rooms. Before retiring, Louis taught Marta to play a card game called Tonk. Marta was a natural and held her own, beating them regularly at their own game. It was well into the wee hours of the morning before everyone headed off to bed.

The next morning Marta arose early and prepared breakfast: bacon, eggs, pancakes, toast, coffee, and orange juice. Additionally, a thoughtful Marta made ham and cheese sandwiches for the guys to take on the trip home. "Gentlemen, this was one of the greatest weekends I've ever had! I'm so grateful to have spent quality time with each of you. Joe, you're like a gentle giant... not at all what one expects from a man who makes his living prize fighting. Tee, you are also special...there is something kind, caring, and generous about you. Squirt, you really do favor Joe a lot... I can see why some people may have gotten you two mixed up."

Tee inadvertently let the cat out of the bag. "Squirt really had a great couple of days in Louisville...he's batting two for two!"

After breakfast, everyone helped clean up. Once the kitchen and dining areas were spotless, Marta walked the men to the car. Before heading off, she gave Squirt the wrapped sandwiches and six bottles of soft drinks. They needed to stop and pick up the rest of their things at the boarding house. Marta made sure Joe and Tee had her private phone number in Barcelona. She encouraged them to stay in touch. The lady from Barcelona, Spain, gave each of them a hug.

"Joe, please let your wife know I said hello. Tee, I would love for you to contact me at my home...if that's all right?"

"Sure...I'd like that too!"

"Tee, before I forget...I want to ask you a personal question. What on earth is your real name?"

Tee smiled. "TaNellie...my real name is TaNellie."

Marta kissed him on his cheek and stepped back, wearing an engaging smile on her face. "Well, TaNellie...don't be a stranger."

The men boarded the car, then drove slowly down the drive, and out of sight. Marta was intrigued by the tall handsome man she'd met only days ago. "TaNellie...the name suits him."

Tee turned to Joe. "She is the most beautiful woman I have ever laid my eyes on. Champ...she scares the shit out of me. I could really love that woman!"

(11) Stable mates...

Six women, all young, all white, and all prostitutes mostly slept during the day and worked through the night. Home was a shared four-bedroom apartment on the third floor of a five-story yellow brick building just off scenic Liberty Boulevard. It overlooked the lush verdure of Rockefeller Park. The upper-class neighborhood enveloped a beautiful manmade lagoon whose small boathouse and still water were perpetually dotted by rowboats for hire. Visitors sat on park benches situated around trimmed grassy knolls. Romantics held hands along the unique patterned red brick promenade encompassing an algae-covered trout-stocked pond. Colorful bobbing floats signaled novice anglers when to pull up sharply on bamboo fishing poles to hook their catch. Located directly across from the lagoon were clay tennis courts. During summer, ladies and gentlemen dressed in pristine white clothing played doubles with a vengeance usually reserved for boxing matches.

The large rooms of the apartment were inundated with fresh air and sunlight reflecting off highly polished hardwood floors. Except for personal items, each bedroom had double beds, mirrored dressers, chairs, and closet space. Shane, whose real name was Ana Whitmore, had been there the longest, having just celebrated her sixth year. The blonde twenty-five-year-old was Ta-Nellie's bottom lady, and as gorgeous as when he first met her. The other girls admired her journeyman approach to business. She was the girl next door who could turn a trick in five minutes and be ready for the next one. After being turned out by TaNellie, she was affectionately known as "Pink Gold." Shane accepted the honor very seriously and her pride was evident. In the life, there are certain rules a whore learns early on and follows to the letter. No stealing, no eyeballing, and absolutely no back talk. The wench must realize the pimp is the end-all and be-all... the daddy. Breaking any of his rules could result in instantaneous retribution. Punishments are based on severity of the infractions and levied corporally or by warnings, which are determined solely at the pimp's discretion. How house members conduct themselves was Ana's responsibility. She was taught the traditional way of doing business, and knew what was expected of her girls. She ran a tight ship and an even smoother operation. Ana was worth her weight in gold, and TaNellie knew it. He trusted her to handle daily activities, and she always did what was expected. If there were discontentment within the stable...it was Ana's to handle.

Justine preferred to be called "Boots." A reasonable explanation for her name may have come from a French fairy tale, *Puss in Boots*, written by Charles Perrault in 1697. In Barbara's case, however, "pussy in boots" was more apropos. She had the uncanny ability to use her sphincter muscle to coax an offering from even the most resistant male. "Honey, time wasted...is wasted money!" she often said after being compensated. "Next!"

Margaret was a true redhead in every sense of the word, from her drapes to her carpet, with freckles in between. Clients called her Peggy Sue because of the large horn-rimmed glasses she wore. Margaret specialized in fellatio with a twist. While performing her act, she always looked deep within the eyes of her Johns. This visual stimulation made her clients cream uncontrollably...making her a trick's favorite. Because she was able to perform almost anywhere-- including cars, alleyways, and doorways--she turned what used to be room fees into profits, making TaNellie a very happy camper. Peggy Sue was proof that men do make passes at those who wear glasses…and will pay dearly for the privilege.

Gert was tall and slender, the newest and youngest member of the troupe. The twenty-one-year-old was from Berlin, New Jersey. She was currently recovering from an overdose of prescription pills. To hear Ana tell it, "If she really wanted to die…she'd be dead right now!" Ana found her lying unconscious in an alley. With help from the other girls, she brought the ingénue home. They welcomed the troubled kid into the fold with open arms. On the surface she seemed well-grounded and contented with her new family. The ill-fated suicide attempt was the result of boyfriend trouble, which was often the case. Her current beau loved more than one girl, which proved a bit hard to take for the lovelorn Gert. Ana was currently teaching her the ropes, and expected that she'd be very productive. Meanwhile, Gert had been coming along steadily.

"She reminds me of myself when I was her age," Ana said. The mother hen shared one of her first professional experiences with the new kid. "Sometimes being a prostitute is its own reward. I remember my first week out…a brand-new 1949 Chevy pulls up. The passenger rolls down his window and I peek inside. 'How much for the four of us?' I size them up. 'How much you got?' 'One hundred dollars!' 'That'll do!' I took the money and hid it someplace safe. They pull onto a side street and I have them all sit up front. I service each one in the back seat. Those little fuckers exploded like popcorn, and I finished in no time at all. Someone adjusted the rearview mirror in such a way…it caught my every move. Those boys played with themselves throughout my entire session…cocks were exploding nonstop. I didn't have the heart to spoil it for them by saying I would have done them all for twenty bucks. After the first time they continued coming by every Friday night. We dated for three months straight, just like clockwork…or should I say cockwork. They sought me out no matter what. The spokesman always handed me a crisp hundred-dollar bill...while the others waited with their dicks in their hands. I haven't made that kind of money for fifteen minutes' work since. On Fridays I still keep an eye out for those boys...I guess they're a lot older now and a helluva lot wiser."

Shirley hailed from Toronto, and she got into the act. She was the spitting image of Mamie Van Doren, the movie star. She consistently made more than any of the other girls, but that hadn't always been the case. "Star," as she was called, used a falsetto voice when servicing Johns. The blonde bombshell encouraged them to imagine themselves fucking Mamie Van Doren. Actually, the sex was phenomenal and the men always expressed their delight with generous tips. TaNellie never took a dime of her extra tip money, and she stayed loyal to him. Shirley was an honest whore, a quality rapidly becoming a rarity in the skin game.

"Whatever happened to honor among thieves? You just can't trust anyone. The night I turned my first trick, I'd been on the stroll for three or four hours without so much as a nibble, when a middle-aged white guy wearing a suit and glasses passed me by. He did a double take, then turned around and came back. 'Miss, I'm not trying to be nosey...but I saw you earlier this evening. Business must be pretty bad tonight, huh?' 'So what are you going to do about it, friend...talk or get laid?' 'I wasn't looking to do anything about it, miss. You just reminded me of someone and I wanted to share who the person is. I just left the Liberty Theater, on 105th and Superior. If you dyed your hair blonde, I believe you'd have more business than you could handle.' 'Why is that?' 'Because you'd look exactly like Mamie Van Doren...the gorgeous starlet, that's why. But who'd know it...because you're hiding behind your dark brunette hair. If you don't believe me, walk with me to the theatre, and you can judge for yourself. You change your hair...get one of those glittery gowns...and you would clean house! You'd be a STAR!'

"I was skeptical at first...but I felt safe, and decided to walk the two blocks to the Liberty. I was floored! He was absolutely right. His advice changed my life for the better. The Liberty was already closed, so I took him behind the ticket booth and sucked him off. When I finished, his glasses were foggy...but he was all smiles. So was I, to tell you the truth!"

" 'Miss, I only have a couple of dollars, but you're welcome to it!' 'Honey, what we just did was on the house. Thanks for your advice!' From then on I was Mamie Van Doren's double. I should have taken his two bucks,' cause I was broke as a dog. I thought better of it, though. I decided to leave well enough alone. I've been making good dough ever since. TaNellie was pleased with my decision to change my hair color, and I'll never forget the old guy with the spectacles. He was the only trick I've ever sucked off for free! You might as well say...he discovered STAR!"

Mary Jo was the least-likely-looking prostitute ever. Even when wearing short skirts, she looked more like a Sunday school teacher...which was precisely why she did so well. Mary Jo wore fishnet nylons and carried a wooden paddle strapped around her waist. She loved using it on naughty submissive boys. It seems the more power her clients wielded in the world, the more they yearned for direction and discipline in hers. Captains of industry regularly sought Mary Jo's services, paying handsomely for her punitive skills.

Mary Jo reflected on her first go round. "It was a disaster... right smack in the middle of April and raining like cats and dogs. I'd just broken a heel running from a vice car. The cop on the passenger side chases me on foot while his partner waited in the car. He catches up to me and snatches me by the arm and drags me back to the black and white. I'm limping along...and we're both wet as hell. His partner rolls down the window and yells out, 'Officer down!' They've got to leave...but before they do...this asshole cop cuffs me to a stop sign. He points his finger, saying, 'Stay put, girlie!' He jumps back into the squad car and they swoop off with lights flashing and siren screaming. Meanwhile the rain is falling so hard that my stringy hair is plastered against my face. Rouge and mascara are running down my neck like crazy. I'm hugging the pole, like I'm slow dancing. Can you imagine how embarrassing it was, making out with the stop sign?

"Just then TaNellie drives up and rolls down his window. I'm crying and he's laughing his ass off. 'Hey, wench--are you trying to catch your death of pneumonia? What the hell you doing cuffed to a stop sign?'

"Between raindrops I explain what happened, and he runs over to get me. He sorts through his key ring and finds a small handcuff key. He smiles and says, 'I'm going have to dock you for lost wages. I can't allow my girls to hang on the corner doing nothing. I'm also charging your lazy ass a locksmith fee!' I'm soaking wet, trembling, still crying...while sneezing my ass off. He takes off his trench coat and wraps it around my shoulders. We drive by Scatter's where he hops into the pouring rain and returns with a pork shoulder dinner for me and a chicken dinner for himself. To my utter surprise he hands me a freshly brewed cup of hot tea and lemon. Then he drives to the house off Liberty Boulevard. "Why don't you go upstairs, take a hot bath, then eat your dinner and drink some tea, baby. You know I was just kidding about charging you for my services. You've already had rough first night. 'Tea Baby,' I want you to stay out of the spotlight for a few days. Clean up the crib...anything to keep busy. That roller's going to be awfully pissed about losing his handcuffs. I'll see you when I see you!' That's the night he nicknamed me Tea Baby!"

Mary Jo glanced over at Gert. She was fast asleep in Ana's

arms. The teen was wearing a subtle smile on her face...a clear indication of how thankful she was after being saved by TaNellie's angels in high heels and short skirts. When all seems lost...nothing beats having friends.

Southern Jim Crow laws afforded TaNellie's girls an immeasurable fringe benefit. When Negroes migrated north during the '30s and '40s in search of higher-paying factory jobs in cities like Cleveland, Detroit, and Chicago, most had never experienced intimacy with white women. Once faced with an opportunity...TaNellie made sure they paid dearly for the privilege. According to him: "When you supply a colored man with a white woman and a white man with a colored woman, you've single-handedly solved America's race problem." His reasoning was basic: "Because every man will have his heart's desire. If you don't believe me, just ask former President Thomas Jefferson, or the first black world heavyweight champion, Jack Johnson! The proof is in the pudding...I mean the pussy! If you don't know, you better ask somebody."

TaNellie cracked himself up, and always laughed before finishing his own jokes, even if others didn't. Say what you will, TaNellie Lafitte Purifoy really knew how to treat a lady. When walking or sitting, he made sure he positioned himself on the woman's outward side. In this way he was able to protect her should the need arise. His old-world behavior had been learned by studying rules of gentlemanly propriety and reading books based on the adventurous exploits of Giacomo Casanova, and the seductive libertine...Don Juan.

TaNellie was a very shrewd businessman, and never sent all of his girls to work at once. He preferred operating more like a factory...sending employees out on hourly shifts. This approach assured the viability of his enterprise in cases of sweeping police arrests. Legal ramifications could send a pimp's profits spiraling downward, costing him a pretty penny. Whenever business became too hot, he'd transfer operations to another location. Since unforeseen occurrences were the nature of the business, he made sure Johns knew where to find his girls. TaNellie often commented, "One monkey don't stop the show!"

(12) The youngster...

Sometimes things happen without rhyme or reason, and in the process often boggle the mind. "Suppose her first mistake was literally her last?'" It's a question TaNellie pondered while curious onlookers gathered around them. He held the newcomer gingerly as she lay near the curb motionless. For the moment, each waited for the city rescue squad to arrive. Any of Tee's more experienced girls would have known better than put themselves into such a dangerous position. Gert, the lovelorn kid from Berlin, New Jersey, didn't know what she was bargaining for. It was her first time walking the stroll alone. Ana had trained the youngster and was certain she was ready to take her maiden voyage.

With neon lights flashing in her eyes, Gert thought about her stable mates, who had shared insights about their first times actually doing the nasty for money. She'd hoped her experiences would be just as memorable. Earlier that evening, a car pulled up and the female driver beckoned Gert around to the driver's side window. "How much money would it cost for us to have a party?" Ana, her mentor, had gone to handle some business and left Gert walking the stroll alone. Surely she would return momentarily... but time never takes a break.

"What kind of party?" Inquired the hooker. The short-haired brunette wantonly eyed the youngster up and down, pleased with what she saw. Gert, an innocent wholesome-looking girl without the harsh rigors the job often causes, continued listening.

"It's my boyfriend's birthday...I want to show him a good time.

Getting it on with a cute girl like you will really turn us both on. It'll be the three of us. So, cutie pie, how much?"

Asking the right questions is paramount when trying to get straight answers from a trick. It's a valuable lesson...one only time and experience can teach. Gert looked around for Ana, but she still hadn't returned. The driver sensed her lack of experience and went for the coup de grâce. "Look, girlie, I'll give you $200 to let me eat your cute little snatch in front of my boyfriend. Maybe we can even take a few photographs...how about it?" The apprehensive first-timer looked around once more... still Ana was nowhere to be found. "Come on, pretty girl...this won't take long...you'll be back in no time flat!"

Gert surveyed the area one final time and made a decision. "Okay...I'll do it!" She got into the back seat of the dark-colored sedan...the driver burned rubber and sped off like gangbusters long before the door had closed shut.

Traveling in the opposite direction at precisely the same time was Colin Dancer...who was shooting the breeze with TaNellie. Tee did a double take, turning his body completely around to be sure. "Man, that looked like Gert! Hurry, Colin, and turn this bad boy around. Catch up with that car!"

Dancer never lost sight of the car's rear lights as it turned onto East 93rd... speeding north toward Liberty Boulevard doing at least 60 mph. In no time at all they were heading west on route 2, toward Lakewood. TaNellie made sure his .32 automatic was locked, loaded, and ready. He knew whoever was at the wheel was up to no good.

"Tee...get me my pistol out of the glove compartment. I think we're gonna need some extra firepower." Colin was a military vet and a seasoned driver.

"Keep your eye on the car, Dancer--don't you lose 'em! I don't want nothing to happen to the youngster!"

"Don't worry, man, I got these punk-ass motherfuckers. They ain't getting away!"

TaNellie's eyes were focused like a laser. He watched their every move like a hungry mouse in a cheese factory. Dancer was already doing 80 mph and stepped on the gas, managing to pull alongside the speeding car. The young female behind the wheel was an expert driver. The man in the back seat had his hand tightly covering Gert's mouth. TaNellie rolled down his window and leaned out, brandishing his weapon. "Pull over, bitch, before I shoot your dumb ass!" She sped up even more, creating distance between the two vehicles.

The woman could have taken Clifton Boulevard toward Lakewood, but at the last second made a sharp left turn instead. On Baltic Avenue, her car came to a screeching halt. The man in the back seat pushed Gert from the car with his foot as they took off. Dancer stopped his car in the middle of the street. Both men jumped out and carried the dazed and confused Gert back to the car. Her jaw and forehead seemed to be in pretty bad shape.

"Colin, let's take her back to our side of town. If the rollers come, I don't want to have to explain a bleeding young white girl in our back seat...not in this neighborhood. We'll call an ambulance later and get her patched up!"

Tee was concerned about the newest member of his stable. "Gert--it's me, Tee. You're going to be fine, so hold on. I'm taking care of you until we get to the hospital!"

Both Tee and Colin were still wired from the frantic high-speed chase. They were thankful to have the youngster. Anything could have happened to her in the hands of those kidnappers. "We're almost home, baby...you'll get some medical attention when the ambulance comes." TaNellie had seen it all during his stint as a pimp. "Those two freak bastards were out for blood...anything was possible. I don't think I'll ever understand this business!"

When they arrived back at the stroll, a crowd had gathered. Tee and Colin placed Gert on the sidewalk with a wool blanket covering her from the neck down. TaNellie cradled her in his arms. "Gert...help will be here soon."

Ana knelt beside them and gave the dazed youngster her marching orders. "When the ambulance arrives, give them your correct name, because you haven't done anything wrong. Tell them you're my play cousin visiting from Berlin, New Jersey. Everything is going to work out, Gert. We're all praying for you."

The police never found the kidnappers. It was fair to assume they'd keep trying until they snatched someone. TaNellie and Ana were sure the youngster would head back home after the incident...but she hadn't yet. She loved her new family and they loved her, too. In spite of all the drama, Gert was going to be all right. It was all that really mattered to Tee and his girls. One thing was certain...the New Jersey youngster finally had her own *first-time* story to tell.

(13) Simone Michaels...

Her phone constantly rang for most of the morning. Every time Simone answered, it was someone trying to sell something. With frayed nerves, she was fit to be tied. The next time it rang she snatched it up with a vengeance...this was war. "What the hell do you want?" she growled.

"Good morning, Simone--Marta de LaCosta. How are you?"

Simone's anger dissipated like melted snow, and her furrowed brow invited a warm smile. "I'm so sorry, Marta...please forgive me? I thought you were one of those God-awful telemarketers. They've been pestering me for most of the morning. Marta, it's been a while since we've talked... how have you been, my dear?"

"I'm just fine, Simone. I was calling because I have something I think belongs to you. I'd like to drop it off if you have the time?"

"Bradford's out of town on business, so it'll just be the two of us." She paused, her eyebrow raised lustfully. "I hope it's not a problem?"

"Simone, don't be silly. How about eight this evening?"

"Great, Marta--I'll be here; see you then!"

It was only noon. Simone raced up the stairs two at a time. She ran into the master bedroom, flung open the closet doors, and immediately began searching for just the right ensemble to wear for Marta's visit. Simone was bisexual and has been intrigued by Marta's aloofness and beauty ever since they met at a political fundraiser. They hadn't spoken in weeks, but she was excited just hearing the young woman's voice. Simone, in her exuberance, hadn't inquired about what Marta had of hers. Not knowing was driving her crazy...but she would just have to wait until eight.

There was so much to be done before Marta arrived. This would be the first time they were ever alone, and she wasn't about to waste the opportunity. Simone retrieved a pair of cocktail glasses from the bar. She sprinkled a crystal powder in one and put both inside the freezer to frost. She acquired the mysterious substance while on safari in deepest darkest Africa. The Michaels paid handsomely for the stimulant, and once consumed it erased all inhibitions and created an immediate craving for all things sexual. The Michaels jokingly referred to their discovery as *Love Potion #9*. Simone loathed being married, and it wasn't because she hated her husband. He was much older than she, and set in his ways. She just wasn't interested in him anymore. She had been enticed by Bradford Michaels' massive fortune and decided to accept his proposal of marriage. Of course she had been happy for a few years, but felt trapped now, and couldn't take it any longer. In her mind's eye, a relationship with Marta represented the freedom she sought, the best of both worlds. Being alone with her this evening would permit Simone an opportunity to fully explore the possibilities of an affair. Her phone rang and she answered seductively, "Hello."

"Hi, my name is...."

"Get lost, you creep!" She slammed the phone down, almost breaking it in the process.

A few minutes after eight, the door bell rang. It was Marta. The front door swung open wide, revealing a stunning Simone in a black sequined top and fitted silk pants with satin mules. Marta was underwhelming in a casually subdued tan suede riding jacket, Levi's, and rough-hewn hiking boots.

"Hi Simone...my, do you look wonderful!"

"Thank you, my dear...just a little something I found lying

about...please come in and have a seat." Marta cautiously followed her hostess, trying not to appear standoffish.

Simone motioned for her guest to be seated in the living room. "May I prepare a beverage for you, Marta?"

"Not tonight, Simone...I'm meeting with friends in thirty minutes."

"Ohhh, how disappointing...you must have at least one quick cocktail with me to celebrate the return of my...what was it you found of mine, my dear?"

Marta reached into her leather clutch bag and handed Simone a sealed white business envelope with her name, in c/o Marta de LaCosta. Simone tore it open and for a few seconds the silence was deafening. An inquisitive look settled upon her face, which Marta noticed immediately. "Is everything all right, Simone?"

"Yes...of course, my dear...everything is just fine." Her curt response unveiled apprehension.

"It is yours...isn't it?" queried Marta.

"Certainly it's mine!"

"Why not try it on, for old times' sake?"

"I'll put it on later, my dear...thanks so much for returning it... where on earth was it found?"

"Joe Louis sent it by courier...after finding it in the rear seat of his Rolls. I knew you'd be pleased!"

Simone's whole demeanor changed and she abruptly abandoned the entire conversation. "Well, I see time is flying by, and I must apologize for completely disregarding your appointment this evening. Marta, if you hurry you can still meet your friends. Perhaps we can get together at another time. I certainly don't want you to be late!" Marta was taken aback by Simone's sudden change of heart.

Simone stood and walked Marta to the front door. "Thanks so much for stopping by... you're such a dear friend."

The young woman said goodbye and walked to her car. Simone closed the door behind her and retrieved one of the chilled glasses from the freezer. She poured a martini and sat in her armchair. After taking a long sip she again picked up the envelope and emptied its contents. The solid gold ID bracelet was encrusted with at least three carats of pavé diamonds. Simone turned it over and reread the inscription. *To the love of my life...BTM.* Bradford Thomas Michaels. Simone knew the bracelet wasn't hers, and wondered who it did belong to. Another relevant concern was how the jewelry had found its way into the back seat of Louis' Rolls Royce. Her husband wasn't due to return until next week... giving her four days to solve the mystery.

Marta slowly backed the '54 Aston Martin out of the drive. While heading east she sequentially shifted manually and began wondering what was really happening inside the forever- scheming mind of Simone. Why did she react so strangely after seeing the bracelet? First insisting upon sharing drinks, then quickly shooing her off to meet with friends? Something was definitely askew with the picture Simone was painting. And why was she so hesitant about trying on the bracelet? Was it because she really didn't own it? Of course, it was engraved with her husband's initials. Marta's mind was working overtime and she wondered if Simone's initials were purposefully left off. If so, it could only mean one thing. Bradford purchased the bracelet for someone else? Marta met her friends as scheduled and was careful not to breathe a word of what had transpired with Simone. She decided to contact Joe the first thing in the morning and get to the bottom of what was rapidly becoming a curiosity.

Marta opened her address book and dialed the Champ's number. After ringing numerous times she was about to hang up when a winded voice answered.

"Hello."

"Hi...is this Joe?"

"Yes it is."

"It's Marta de LaCosta, in Louisville--how are you?"

"I'm fine, Marta...what a pleasant surprise. I was sparring in the ring...how are you?" "Just fine, Joe...sorry to bother you so early, but I need your help."

"Sure, Marta, anything...what can I do for you?"

"Yesterday I presented the bracelet you sent Simone Michaels. Even though it was engraved with her husband's initials...I'm not so sure it belongs to her. Do me a favor, Joe, and check with Squirt...maybe he can shed some light on how it got into the back seat?"

"Hold on, Marta...I'll put him on the line and you can ask him yourself. Just a second, please."

Soon the receiver was picked up. "Hi, Miss Marta...this is Squirt." She explained her dilemma. "Well, ma'am, I was in the back seat of Joe's car...with someone other than Simone. But I haven't spoken to her since leaving Kentucky."

"Do you remember her name?"

"Sure, ma'am...she's the same lady who owns the Negro boarding house where we stay during Derby week. Her name is Viola... the same as the boarding house."

"Thanks so much, Squirt...you've been very helpful. I'll call you guys if I have any further questions. Thanks again...and be sure to tell Joe I said goodbye!"

"I will...goodbye, Miss Marta."

After hanging up, Marta got into the car and headed toward Louisville, where the boarding house was located.

The establishment sat some twenty yards back from the highway. She turned left onto a horseshoe drive, which wrapped around a large grey and white wooden framed structure. It was in a middle-class Negro neighborhood. A lit white neon sign spanned the picture window facing Moss road and simply read: Viola's. Marta parked the car and walked in the main entrance and up a few stairs to the front desk. The first floor of the boarding house hummed with activity and smelled of bacon, sausage, and eggs...all the things Marta loved. She noticed a number of well-dressed colored guests seated at cloth-covered tables, eating and conversing inside the demure dining room setting. An elderly white-haired gentleman in his seventies smiled pleasantly, asking. "May I help you, ma'am?"

"Why, you certainly can. I'm Marta de LaCosta. Can you please direct me to Viola Darden?"

"Yes, ma'am...it would be my pleasure. Please wait here, ma'am, and I'll fetch her directly...be right back."

In almost no time at all, the gentleman returned, accompanied by a striking-looking Negro woman about thirty years old. Her skin was café au lait in color, and blemish-free. After introducing themselves, Marta followed her into an office where she was offered a seat.

"Miss Darden, thanks so much for seeing me without an appointment. I'll try and be brief and keep my comments as delicate as possible." Marta scooted her chair a little closer to Miss Darden's desk. "Have you lost anything lately, perhaps something personal in nature and quite expensive?"

Viola responded immediately, "Why yes, I have...a diamond bracelet. I lost it during Derby Week and I haven't the slightest idea when or where it happened. I did attend the Derby and assumed I was a victim of pickpockets. Silly me...I shouldn't wear it as often as I do...but it is so nice I can't seem to stop myself. Why do you ask, Miss de LaCosta?" Viola's tone was subtle... but suspicious.

"Well, it just so happens I know where it is. Now this is personal, Miss Darden, but I must ask...can you please tell me where you purchased the bracelet?"

Viola seemed uncomfortable, but answered the question any-way. "Yes... it was given to me as a gift by a friend."

Marta continued. "Would your friend's initials be...BTM?"

"Yes...why?"

"I just wanted to be sure, Miss Darden."

Viola had a few questions of her own. "Where was the bracelet found?"

"Inside a Rolls Royce belonging to a friend of mine...Joe Louis. Miss Darden, does it ring a bell?"

"It certainly does...I have a friend who works for the Champ. His name is Mauzy...but everyone just calls him Squirt. He and Joe come to my place once a year. I've dated Mauzy before...most recently during Derby Week."

"I'm going to give it to you straight, Miss Darden. Joe Louis sent the bracelet to me after finding it in the back seat of his car."

"Why would he send it to you?"

"The initials on the back led him to believe I knew the owner... but I didn't. I mistakenly gave it to Simone, Bradford Michaels' wife. I knew something was wrong, based on how she reacted when I gave her the bracelet. I phoned Joe soon after leaving her home. I was determined to get to the truth. Simone has the bracelet now."

"So when can I have my property back? After all, Bradford did buy the bracelet for me. I need to share something with you, Miss de LaCosta. We keep our relationship a secret because of his mar-riage, not to mention the racial aspects. Bradford loves me...we even own this restaurant together."

"Miss Darden, I want to help you get your bracelet back, and I have a plan I think will work with no questions asked."

Viola leaned inward. "That's great...how will I know if your plan succeeded?"

"Give me a few days and I'll contact you. Don't mention our conversation to anyone...just leave it all to me."

The women shook hands and walked to the parking lot. "Thank you so much for your help, Miss de LaCosta."

"Please, Viola... just call me Marta. I'll talk with you soon... goodbye."

Marta called Joe and explained everything, including all the sordid details. She shared her plan and asked his cooperation.

"I'll take care of it immediately, Marta. I'll send it out airmail special delivery, but you'll have to wait a couple of days. Let me know when she contacts you...I want to be kept in the loop. Good luck!"

"I will, Joe--thanks, bye!"

Simone called Marta that evening. "I just received a call from Joe!"

"Who?" asked Marta.

"You know, Joe Louis, the heavyweight champion. He's sending me an autographed picture. He sent the bracelet by accident. It belongs to a friend of his...Booker T. Mitchell...he was named after the famous Negro, Booker T. Washington. He wants you to pick it up and send it back. I told Joe I'd check my schedule. He actually wants to spend time with me and Bradford on the links... if we can find some free time. He's such a wonderful fellow. I'm so happy I had the chance to spend some quality time with him during Derby Week. Marta, I'm sorry about the small matter concerning the bracelet the other day. Thanks so much for understanding--talk with you soon."

After picking up the bracelet, Marta delivered it to the rightful owner. Miss Darden was thrilled to finally have her bracelet and tried it on immediately. She and Marta talked for hours over dinner right in the boarding house dining room. Marta had never tasted anything to compare with Viola's soul food. She savored the thick smothered pork chops, mashed potatoes and gravy, collard greens, peach cobbler... not to mention the corn bread sprinkled with bits of whole kernel corn inside. In Marta's own words, *"La comida es muy sabroso!"* [The food is very delicious indeed!] They washed it all down with ice-cold southern-style sweet tea with a mint leaf and slice of lemon. Marta used the opportunity to caution Viola concerning Simone's unpredictability. She warned the beautiful woman to always be wary concerning clandestine activities with married men.

As promised, Marta contacted Joe Louis. He thought her story about Simone was so hilarious that he could barely stand it. "Oh, I wish I could have been there! Marta, you have a remarkable talent for putting folks at ease. Your sense of humor is great...let's just say you're a real beautiful and funny person. It's always a pleasure speaking with you, whether on the phone or in person. Thanks for filling me in on Simone--she is one weird character. I guess it takes all kinds to make the world go 'round! I'll talk with you soon. Oh, Marta...before I forget...I wanted you to know Tee was very impressed by you. I've known him for some time, but I want you to maintain your distance. There's more to Tee than meets the eye. So long, Marta...and good luck!"

She was confused by Joe's advice and wondered what he meant by "more than meets the eye." She decided to have a dear friend who owned a detective agency look into Tee's carryings-on. Raul would be delighted to snoop around Cleveland to see what could be uncovered. Marta's gut feeling was seldom wrong and revealed a kind and caring man. Could she have been mistaken about the handsome gentleman with the unusual name and intriguing smile?

(14) Dossier...

Marta pondered quietly, running her index finger repeatedly along the crisp edges of a large manila envelope. It had been sent to her by Solutions Detective Agency, which was owned by Raul Montoya, her childhood friend. He has sold hundreds of agency franchises throughout the world. Marta continued toying haphazardly with the envelope while contemplating its contents. "Ouch!" A paper cut prompted the injured finger in her mouth, seeking soothing. She bandaged the annoyance and read the dossier.

TANELLIE LAFITTE PURIFOY
Born May 20, 1928
Glenville Hospital, Cleveland, Ohio
Mother, Bessie Mae Purifoy
Father, Frederick Douglass Purifoy

Eight months after arriving in Cleveland, Ohio, from New Orleans, Louisiana, Bessie Mae Purifoy gave birth to TaNellie L. Purifoy, a healthy seven-pound, three-ounce baby boy. The single mother is the custodial parent. A nationwide search for a death certificate in the name of Frederick Douglass Purifoy came up with negative results. Therefore it is assumed the father is still alive and living somewhere in the United States. According to Bessie Mae's friends and acquaintances there has been no indication the father has ever visited mother or son. Miss Purifoy is in her fifties and currently owns a chain of Negro beauty shops called Dixie Princess. The salons are located in northern and southern cities. The company has the highest market share in the Negro hair care market. According to the United States Department of Revenue, Miss Purifoy is considered wealthy and her tax liabilities are currently at 000 balance.

During the child's formative years, mother and son occasionally found themselves without a roof over their heads. Sleeping in doorways and park benches was the rule for weeks on end. Their only sustenance came from government cheese, powdered eggs, and dried milk dispensed by church-sponsored soup kitchens.

Bessie Mae's circumstances changed drastically after a chance encounter with Ruby Dandridge, mother of entertainers Dorothy Jean and Vivian Dandridge. Ruby was so impressed by Bessie Mae's hair styling skills that she sent her talented daughters to her whenever they needed their hair done. Vivian and Dorothy Jean loved Bessie Mae's expertise and often took her along when performing on the chitlin' circuit. As a result, Bessie's clientele grew by leaps and bounds. Soon the young mother saved enough money to open her very first salon. She lovingly referred to her son as Tikey and tried embodying her ethics, determination, and God-fearing spirituality inside him. During his elementary training, the boy attended six public schools. This was the result of constant relocating. When he reached junior high, they were finally able to live in a stable home. Their wandering period had at last come to an end. TaNellie graduated from Glenville High School at the top of his class. Bessie Mae had great expectations for her son, hoping he'd become a lawyer or even a doctor. As with most his age, the eighteen-year-old considered his mother old-fashioned and behind the times. Her patience and easy manner were viewed as contentment with the status quo. TaNellie was misinformed by youthful naivete.

TaNellie is a born leader. He was comfortable with expressing his own wishes but found it increasingly difficult to obey authority. At Central State University he dropped out just twelve credit hours prior to receiving his degree. Rumors suggest he left after being disciplined for pandering and gambling. School and police records haven't substantiated those rumors. Upon his return home, a heartbroken Bessie felt it necessary to oust him from her home until he obtained his degree. She referred to her decision as tough love.

Without monetary funds or a place to stay, TaNellie struck out on his own and has been estranged from his mother ever since. He has no criminal record; however, he has been observed in the company of those who do. For the past five years he's been seen with a variety of white female prostitutes. Subtly put, he thinks of himself as a gentleman of leisure... a more graphic term is pimp. Among his circle of friends TaNellie is viewed as well-to-do and has vowed to earn $1,000,000 before leaving the life. He finds solace with celebrity types, including professional athletes, politicians, and those in the entertainment world.

Attached please find a number of photographs taken during a month-long investigation. For thirty days our detectives have compiled photographic evidence, observed from a distance, of the subject's most recent activities. Marta, I certify that the report contained herein concerning TaNellie Lafitte Purifoy is an unbiased view based on information compiled from research, observations, and numerous first-hand interviews.

Warm regards,
Raul Montoya, CEO

Marta didn't know what to make of the agency photos. The facial identities of those in the black and white photos were blacked out. Only those of TaNellie were identifiable. Their secret nature, based solely on the graininess of the photos seemed to reveal a seedier side of the man she met in Kentucky. Generally speaking, Marta's intuition was seldom wrong. Could it be that TaNellie's charm was an act--a diversion of sorts, a calculated ruse to snare unsuspecting women, thereby trumping Marta's basic human instincts?

Even though she had been cautioned by Joe Louis, Marta found it difficult to believe Tee was part of a vast underworld plot that exploited women for money. For the first time in her life, she wasn't sure of what to do. She wished there were tape recordings accompanying the pictures, enabling her to hear his conversations. Maybe in a day or so she'd be able to make sense of the dossier provided by Raul Montoya. Until then, she'd have to do some serious soul-searching. Reading about alleged actions is one thing, but caring about TaNellie the way she did made it a brand-new ball game.

(15) Word on the street...

With cupped palms shading his eyes, TaNellie peered past the reflection of the sun- drenched front window and into Cotton's Top Barber Shop. The eighty-year-old tonsorial expert, Ezekiel Cotton, was seated in the chair nearest the window. His legs were crossed exposing his banlon socks and new captoe shoes. He was reading yesterday's *Cleveland News*, Final Stocks edition. Of the three local newspapers, it was the only one to feature both horse racing results and daily policy numbers. Zeke zeroed in on the words...what stocks did. A quick calculation revealed three digits: 687 was last night's number. TaNellie knocked on the glass and was about to move on when the old man looked above the rim of his spectacles and hurriedly beckoned him inside. The two shook hands.

"Hey, old timer...what's new?"

"Hello, Mr. TaNellie--how've you been, sir?"

Zeke stood, folded the newspaper, and dusted off the seat with a whisk broom. "Why don't you sit down right here, son, and I'll give you a shave?" The barber lowered the volume on the Indians radio broadcast, and looked around his shop making sure they were alone. "I got a few words to share with you, Mr. TaNellie."

Tee placed his fez on the hat rack and sank into the comfortable barber's chair. Zeke wrapped a sheer paper strip around his neck, then draped a white cutting cape over his chest, securing it with a chrome-colored clip. Cotton pulled his favorite leather strop taut and sharpened the straight razor with multiple back and forth motions. Afterward, he mixed a cupful of hot lather and everything was good to go. Zeke reclined the chair and carefully spread the warm foamed soap onto Tee's face and proceeded with the shave.

"Mr. TaNellie, there was a gentleman here last week asking some personal questions about you."

"What kind of questions, Zeke?"

"Questions about your character, and things of that nature."

"What did you tell him?"

"Wasn't nothing to tell, but I will say this, he wasn't the police. He didn't show a badge--and you know cops, it's the first thing they do. Naww, I think he was just interested in the type of person you were."

"What'd he look like?"

"He was a clean-cut colored fellow, about thirty or so."

"Where did he go after he left here?"

"Don't rightly know, Mr. TaNellie...he could have made a few more stops down the street. You might want to ask the other folks directly."

Tee didn't put too much worry into people asking about him, just as long as they weren't rollers. TaNellie sank lower into the barber chair, relaxing comfortably while enjoying his shave. In Zeke's hands the razor seemed to glide effortlessly over every nook and cranny of Tee's chestnut- colored skin, dispatching stubble with each stroke. TaNellie's nostrils flared ever so slightly, sensing peach brandy on the barber's breath. Ezekiel's adeptness and calming bedside manner caused TaNellie to fall asleep right in the chair...where he dreamed of a time when he was a very young boy.

When Zeke finished smoothing on witch hazel, he applied a few sprinkles of Canoe cologne to Tee's face. The old man stocked it at the pimp's request. Cotton just happened to glance up in time to see the stranger who'd asked all the questions. He was walking down the street, dressed in a brown sports coat with khaki trousers. The man was carrying a brown leather 35mm camera case. Zeke leaned closer to his client's ear and whispered, "Mr. TaNellie!" He pointed. "That's the man, over yonder...he's the one who was asking about you."

Tee got up while Zeke carefully removed the clip and cutting cape from around his neck. With squinted eyes, TaNellie continued staring intently. "You sure, Zeke?"

"Just as sure as Lincoln freed the slaves!" Tee left his fez on the hat rack and waited a few seconds before he opened the shop door. When the opportunity availed itself, he slipped outside and followed the stranger.

TaNellie moved slowly along the south side of the street, deliberately shortening his steps to avoid getting too close. The stranger went directly into the dime store and headed for a bank of telephones toward the rear of the establishment. He waited a few minutes for an empty booth, then stepped inside and made a call. Meanwhile Tee took a seat at the end of the lunch counter, ordering a powdered donut and a cup of coffee from Sally. After a short conversation, the man hung up the phone, checking the coin return in the process. He nodded, courteously smiling as Sally tended to a customer. Tee watched him leave the premises, then followed. The man walked half a block and got into the passenger's side of a black Ford, and rode off. TaNellie was close enough to jot down the license number. Later he passed on the information to a buddy, who promised to have it checked out.

It rained throughout the night. There is nothing more disconcerting to a pimp than seeing his wenches standing in a downpour holding umbrellas with not one red cent to show for it. The next morning, after a broken rest, TaNellie awoke from a recurring dream. He pondered the dream's meaning while staring outside at ominous dark clouds. The staccato flashes of light quickly followed by rolling claps of thunder continued moving eastward at a rapid pace. Tee had dreamed about his sixth birthday. He remembered holding his favorite childhood treat: orange cupcakes wrapped in cellophane. Earlier that day, Bessie had spent her last dime for a package of two Hostess cupcakes. She gave him one cake for later, then put a lit match in the other cake while singing "Happy Birthday" before it died out. When night fell, they huddled together in the rear of an elementary school building. Bessie Mae held Tikey's hands while reciting a children's prayer: "Now I lay me down to sleep." As they curled up beside a metal door stenciled with the words "Boiler Room," it began to rain. Soon Tikey was soaking wet and nestled even deeper into his mother's bosom. He sobbed as raindrops masked his tears. Little Tee had no way of knowing his mother's tears were flowing as well. At that moment, on May 20, 1934, Bessie solemnly promised "We'll never again be without a roof over our heads!"

TaNellie missed his mother and wanted desperately to see her again. He wanted to feel Bessie Mae's arms around him. With the lucid dream still fresh in his mind, he did something shocking even to him. He sat at the dining room table and wrote a letter to the Chancellor of Central State University. Tee requested he be allowed to re-enroll in school via correspondence courses to complete his degree. After getting dressed, he went directly to the mailbox nearest his apartment and dropped the envelope into the slot. Wearing his trademark fez, he stood silent for a few seconds, rubbing the olive-green letter receptacle like a crystal ball. A myriad of positive thoughts raced around in his mind like cars at the Indianapolis 500. If ever there was a chance to right a wrong, getting his sheepskin was truly the opportunity. A wonderful feeling surged throughout his entire body, leaving him with positive visions concerning the future. After contemplating what might be, as a result of his actions, TaNellie purchased a newspaper. He stopped by Juanita's southern cuisine restaurant for breakfast. As far as he was concerned, nobody in Cleveland cooked as well as Juanita.

As usual, her place was jam-packed with a diverse crowd representing people across the city and from all walks of life. "Hey, Tee! Got a booth all set up for you right over here, baby!" The owner was a petite, yet shapely woman, in spite of her vocation.

"Thanks, 'Nita... I see business is good!"

"When you serve the best food in town, business is always good!" She slid into the seat across from him. "Hope you don't mind me sitting here for a second. I got some holler for you."

TaNellie quickly responded, "Yeah, 'Nita--somebody's been asking about me...I heard already."

"How'd you get the word so fast?" she asked, astonished. "He just stopped in!"

"I've got my ways. Let me school you to something, 'Nita... trying to one-up me is like sneaking daylight past a rooster...it ain't possible!"

Juanita laughed heartily. "Baby, I'm scared o' you!"

"Let me have my usual breakfast fare, 'Nita...with a tall glass of buttermilk on the side."

"Coming right up, honey!"

TaNellie sat back in the booth and stretched his long legs while opening the paper to the sports page. "INDIANS TAKE DOUBLE HEADER FROM TIGERS!"

(16) Quizas...

—

TaNellie's buddy, a police officer, gave him the requested DMV information about license plate AB 2820. It was a Hertz rental car paid for by purchase order # 110749 from Solutions Detective Agency of Cleveland, Ohio. Their parent company was located in Barcelona, Spain. Señor Raul Montoya was the organization's president and CEO. Tee thanked the friend for helping, and gave him a fifty-dollar bill for his trouble. TaNellie never shied away from paying for services... it was just the price of doing business. When he noticed Barcelona listed in the information, he immediately thought about the beautiful Marta de LaCosta. *I wonder if she had anything to do with the man who asked all the questions? Perhaps I'll give her a call later on when I get back to the crib. Nothing major...just to say hello...maybe she'll tip her hand.*

TaNellie lived in the small municipality of Bratenahl in a luxury apartment building overlooking the shores of Lake Erie. He shared the spacious suite with Ming-toy, his spoiled but lovable Chinese Crested. It was early morning in Barcelona...7:06 a.m., to be precise. TaNellie couldn't care less and dialed the operator anyway.

"Number, please?"

"Long distance please, operator."

"I'll connect you, sir--one moment please!"

"Hello, long distance operator, please dial Miss Marta de LaCosta at 111-4398."

"It's ringing, sir."

"Thank you, operator."

The phone continued ringing...finally she picked up. "Hola."

"Hello, Marta...it's Tee, in Cleveland...I'm so sorry for waking you up this early."

"Tee, don't be silly; I'm in bed planning the rest of my day... this is just normal procedure for me, but thanks for being so considerate. I trust nothing's wrong?"

TaNellie hadn't known until this very moment how pleasing it would be to hear her alluring voice again. "Marta, everything is fine. I was thinking of you and decided to call. It's been a while and I wanted to make sure you didn't forget about me!"

"Tee, how dare you even think such things? How often does a woman win a $1000 bet from a pimp?"

TaNellie laughed. "Who told you I was a pimp?"

"Like they say...where there's a will there's a way!"

TaNellie responded jokingly, "I assume you're referring to Spain's answer to the great detective, Sherlock Holmes--Raul Montoya, the CEO of Solutions Detective agency!"

"Oh my, Tee...you're really good! Raul and I have been friends since childhood."

"Marta, all you really had to do was ask, saving yourself some money in the process."

She sat up straight, her body against the headboard, while positioning fluffy down pillows into the small of her back. "Sorry...I just like doing things my way!"

"Don't we all..." replied Tee. TaNellie cleared his throat. "So, Marta, what is it you do for a living?"

"Funny you should ask," she joked. "My father was in Spain's diplomatic corps under Generalisimo Francisco Franco. Dad never became a rich man, but was able to leave me a sizable trust fund when he died. My portfolio increased after I traded in stocks and bonds along with some smart blue chip investments. Tee, what's the term used in your profession...it has something to do with gentlemen?"

Tee thought for a few moments. "You don't mean gentlemen of leisure, do you?"

"*Exactamente! Ahora me doy la gran vida*! [Exactly! Presently I'm living the great life!] It seems you and I are similar in so many ways."

"Marta, please answer a question for me. What does the word pimp mean to you?"

She spoke extemporaneously. "It's a word which describes a professional leech. It has negative connotations...and identifies a man who mistreats and uses women. After which he has the nerve to confiscate her earnings. In a word, Tee...." Marta collected her thoughts. "A pimp is a cad! You did ask."

"Marta, do you really think I'm as bad as all that?"

"Let me be honest with you, Tee. I was extremely disappointed to find out how you made your living, especially after feeling a subtle attraction toward you...since our very first meeting. You were quite chivalrous then...a perfect gentleman."

"Marta, when I was at the Derby with Joe Louis, I felt comfortable enough to be a perfect gentleman, to use your phrase. It's my *raison d'être*. Marta, I'd love to spend some quality time with you...and unmask myself...the parts of me I keep hidden as a result of my profession. I'm sure you have a lot of things to do today. Promise me you'll think about what I said. We can make arrangements to see each other--what do you say?"

Things were moving rather quickly for Marta, and she abruptly ended their conversation with one word: "*Quizas!*" She quickly hung up.

TaNellie had to wait until the library opened to find a Spanish dictionary. He immediately delved into the pages, his heart racing. His brown eyes kept pace with his fingertip as it slid down the

Q's at breakneck speed. "Quiteño...quito....Ahhh here it is...qui-
zas. It means maybe or perhaps!" The pimp was elated, blushing
like a child with a report card full of A's. "Wow...she said maybe!"
He couldn't remember having been so gratified by such a simple
word...which Marta chose to close their conversation. He repeated it over and over until it was committed to memory.

Marta de LaCosta had hung up the phone by design...it was
her defense mechanism. No way did she want Tee getting inside
of her head. "After all...he is a pimp!" Marta had some decisions
to make. Was she or wasn't she going to allow this man into her
life? Just being on the phone with TaNellie for just a short time
already resulted in her tentatively agreeing to get together...alone,
no less. He was a very charming man whose voice was smooth
and disarming. It oozed assurance whether speaking the truth or
a load of bull. TaNellie was a silver-tongued devil if ever there
was one. He always knew just what to say and what to do. Marta
wasn't usually attracted to bad boy types. She found them to be
self-centered, egotistical, selfish, and above all... narcissistic. Tee's
good looks notwithstanding, he'd managed--with her help, of
course—to visit her most sacred place. It was where she felt most
vulnerable...the heart. The more she said no... the more her heart
responded affirmatively. Soon she threw caution to the wind.
Marta was ambivalent about sharing her personal feelings with
Tee. One thing was certain, however; she had passed the point of
no return. In spite of all the logic in the world, the fact remained:
she was smitten with a pimp.

(17) Good news...

Dear TaNellie L. Purifoy,
It is with great pleasure that I inform you, Central State University has decided to grant your recent request. Our records indicate you need twelve credit hours to complete your graduation requirements for a degree in the Liberal Arts.

We invite you to register for our next quarter and attend classes here on our campus in Xenia, Ohio. This is a slight variation from the correspondence courses you wanted; however, this avenue will afford you and your family an opportunity to experience the excitement and pomp of witnessing your graduation ceremony first hand. If this is agreeable we look forward to seeing you soon.

Sincerely,
William L. Jeffries
Chancellor, Central State University

Tee was pleased with the reply from CSU. He looked forward to moving in a positive direction. He couldn't wait to share the news with his mother. He imagined her surprise and satisfaction upon receiving an invitation to his graduation. For as long as he could remember, college was all she ever dreamed of for him. Bessie knew education was the key to a successful life. She never failed to drum her expectations into her son. If Tee proved unsuccessful, it wouldn't be because she hadn't tried.

Tee loved games of chance, and played poker with his friends a few times each week. Every outing included the most hilarious embellished tales ever told. Each story grew in farcical content, as if filled by helium. TaNellie's focus was on Dancer's hands, as he dealt the Bicycle brand cards. Tee dragged them in closer: red side up, and one at a time. He used this lull to scrutinize the faces of those around him. methodically searching for dormant tendencies, such as a tell...anything to give him an upper hand. Short Stack was the easiest--an open book, who always smiled sheepishly when dealt a decent hand. The little fellow just couldn't help himself. He might as well have left his cards exposed. Pimp-or-die, on the other hand, stuttered when placing bets... unless his hand was promising...at which time he was cool as a cucumber. The most advanced player among Tee's circle was Ginger Ale, whose real name was Vernon. He was great at bluffing because his mannerisms and poker face were always difficult to discern. Ginger Ale would cheat at cards in a second if he thought he could get away with it. Needless to say, during game time...he was watched closer than a fox at a hen convention.

Last but not least was the handsome Colin Dancer, a boss gambler from Port of Spain, Trinidad. He started playing cards for money at the age of nine years old. Dancer knew every rule according to Hoyle, and a few streetwise axioms of his own. Whenever the cards didn't quite pan out as planned, he recited a short gambler's poem: "The saddest tale on land and sea...is pleading with the dealer not to pass by me!" Dancer always cracked himself up and laughed louder than anyone at his own jokes. Before play began, Dancer started his ritual. "You young boys got a lot of gall... calling yourselves poker players. You boys ain't done nothing... ain't been nowhere except for Cleveland. You motherfuckers still doing the pussy...while grown folks is fucking. Short Stack, you little bastard, I bet you came over here on a bicycle even though a tricycle is more your speed. Shit...when I was you boys' age, I was already a war veteran. I've seen Europe, and been to China. Hell, I even carved my name on the Great Wall, as a matter of fact, I was in *Bagdad*... when you baby-cereal-eating motherfuckers were still in your *dad's bag*! That's right, I said it. Now if you boys really want to learn something...just sit back and relax while the Dancer goes to work. I'll show you bucks how poker's supposed to be played! Now you broke-ass motherfuckers ante up! This is going to be fun...I can hear those weak-ass knees of yours knocking right now! Short Stack, you might as well leave your wallet with me...you little fucker! Ha ha ha ha!"

Tee cut in. "Hold it Dancer! I'm still searching my pocket for some small bills for you small-time poker players. Besides, Dancer--always remember good things come to those who wait."

"That might be true for you pimp types, but inventor Thomas Edison said, and I quote... 'Good things come to those who *hustle* while they wait!'"

TaNellie bogarded (cut in) once more. "Thomas Edison was a natural-born pimp. He's got the whole world working for his ass. In case you boys didn't know, he stole the light bulb idea from me. I'm kicking his old ass when I see him again."

Dancer was ready to play some cards. "Okay, let's get this show on the road! That's enough with the bullshit, motherfuckers! Ante up...or get the fuck up. I don't know about you boys, but I got places to go and things to do!"

TaNellie had played with some of the best card sharps in the Midwest during his short career. He knew a wide variety of hustlers...hookers, too...who played poker like nobody's business. Some were very good, while others were just mediocre, but he learned from each of them. Most in his group handled big bank through the years and were really down...copacetic hustlers. The more enterprising players were entrepreneurs with a variety of business interests such as restaurants, bars, cleaners, convenience stores, and apartment buildings. They viewed these investments as something to fall back on after retiring from the life. There were also those who pimped and gambled well into their sixties and seventies. Unfortunately, pimping still remained a young man's game, and old timers were just tempting fate. Everyone knew sooner or later the axe was going to fall...usually when they could handle it the least. Some hustlers stay in the life for the love of the game...like athletes. Still others continue chasing the big score, the pie in the sky, or the chicken farm. Each one is still hoping for the ultimate payoff that will give them a carefree life. In the case of a few unfortunates...for whatever reason...the life has caused many a player to sing his swan song before slipping off into obscurity. They become burdens on society, barely able to remember who they are...or once were. Youth is fleeting and time flies even when everyone is having fun and spending money like there's no end in sight. Hard living, too much drinking and carousing eventually take a toll. The life teaches even the hardest heads cruel lessons. There's nothing more pitiful than a life wasted on a bullshit tip. Once-vibrant men and women become discarded detritus and find themselves in rat-infested buildings, crazy as Betsy bugs. "Oh, what a tangled web they once weaved!"

In a very real sense, TaNellie was one of the lucky ones. He kept his girls in line using brains and intellect, as opposed to fists and fear. His wenches were a part of his stable because they wanted to be, and not because they were forced. This allowed him to be fair-minded and flexible when it came to his operation. Take the average pimp, for instance...who falls victim to the Master's plantation mentality and deals harshly with his wenches like slaves. These pimps have replaced old Master by physically abusing their charges with harsh punishments, like a God-given right. From a strictly business standpoint, cosmetics can hide only so much.

Violence is just plain bad for business. Eventually Johns look for unbruised, prettier girls to fulfill fantasies. Hustlers who beat a woman into being a hoe may as well be a lion tamer wearing a pith helmet and carrying a whip, wooden chair, and loaded sidearm in a wild animal circus act. As a result of his abusive tactics, he becomes paranoid. It's highly probable he's an insomniac who hasn't slept soundly in years. He is always keeping an eye out for a disgruntled wench seeking revenge. His greatest fear is waking up dead. Tee always cautioned those bullying types by saying, "Mark my words, when you're sleeping under those warm covers on a cold Sunday morning and smell bacon grease, don't think you're about to eat breakfast. You'd better haul ass while you can! If you motherfuckers think you're dark now...try wearing some hot grease on your crispy black asses!"

Tee's friends burst out into laughter...like magpies. Short Stack put his two cents' worth into the mix by rejecting Tee's theory. "Negroes, please! I wish some scandalous-ass hoe would try and pull some bullshit like that on me!"

Deep down inside, every pimp knew Tee was right. After all, the law of averages clearly stated that everyone had to fall asleep sooner or later. It just made you wonder how long must literary scholars repeat what men already know: "Hell hath no fury like a woman scorned."

TaNellie stopped by the stable before his morning constitutional. He wanted to see Ana and get an update on how things were going. He always varied his visits and never announced himself beforehand. He loved Ana and often shared his innermost feelings with her. At the last minute, he decided not to speak about college. "Those bitches would think I've gone and lost my ever loving mind!" He always looked forward to seeing his bottom lady. Only God knew where he'd be, if it wasn't for Ana. TaNellie kept a key to the apartment, but always knocked prior to entering. As he walked down the hall, he heard the distinctive sounds of raised voices. Upon sidling closer, he was able to hear the gist of the conversation. It seemed as though Ana was arguing with one of the girls about missing earrings. When Tee heard glass breaking, he quickly opened the door and found himself smack between two women.

"What the fuck's going on?" he shouted. Ana's knuckles were pure white, as she tightly gripped a butcher's knife. The other woman was a Negro, who was holding a double shot glass like a baseball. She'd already thrown one glass but missed, chipping the wall. "Ana...who the hell is this bitch?"

Before she responded the woman answered--rolling her eyes at Ana in the process, and loosening her grip on the shot glass, "My name is Rae...and this snow Jane is trying to steal my man!"

"Who the fuck is your man, bitch?" Tee asked.

The slim brown-skinned woman threw her head back and proudly proclaimed, "Short Stack is my man!"

Tee seemed perturbed by the stranger's effrontery. "Ana, what's this all about?"

"This crow Jane thinks I want her fucking man. She says he gave me a set of diamond earrings he bought for her. Tee, I don't even own a pair of diamond earrings--and besides...I wouldn't accept shit from her chili pimp if my life depended on it!"

"Rae...is that your name, bitch? Let me hip your dumb ass to some facts!" TaNellie reached inside his coat pocket and gave Ana a black velvet jewelry box. "Open it up, Ana...those belong to you!" Ana beamed her satisfaction. It was a gorgeous set of diamond earrings, at least a carat and a half apiece. "Look, Mae...I've got those rocks because I won them fair and square from Short Stack two nights ago. Now I'm not saying you don't have a beef. But it's not with my wench. You need to go and talk to Short Stack... with his non-gambling ass. Now you saw me give those earrings to Ana...that means they're hers! So do me a favor and take your narrow simple ass back to your chili pimp and tell him what happened. If he has a fucking problem, he can deal with me!"

The woman just stared blankly into space. "That's right, Rae... I said it...I meant it...and I'm here to represent it! Now tell your pimp what I said."

The woman dropped the empty shot glass onto the floor and left with her tail tucked between her legs like a stray pussycat.

Ana was relieved. "Tee, I'm sure glad you came by when you did...I was about to slice and dice that wench!" Ana was trembling, still pumping adrenalin after the confrontation with Rae. TaNellie tried his best to calm her, and warmly embraced the pretty blonde.

"I've got your back baby...it's my job...it's why we need each other." He pivoted in midstream. "Before I forget, how do you like those diamond earrings?"

"They're exquisite, daddy...and I love you for giving them to me!"

TaNellie paused and glanced into a couple of empty bedrooms. "Baby...where's the girls?"

"They'll be back soon, Tee...I let them take the car to Juanita's. They deserved a real sit- down breakfast for a change. I knew you wouldn't mind."

Tee gently embraced his favorite gal. "Not at all, Ana...you've got those bitches working like they mean it. They're on the good foot right now, and performing more tricks than a magic act."

He opened the velvet box and placed the earrings into Ana's lobes. "These diamonds express just how much I appreciate your fine pink ass!" After Tee's timely display of affection, he briefly kissed Ana on the lips and she was good to go. The jewelry proved to be a real game tightener and just what the doctor ordered. TaNellie was a master manipulator, and everything he did was to enhance his perceived image. "Say Ana, let's go over to Juanita's for breakfast too-- steak and eggs would hit the spot!" He winked at her, then smiled. "It's on me!"

A few days later, TaNellie met with his associates for another round of poker. Short Stack's absence was the topic of conversation for most of the day. "Tee...I know you heard about your boy... Short Stack!"

TaNellie's eyes were fixated on his hand. He pulled the cards close to his chest, spreading them apart ever so slightly for a sneak peek. "Naaw, Colin...I haven't...what about him?"

"Tee...the little motherfucker was found sitting inside his 1949 Plymouth convertible...dead as a sonofabitch, with a bullet hole right between his wide-open eyes. His pockets were turned inside out and every piece of his gaudy-ass jewelry was missing. The rollers don't have a clue about what happened."

TaNellie was appalled at just how quickly life's fortunes could change. "Damn...we were playing cards with him just last week!" TaNellie never mentioned the altercation between Ana and Rae. "Sometimes it's wise to leave well enough alone." Besides, what his friends didn't know couldn't hurt him.

It had been two weeks since Short Stack's untimely demise. The rollers wanted to question his associates to help shed light on who may have killed him. It was just routine, but TaNellie was asked to stop by second district police station on 21st and Payne Avenue to answer some questions. Tee entered the station sharp as a tack, wearing a navy-blue suit, polka-dot tie, and kiltie alligator loafers. He was taken to a small office on the first floor. Shortly afterward...a captain with a ruddy complexion entered the room and took a seat behind his desk directly across from Tee. "Good afternoon, son...is there anything I can get you, before we proceed with the interview concerning the death of Mr. Perry Wilcox...aka Short Stack?"

TaNellie slouched in his chair, shaking his head in the negative. "Captain, please feel free to call me TaNellie, or Mr. Purifoy. I don't like being referred to as son...if you don't mind?" The captain continued perusing a folder with Tee's name handwritten across the cover. "Are you TaNellie L. Purifoy... born May 20, 1928 at Glenville Hospital to Bessie Mae Purifoy?"

"You tell me, Captain...you've got all the answers you need right in front of you."

"Answer the question, son!"

TaNellie was becoming irritated with the captain's insistence on using the word "son." He sat up straight in his chair and reiterated, "Captain, I've asked you nicely not to use that word. You don't know me well enough, so please don't call me son again!"

"I'll call you whatever I like, Mr. Purifoy. So you can take it or lump it...and here's why. My name is Captain Dale Murphy...I was just a sergeant when I helped bring your sorry ass into this world. I remember May 20, 1928 like it was yesterday. You see... SON...it was my men and I who escorted Councilman Thomas W. Fleming and your mother Bessie Mae safely to the maternity ward at Glenville Hospital. Once there, we also assisted Doctor Champion and Arnetta Houston, the midwife, in delivering your ungrateful ass. I don't think you realize just how close you came to dying that morning. Breech births have come a long way since then...but they're still life-threatening and are a harrowing procedure. We all worked as a team that morning and pulled off a nearly impossible task by saving your life. So don't you dare crack wise with me, son. I am your father... me and the other four Irish officers who helped bring you into this world. It was Bessie Mae, your own mother, who gave us the honorary title of Father...so like I said son, you can either take it or lump it!

"Now this interview is just a formality, so the sooner you answer my questions, son...the sooner you can leave. Perry Wilcox's girlfriend said you took some jewelry from the late pimp. You're not a suspect, but if you want a lawyer...give me the name and I'll contact him for you. If not, just answer my questions and you'll be free to leave."

TaNellie felt like two cents and apologized to the captain. "I'm sorry...I acted like an asshole. I've never been in trouble with the law. I didn't know what to expect, so I was a bit on edge."

TaNellie told the captain about the confrontation between Rae and Ana. He also copped to the fact he won a pair of earrings in a card game days before the man was killed. The captain seemed satisfied, but wanted to interview Ana as well. He offered to accompany TaNellie to the apartment near Liberty Boulevard to take a statement from her. This would ensure that there wasn't time for collusion between the two. After Ana made a statement in writing, all was well. "TaNellie, be sure to give your mother my best...I hope she's doing fine."

"I certainly will, Captain Murphy...thanks!"

(18) Cleopatra Wisdom...

Miss Cleo sighed...she figured it was gonna be another one of those hundred-degree-plus days. New Orleans was running neck and neck with Hell—each vying for control of a city full of trapped souls. Even lifelong residents found it hard to endure the extreme discomfort caused by the heat. They took great care not to stray too far from shade or ice-filled jugs of sweet tea. Heat waves rose up from parched earthen roads like the scent that breaks from a frightened skunk's backside. "How many days this awful heat gonna be with us, Miss Cleo?" asked the old man, removing his crimped weatherbeaten straw hat, exposing a bald head. Using a pocket hanky, he dabbed the sweat from his pale cranium. The old man looked like two different people...his hat covering a white one...while below the brim line he looked damn near like a Negro...a very dark one, at that.

"I suspect it's gonna stay just as long as it wants, old man. And when it's done hanging 'round here, it'll move on down the line. You can put that in your pipe and smoke it!"

In the entire State of Louisiana, Miss Cleo was probably the only Negro whom whites addressed as "miss"--with a small m, of course. In the land of Dixie, coloreds were usually called by their first names. Occasionally it was aunt, uncle, and even boy or missy, and it didn't matter how old they were. It was no small wonder every Pullman porter working for the railroad was always referred to as George...in spite of their real names. A. Philip Randolph, the colored President of the Brotherhood of Sleeping Car Porters, was quite possibly the only exception to the rule.

Miss Cleo's thoughts seemed a million miles away from the sun's scorching rays. She was preoccupied with her friend Bessie Mae Purifoy...and missed their long chats after church services. Cleo wondered how she was coping with the terrible loss of her family. Somewhere within the wake of that unexpected disaster was a glimmer of hope amidst the sadness. Authorities had listed Bessie Mae among the dead. Cleo hoped the error in news reporting would satiate those responsible for the terrible loss in New Orleans and afford her time to find a counter spell. Miss Cleo was revered far and wide as an extremely gifted spiritualist who got results. She worked arduously every night in a candlelit back room of her small home. She scoured through hundreds of handwritten notebooks full of spells with the patience of the Hebrew Job. Her collection numbered well into the thousands and consisted of recipes, potions, rare plants, roots, herbs, spices, animal parts, talismans, and other bits and pieces of important information. Cleo also had a box of 3x5 cards buried in a secret location somewhere on her property. She had been given them by her mentor, Sister Henrietta Raymore, who lived to be 100 years old. Miss Cleo never used the cards, and until this very moment had all but forgotten about their existence. These were special cards and contained evil spells to be used only in matters of life and death, as a last resort.

Miss Cleopatra Wisdom waited for nightfall...then stepped outside and into the hot, still darkness amid the sounds of chirping crickets and croaking frogs to retrieve her inheritance: Henrietta Raymore's treasure trove. She walked quietly toward a large spiral willow tree. As she knelt down beside its broad trunk, an eerie yet familiar voice startled her. "Miss Cleo!"

Her eyes widened, then focused in on a hunched-over, shadowy figure. "What you doing out here, old man?" she asked.

He clicked on his penlight. "Searching for night crawlers...
you?"

"The same thing...now get on away from here and do your
searching on someone else's property. Go on...get, before I turn
you into a garter snake!"

She waited for the old man to leave, then dug precisely one
foot beneath the soil using a small shovel. Cleo carefully cleared
away dirt from around the metal box, pulling it up from its tomb
by a wrought-iron handle. She cleaned it off with pumped spring
water from her well...then took it inside and headed directly for
the backroom. She lit an old kerosene lamp and perused the cards,
which were listed in alphabetical order. When she was halfway
through the B's, she noticed a card titled Boomerang...with a skull
and crossed bones stamped in India ink on both sides of the word.
The records indicated it should be used for countering dangerous
spells and hexes. It contained rare ingredients, which supposedly
administered the same fate to those who had initiated the original
hurtful hex. In a word, it possessed boomerang capabilities--or
more specifically, the instigator reaped what they sowed. Sister
Raymore's recipe was as powerful a counter-curse, if ever there
was one, and impossible to trace. Once activated, it instinctively
sought out the originator of the spell, rendering them null and
void forever...dead! A key component in this voodoo spell is an
extract made from the petal of a corpse flower, technically known
as *amorphophallus titanum*. Its unique scent mirrored decom-
posing flesh and attracted carcass-eating insects to the evildoer
in much the same manner that common house flies are drawn to
a dead corpse.

Miss Cleo worked until daybreak precisely measuring, reciting
incantations, and cooking ingredients until her home reeked of
the netherworld. Finally her work was finished, and she was more
exhausted than ever before. Any slight deviation from the recipe

would cause the spell to backfire, causing death to both Cleo and Bessie Mae. Since there was no way to test the mixture, the proof would have to be in the pudding. It was time for a nervous Miss Cleo to utter the final evocations. She sipped some sweet tea to quench her dry throat.

"I call upon goodness and mercy to overcome the evil which has been wrought against Bessie Mae Purifoy and her descendants. Strike down the evil ones and protect the righteous. I ask this of the ancient ones in the name of all that is good!"

Cleo placed the concoction into a saucepan and turned the stove's burner on high. She quickly brought it to a full boil, and as the steam filled the kitchen it began to sputter and give off sparks and popping noises like it was the Fourth of July. In less than thirty seconds, it evaporated into nothingness. Miss Cleo looked inside the pan, and pursuant to her instructions, it was empty and dry as a bone. Unfortunately she still had no way of knowing if the spell would work or not. Cleopatra Wisdom had followed the directions explicitly, and waited for a sign.

The following Sunday morning--almost a week to the day that Miss Cleo had prepared the recipe--she walked to Saint Joseph AME Church with a few of her friends. The church was a quarter mile away, which proved quite enough time for some of the girls to dish the dirt about different members of the congregation. Miss Cleo had been baptized in the very same church by the Reverend William Ward, who still presided over the congregation. His first wife had died mysteriously five years ago, at which time he married Irene Ward. She was new to the church and was thirty years his junior. She was a beautiful young woman who smiled incessantly. Most of the female members of the congregation were certain she had roving eyes, and watched her like a hawk. Miss Cleo never put much stock in gossip, and always gave Sister Irene the benefit of the doubt.

The choir had just finished singing "What a friend we have in Jesus." The service was about to begin when a late arrival opened the front door of the sanctuary and was followed inside by an onslaught of thousands of swarming flies, completely darkening the entrance. They gathered en masse and flew high above the parishioners...circling the church's ceiling. The house flies continued buzzing and searching for what seemed like an eternity, before finally lighting upon Sister Irene. In seconds, the woman's shocked face was completely engulfed by the intruders. Her screams were muffled as hundreds of flies simultaneously entered her every orifice. The reverend tried to help, but Irene panicked and pulled away, running from the church. A dumbfounded flock looked on in horror as Sister Irene grabbed her throat with both hands while choking and screaming for mercy. She begged Heaven to save her. The young preacher's wife ran blindly down the dirt road as fast as she could with thousands of flies in hot pursuit. Finally she stumbled and fell to her knees in anguish, with her eyes revealing the horrible truth. Every one of those flies entered her body and began ingesting her being from the inside out, leaving a pile of steaming skin and bare bones behind. The entire uncanny process took less than ten minutes, and smelled like death warmed over...the same fragrance as the corpse flower.

Miss Cleo was a true believer in her chosen endeavor, and was taken completely aback by the spectacle she witnessed in church. The woman responsible for the deaths of many innocent people was finally exposed to the entire congregation. Justice was meted out swiftly to Irene Ward, who was also suspected of killing Reverend Ward's first wife. There were still so many unanswered questions, starting with why the Purifoys had been targeted in the first place. Perhaps time would reveal the mystery...or maybe not. Cleo never spoke to anyone concerning why or how Sister Irene met her demise, but would remember it like yesterday...for the rest of her borne days.

When Cleo returned home from church, she addressed a postcard to Bertha B. Goode c/o Councilman Thomas W. Fleming in Cleveland, Ohio. She would be sure and give it to the postman when he made his rounds. Miss Cleo jotted a personal thought on the card: "All is well that ends well!" She placed the penny postcard on the davenport, again reminding herself to give it to the postman.

When he arrived the next day, Miss Cleo was on the front porch sitting in her rocker. She handed him the postcard and smiled as he removed the crimped weatherbeaten straw hat from his bald head, asking, "How many days this awful heat gonna be with us, Miss Cleo?"

"Don't know, old man," she answered. "And I don't rightly care. How long we known each other, old man?"

"Thirty years, easy...I expect...since I started delivering mail to the parish...why?"

"I suspect it's about time I knew your given name."

"It's Freddy, Miss Cleo...Fred Bradley. Does knowing my proper name mean we're friends?"

Cleopatra rolled her eyes. "Not even close, old man. Ask me again in thirty years, and I'll let you know then."

After giving her all in the Purifoy ordeal, Miss Cleo's reputation skyrocketed. She had helped a good friend, expecting nothing in return. It's a special person who risks all to save another. Cleo knew the universe was just, and would sort itself out in due time...like it has for thousands of years. Cleopatra Wisdom slept contentedly for the first time in days, and so did a relieved Bessie Mae Purifoy. Meanwhile, the heat wave left New Orleans on the very same evening, moving on down the line for another more deserving city.

(19) Peppermints...

Bessie Mae firmly gripped the gentleman's hand and shook it vigorously like she meant it. "Mr. Silverman I want to thank you for all you've done. You mark my words—this beauty shop is just the beginning!" Ishmael Silverman smiled graciously, reciprocating her thanks with an embrace. The pair continued touring the 950-square foot storefront with Tikey—her young boy. It was an ideal location right on the Number 38 Cleveland Transit (CTS) System bus line. The partially integrated Polish neighborhood was sprinkled with working-class coloreds and some newly arrived Puerto Ricans...with each group searching for the American dream. "Once this space receives a fresh coat of paint and some elbow grease, Mr. Silverman, it'll be known as the Dixie Princess Beauty Salon!"

Tikey whispered in Bessie Mae's ear, "Momma...does this mean we're gonna live inside here?" Even her young son realized sleeping in a storefront was better than being outside.

"Shhh, honey...Momma's gonna talk to you about that later."

To her son, Mr. Silverman resembled jolly old Saint Nicholas, because of his rotund frame and white beard. He wasn't a very old man, perhaps in his early fifties, but to a six-year-old he was older than dirt. The boy didn't remember Mr. Silverman ever removing his hat...not even inside a house. His large black fedora forever rested precariously on the back of his head, exposing long wavy hasid locks, called payot. They looked like sideburns, only different and with a lot richer history.

Bessie Mae was well aware of his unrequited glances, but still managed to maintain a formal yet cordial relationship with the divorced man. Tikey liked Mr. Silverman. He always carried a pocketful of cellophane-wrapped peppermints. He would dole out the sweets whenever the little boy answered a tough question. "Okay, young man, how many eggs are in a baker's dozen? Think hard, son; we went over this last week."

Tikey answered confidently and quickly. "Thirteen, sir!"

He smiled...then quickly opened his palm. The man patted down his pockets, carefully repeating the process with a puzzled expression on his face. "Oy vey! I think I'm out of peppermints... there's just too many smart kids around these days."

Tikey lamented, "It's okay, Mr. Silverman...you can owe me two next time."

He patted his pockets once more. "Aha!" he exclaimed. "Here's a peppermint! It was hiding in the corner of my pants pocket all the time."

He extended the candy. "Here you are, young man...this one's for you...and I'll still give you two the next time!"

"Thank you, sir!" answered the boy, quickly unwrapping the candy before popping it into his mouth. Tikey wadded the wrapper, jamming it way down inside his jeans pocket until he felt a penny... a button...and his favorite cat's-eye marble, which he called "Kitty."

Bessie Mae first met Ishmael Silverman at the Hotel Statler laundry room, where she worked as a day laborer. He was the featured speaker at a large gathering of executives. Ten minutes before he was to go on... someone accidentally spilled coffee all over his white shirt. He was immediately rushed to the laundry room, where Bessie Mae was given the task of removing the stain. Without a second to spare, she gathered baking soda, vinegar, and salt and went to work. After eliminating the stain, she blotted the remaining wet spot, then quickly ironed it dry.

"Great Caesar's Ghost!" The speaker was astonished, to say the least. "You did an excellent job, young lady...excellent; the stain has vanished. Thanks so much, miss...?"

She curtsied. "Bessie Mae Purifoy, sir." He reached inside his pocket.

"Here...Miss Purifoy, take my card, and if you ever need anything at all, please contact me!"

He tipped Bessie five dollars before making it back to the gathering, just in time to hear his name being called to the podium. Once on stage, he smiled genuinely while stroking his neatly trimmed beard. Ishmael Silverman's reputation preceded him and he was welcomed by a thunderous standing ovation.

"Thank you...thank you for such a warm round of applause. I'll do my best to prove worthy of such a spirited welcome. As I look out among you, I see nothing but smiling faces. It's hard to imagine most of you are still smarting from events which took place some years back during the market crash in 1929. Gentlemen, that's exactly why I'm here." He smiled sheepishly. "Not to mention the extremely large fee I was given to help nurse your wounds and bring each of you back into the world of financial health. Please be advised, if there are no objections, I'm going to remedy what should never have occurred in the first place. If you gentlemen double down this evening, I'll guarantee you'll be back in the black before you know it! Or I'll happily refund double your money back. Now let's see about getting you men back on track!"

The room immediately filled with energetic and sustained applause. Ishmael Silverman did not disappoint in the least. He'd delivered his remarks hundreds of times, using only the most carefully chosen words. Silverman had the innate ability to glean information from an audience, and then come up with the obvious explanation for resolving their problems...sure fire tips on even more stocks. He incorporated his solution into an hour-long motivational presentation. He boasted of amazing results, and guaranteed that at least 90% of participants would triple their investments in a matter of months...some even sooner. Suffice to say, Mr. Silverman enjoyed what he did...and was completely booked across the country year-round. He offered hope to those who desired to be successful. Then he rode the swell of their desire...all the way to the bank. At the end of his presentation, he was routinely deluged by hundreds of investors, each wanting to take part in his apparent successes. Upon closing...to even greater applause than before...he momentarily glanced down at his shirt and smiled...when thinking of Bessie Mae...the colored girl.

The large man often shared his childhood experiences in Austria with Bessie and her son. But the tale he was about to tell was going to be a lot different from the others. He spoke of the time his father escaped from an internment camp during the Great War. His father Manny—along with eight others—each suffering from a host of maladies, hungered for freedom. On a dark night, luck appeared to be with the men as they crawled stealthily past armed guards and attack dogs. Under the cover of darkness, the group managed to slide beneath yards of barbed wire unnoticed... and fled the compound. They had gone just fifty yards in a feeble dash toward freedom when loud sirens and huge spotlights alerted soldiers. Manny took charge by encouraging the men, hurrying them along and whispering within earshot, "*Mach Schnell*! [Hurry!]" over and over as they continued running. Their best chance for escape prompted them to intersperse among the tall pines, only a hundred yards from camp. Manny exalted his friends to continue running. "*Mach Schnell! Mach Schnell!*" Their infirmities were many and it was becoming increasingly more difficult with each step for them to keep up. Manny's fast pace was taking its toll on the prisoners. "*Mach Schnell!*" he said again and again.

Suddenly...0815 light machine guns began uttering the very

succinct language of death. Manny dove for cover and continued crawling onward, asking the others to do the same. "*Mach Schnell!*" he cried. "*Mach Schnell!*" Enfilading 7.92mm bright-orange tracer rounds tore into trees and bodies alike...indiscriminately mowing down everything within their path. "Ta ta ta ta ta...too too too too....ta ta ta...too too too" brass shells pinged like chimes until the red-hot barrels of the 0815s ceased their deadly chorus. Clouds of thick smoke from the guns, and German voices permeated the air and in every direction. Manny kept moving even though the aches and pains of his body pleaded for him to stop. Hours later, his legs were moving much slower. He was spent...but inched forward nevertheless. His heart was racing like crazy—he was certain its distinct beating could be heard by the soldiers. Finally, after four days and four nights of being constantly on the move, he made it to safety. When "The war to end all wars" was finally over, Ishmael's father was never the same fun-loving man he once knew. A shell of his former self, he was withdrawn and felt the guilt of a survivor...a common affliction when witnessing the carnage of war. Manny was compelled to revisit his slain brethren via the far recesses of his mind's eye and the lucid nightmares from which he never escaped.

On a day when all seemed right with the world, shortly after the family finished a modest supper, Manny presented his son with a gift. It wasn't his birthday...nor was it a celebration honoring good marks in school. On this day, Ishmael received his very first stick of peppermint. Manny had always wanted a better existence for his son, and seeing him smile occasionally was the best he could offer. He apologized at length for not being the husband or father he'd hoped to be.

"Ish-dalah, my son...a piece of peppermint will help cheer you up during trying times!"

His son had never tasted peppermint before and didn't know

whether to bite, chew, or nibble the striped red and white candy. He tried it, and to his surprise—felt cheery inside as his father predicted. But the best part of all was its exquisite porous taste. Often the importance of an event goes unnoticed during its greatest impact. The stick of candy was to be a father's legacy to his son. Manny was--and is--the reason Ishmael Silverman currently passed out peppermints. They always brightened the smiles of those who received as well as those who gave.

Later that evening, his parents retired and Manny suffered a terrible nightmare...the worst yet. He was sweating profusely, thrashing his arms about while tossing and turning uncontrollably. He screamed at the top of his lungs, "*Mach Schnell!*" The severity of the nightmare prompted his wife to send Ishmael to fetch water from the well. His mother continued to apply cold compresses to his father's forehead in vain. "*Mach Schnell!*" he kept saying over and over. "*Mach Schnell!*" After what seemed like hours, Manny suddenly relaxed and his body was no longer spastic. It was as if nothing had ever happened. Manny had suffered from seizures ever since escaping from the internment camp, and now his demise seemed near. Everyone held hands and prayed for Manny. With closed eyes, he appeared to be at peace, and a slight smile graced his lips briefly as he whispered "*Mach Schnell*" for the very last time. Emanuel Silverman's life ended that night... but so too his pain. After Manny's burial, his friends sat Shiva for seven days.

Those events happened such a long time ago. Ishmael Silverman never told his father's story to gentiles before, and he was still visibly shaken. Tikey suggested he try a peppermint to help him feel better. "It's a wonderful idea, Tike-alah...I'm surprised I didn't think of it myself!"

After becoming an American citizen, Ishmael continued corresponding with his family by mail. An alarming trend had developed by 1936. In letters he received from Austria and Hungary, a bleak picture emerged. Jews in those countries faced another powerful nemesis. Ishmael was cautioned not to visit his homeland because things were worse now than ever before. Even living under the regime of Kaiser Wilhelm II--whom most deemed responsible for the world war and Germany's hatred toward Jews--couldn't compare. This newest menace had risen from the rank of corporal in the world war, and was now chancellor of a political party referred to as the Brown Shirts. Nazi party members were poised on the brink of controlling the Weimar Republic.

In 1931, the International Olympic Committee awarded Berlin the bid over Barcelona to host the 1936 summer games. With worldwide attention focused on Germany, Hitler hoped to prove his theory of Aryan superiority. The United States openly debated whether or not to attend the Olympics. Among those supporting a boycott was Jesse Owens, the Ohio State University famous track star. In time, he and others relented and decided to compete. After Jesse's remarkable five gold medal winning performance, the Führer left the stadium rather than honor a Negro... it was the snub heard around the world. Following the Olympics, Team USA was invited to meet with President Franklin Delano Roosevelt at a White House reception. Ironically, when Owens and his fellow Negro athletes decided to compete at Berlin, they dispelled Hitler's assertions of white superiority. Without any viable reasons, Jesse Owens and his Negro track and field teammates were not given invitations to meet with Franklin Delano Roosevelt. America's colored athletes were indeed snubbed by both friends and foes alike.

(20) Juggernaut...

Almost immediately, word spread about the Dixie Princess Salon--especially after the Dandriges began frequenting the shop. People took special note of how well the entertainers dressed, and their beautifully coifed hair styles always appeared freshly done. It was only natural for those in the neighborhood to emulate the sense of style exuded within the family. Ruby, along with daughters Vivian and Dorothy Jean Dandrige, were well-known in show business circles. They traveled across the United States singing and dancing up a storm while wearing the latest designs from the haute couture houses of Paris and Rome. If Bessie Mae Purifoy's well-honed skills were good enough for the Dandriges, they were surely good enough for regular folks. Bessie's beauty shop was just what Cleveland needed. It was a reasonably priced salon possessing the practical knowledge and ability to work on every type of Negro hair, ranging from fine to coarse. Although her salon was small, it was always packed with patrons. GJay, her roomie at the Phillis Wheatley Association, continued supporting her friend, but was never charged for services. Bessie felt were it not for GJay, she would have never opened a beauty shop. The salon was just barely large enough to house a restroom, which was kept spotless...and the personal room containing a rollaway bed and galvanized tub for bathing. Cooking simple meals was performed on a two-burner hot plate. The salon's popularity caused Bessie Mae to set her sights on additional salons.

The Purifoys planned on living in the shop until enough money had been saved for a kitchenette apartment. Mr. Silverman owned property all over greater Cleveland, and she was certain he'd find something reasonably priced and close to the shop. Business was brisk and Bessie rose early every morning and went to sleep late each night. She was determined not to let any client's hair go untreated. Bessie even came up with a special slogan and hired a sign painter to put her idea on the large front window just below Dixie Princess: *"We treat you and your hair like Royalty."*

From her back room, Bessie Mae could hear the bell just below the transom clang when the front door opened. She peered into the salon and confirmed, "Be right there, Miss Jenkins!" The nice looking red bone sashayed inside the shop, took a seat, and leafed through magazines to pass time. "Not to worry, honey," she said, "I'm not going anywhere!" Miss Jenkins was on time for her appointment and really seemed to be enjoying the summer. The thirty-year-old didn't miss a chance to flaunt her sensuous flat ankle wrap sandals. Woven leather straps crisscrossed the ankles and clung to her shapely calves like vines climbing a post. An immaculate pedicure, lacquered in dog dick red nail polish, iced the cake. Lola was a vamp and reveled in attention garnered from men and women...no matter their age, color, or station in life. If the truth be told, she was a tease, roused intensely by her most base instincts: sex.

Tikey loved the scent of Miss Jenkins' perfume. He scratched his head when noticing a dark purplish hue seemingly embedded in her skin. The coloring began just beneath her shin ending below the ankles. The boy queried Bessie, "Momma...why does Miss Jenkins have a strange color on her legs...is her skin coming off?"

She chortled loudly and when Lola glanced up momentarily, Bessie faked clearing her throat. "Ahem...shhh Tikey... her skin's not coming off..." she whispered. "Miss Jenkins works hard for her money at a company called Paramount Distillers on the west side. She has a very interesting job."

Her son was more puzzled than ever. "What kind of interesting job?"

"Well, Tikey...every day when Miss Jenkins reports to work she removes her shoes, then dips her feet into a special solution. She has to clean them thoroughly with a bristle brush before getting started. Lola and her co-workers trample barefoot on mounds of grapes until they turn to liquid."

"Momma, does Miss Jenkins really get paid for stomping on grapes?"

"Yes, son...people get paid for doing all sorts of things nowadays. When you're older... you'll realize just what people are willing to do...say...or pay...for the things and services they want."

"Momma, what do they do with the liquid when she finishes work?"

"After the company removes all of the impurities, they make a fine-tasting wine for public consumption."

Tikey couldn't believe his ears, as evidenced by his scowl. "Yucky...people drink what she puts her stinky feet into!"

"Tikey...it's a long story...and I don't have time to explain now. Why don't you go and do something constructive while I take care of Miss Jenkins' hair? Now scram before I put you to work!" The boy quickly left the shop and toured the neighborhood, soaking up all the urban sights and enjoying every moment.

Bessie Mae's meteoric success continued rocketing skyward. She and Tikey were now living in a nice two-bedroom apartment in Cleveland Heights off Taylor Road. For the first time since arriving in Ohio, the woman from New Orleans had a firm grip on destiny. Events in her life changed after a postcard given her by Councilman Fleming arrived. It was addressed to Bertha B. Goode and included a coded message sent by Miss Cleopatra Wisdom: *Passed spelling exam with flying colors. All is well that ends well.*

World War II was in its second year and Bessie's business

was booming. With most able bodied men in uniform, factories were hiring women in record numbers. After working long shifts, "Rosey the Riveter" types looked forward to shedding overalls for movie star duds and leading lady good looks. With silk and nylon being rationed for the war effort, Bessie catered to clients' every whim and regularly drew seam lines down bare legs with an eyebrow pencil, creating instant stockings. Bessie Mae was willing to do anything to satisfy customers. By the time her son turned thirteen years old, Bessie owned five Dixie Princess Salons. She handpicked and trained stylists in her methods of fixing hair. Once licensed by the state, Bessie rented them booth space, and also charged school tuition for her hair styling secrets. Each shop was doing well and Bessie thanked God for delivering her to Cleveland. Tikey was tall for his age and was experiencing growing pains. At thirteen he preferred to be called by his given name: TaNellie. Bessie Mae obliged him, even though she found it difficult to drop his nickname entirely. Young Purifoy's future good looks were becoming evident, something his mother witnessed first hand, after the curious glances from her clients lasted well beyond what she considered appropriate.

Miss Purifoy's income was modest when compared to Mr. Ishmael Silverman's. He was making money hand over fist. Their platonic friendship has flourished through the years. The Wall Street insider often shared unsolicited advice concerning stock investments, which Bessie never acted upon. He was a strong influence in Tee's life, a father figure of sorts, according to TaNellie... and a man who knew how to make lots of money in various ways.

"Bessie...you're doing very well for yourself now. I think it's high time you made arrangements for your future, as well as Tikey's. Why don't you invest a little money and buy some shares in a company I've been researching for quite a while? If you follow my lead and purchase, say, one hundred shares...you'll triple your investment in less than ninety days. Now I ask you, Bessie... do you know of another opportunity that'll virtually guarantee a three thousand dollar return practically overnight?"

Mr. Silverman never insisted on her participation when it came to buying stocks. Circumstances were different now, and she sensed desperation in his voice. She mulled over his suggestion and was reminded of the time her father told his children, "If something seems too good to be true...it probably is!" She decided to stall. "Mr. Silverman...why don't you let me think about it for a while? A thousand dollars is a lot of money, and I want to be positive before making decisions concerning stocks and bonds."

Ishmael wavered, but was disappointed. "Suit yourself, Bessie Mae...just let me know when you're ready to move forward and I'll take care of everything. Remember...time's a-wasting."

It wasn't the first time he had encouraged her to play the stock market, and it wouldn't be the last. Bessie had always maintained a strong work ethic and was raised believing that with hard work, folks always received their just due. She compared stocks and bonds to gambling, while hoping to reap a harvest without sowing any seeds.

Bessie asked TaNellie to open the shop. Lola Jenkins was scheduled to arrive at 8:00 Saturday morning. Bessie called her client and asked if she would mind coming in at 9:00 instead.

"Not a problem, honey...I'll see you at nine!" When the number 38 bus dropped Tee off the next morning, it was almost 8:00 a.m. He looked around the outside of the shop to make certain everything was in order before entering the salon. He observed the importance of taking precautions from his mother. Bessie had once been accosted and had since realized criminals always pick their victims...she continued to practice safety first!

TaNellie turned on the lights and was just about to lock the door from the inside when Miss Jenkins' breasts pressed against the plate glass door. She caught him completely by surprise and he quickly glanced into her cleavage before catching his breath. Her warm greeting was accompanied by an inviting smile. "Good morning, Tikey...how are you today?"

"Oh...hi...Miss Jenkins...I'm fine. It's my first time opening the shop and I'm a little bit nervous!"

Lola smiled slyly. "I was wondering why you were at the shop. Where's Bessie...is everything okay?"

Her calming voice caused him to relax. "Things are fine, Miss Jenkins...she's just taking care of some business with her accountant." He quickly added, "She'll be back around 9:00 if you want to wait!"

Tee decided to use this opportunity to inform Lola of his recent decision. "Miss Jenkins... can you please do me a favor?"

"It depends on what it is, Tikey."

"I wonder if you'd mind calling me by my first name?"

Until now, she had thought Tikey was his first name. "You mean Tikey is not your first name!"

"No...it's just a nickname...my real name is TaNellie." Her cunning eyes were mere slits, delving deep into his most latent desires. Lola slowly moved in closer, violating his space with her every step. She put her thumb into her mouth. "TaNellie, mm-mmm...what a delicious-sounding name. It seems to fit you like a warm glove. You're practically all grown up, and I'm sure the ladies are really going to love you. Tell you what, TaNellie--that's what you want me to call you... isn't it? I'll do whatever you want on one condition."

"What's that, Miss Jenkins?" She was close enough to smell the corn flakes on his breath. She placed her finger on the tip of his nose and whispered, "You'll have to call me Lola and do whatever I say--is that all right, TaNellie?" She was as close as a second skin.

"Sure, Miss Jenk...I mean Lola. I guess it's okay!"

"TaNellie...I'll assume that's a long...big...fat...yes!"

He stumbled backwards, nearly tripping, but was blocked by the backroom door. Lola's warm breath quickened as she pressed nearer. "TaNellie, how do you like my perfume? It's called La Trampa [the trap] and it's from Spain. I haven't the foggiest idea of what it means." TaNellie's nostrils flared as he tentatively sniffed the nape of her neck...he was enthralled. A rapturous vulgarity surged throughout his body, reminding him of those recent wet dreams he'd been experiencing. There was no turning back now, for either of them. The woman steadied herself against his firm body with her left hand. With her right one she reached under Tikey's arm and around his waist, opening the door. No words were spoken as she backed him onto an unfolded rollaway bed. She forced her body onto his and they fell onto the thin grey striped mattress. Lola's back arched and her groin writhed firmly against his virgin prick. Young TaNellie was solid as the Rock of Gibraltar and they acquiesced to the inevitable. It was an experience he'd never known. "Stand up TaNellie!" she cajoled, then carefully unbuttoned his jeans. Lola was fully clothed while performing acts he hadn't imagined possible. TaNellie was in such a state of arousal the veins in his penis bulged over like a pan of freshly baked hot bread. He'd just visited a place he never knew before, and couldn't wait for the next round.

Miss Jenkins owned Tikey's newly discovered manhood. Not only was she experienced... Lola was a fucking expert. Not in his wildest dreams could he have imagined such sensations. After his initial orgasm, she continued with her aggressiveness until TaNellie experienced three more orgasms, each climax more satisfying than before. Tikey lay spread-eagled on his back... pleasantly exhausted...but not knowing what to do next. Lola returned from the washroom with a warm wet cloth and cleaned the youngster's still-erect penis. She reached into her purse and counted...one, two, three, four, five silver dollars.

"Honey, open your hand...these Bo dollars are for you. I don't have to tell you how your mother would feel about this if she ever found out...so let's just keep it a secret, okay?"

"All right, Lola, if that's what you want."

She cautioned him, "It's best to continue calling me Miss Jenkins...and I'll be sure to call you Tikey. TaNellie and Lola should be used only while we're being intimate...agreed?"

"Yes, Miss Jenkins." He stood and struggled to button his fully expanded jeans. Lola left the shop at precisely 8:45 a.m., having set a sexual standard few could equal. She returned fifteen minutes later as if nothing had ever happened. She was on time for her appointment with Bessie Mae.

"Hey honey...you ready for me?"

(21) House of cards...

~

Most people can remember sitting at the breakfast table and suddenly being overwhelmed by a newspaper headline. Such was the case for Bessie Mae Purifoy. Young TaNellie had separated the color Sunday edition funnies from the rest of the paper to read his favorite comic, *Terry and the Pirates* by Milton Caniff. Bessie was having her coffee, and almost choked when gulping down the hot liquid upon seeing the bold typeface: ISHMAEL SILVERMAN INDICTED! Bessie read each word carefully, and afterward re-read the entire article, hoping the reporter had made a terrible mistake. According to the *Cleveland Plain Dealer* newspaper account...*Silverman had been running a Ponzi scheme for almost three years. This wasn't a new swindle...it was named after Italian businessman Charles Ponzi. Things began to unravel for Silverman when a series of large payments promised to clients was not honored. This led to their widespread panic and caused them to involve the police. Silverman has gone into hiding and currently his whereabouts are unknown. Rumor suggests he may have fled the United States and returned to Austria. Some have expressed serious doubt in the unsubstantiated claims based primarily on Mr. Silverman's Jewish heritage and Nazi control of Austria. The Cleveland Police Department requests persons who have knowledge of Mr. Silverman's whereabouts to contact them immediately.*

Tikey looked up from the comics after hearing his mother groan her concern. "What's the matter, Momma?"

"Well, son--it seems our friend Mr. Silverman has got heaps of trouble on his hands."

"What kind of trouble is heaps?"

"It's the kind that'll land him in jail if he's not careful."

"Momma...I thought only bad people went to jail. Mr. Silverman is a nice man; you said so yourself!"

Bessie thought long and hard before answering her son. "Tikey...let's just wait for a while, at least until we have all the facts. I'll try and answer all your questions then, okay?"

"Sure, Momma...but does that mean we'll never see Mr. Silverman anymore?"

"We'll just have to wait and see, son. It might help if you keep him in mind when saying your prayers."

"I will, Momma...I promise."

Just the other day while Tikey was returning home from the grocery store, he saw police beat a man over the head with billy clubs after he was caught stealing in Tom and Randy's market. "I hope they're not going to hurt Mr. Silverman too?"

Other than a few teachers, Ishmael was one of the few adults in TaNellie's life to take an interest in him. Usually Silverman imparted his vast knowledge to try to teach the boy positive ideals of what it meant to be a good person and a solid citizen. Tikey remembered recent conversations concerning life, and how even people from different backgrounds have the same desires, needs, and goals. Silverman was among the first to clarify that death was an inevitable part of life. He explained how all creatures large and small must leave this world through the same portal: death. He briefly touched on fate, and believed there was a preordained plan determining a person's lot in life. Tee imagined in his mind that if what Mr. Silverman said was true, his fate...or punishment for breaking the law...was already written. This all seemed a bit overwhelming and he decided to heed his mother's advice and pray for the man they called friend...at least until all the facts became known.

TaNellie loved his mother dearly...more than anything in the whole wide world. Later it troubled him to see his mother crying while lying down on her bed. "What's wrong, Momma? Did I do something? Is there anything I can do to make you feel better, Momma?"

She slowly shook her head no...then sank even deeper into the pillow. Bessie had always displayed strength during most matters, but today was different. She seemed lethargic and distant, with a faraway look in her eyes. The boy put his palm on her forehead to feel her temperature, something she'd done many times for him when he was out of sorts. She wasn't hot to the touch and he wondered aloud, "Can I give you a massage, Momma?" Tikey didn't wait for an answer. He ran his fingers upward from her furrowed brow to the top of her forehead, then around her crown to the nape of her neck, where he massaged her scalp and reversed his course. His subtle fingers revitalized her blood flow as well as her spirits. Soon Bessie felt much better and began speaking to her son in a way she never had before...like a friend. She broached a subject which was seldom talked about around him.

"Well, Tikey... thanks so much for looking after me. I've been moping around the house all day long just feeling sorry for myself. I think it's because I really do miss Nawlins. I haven't seen hide nor hair of a familiar face since before my family passed away. I've been thinking a lot about your father, too. Only God knows just how much I've yearned for his company." Tee just stared attentively at his mother while she expressed herself. "Sure we had our ups and downs, but it never stopped me from loving him." Tikey sat motionless, seated at the foot of her bed. "Son...I want you to know your daddy wasn't perfect...who is? But he was a beautiful and generous human being, inside and out. I loved him more than life itself...I still do. I don't like to talk about him, because most times I just can't bear all that's happened. I will say this, son... there hasn't been a day that goes by when I haven't looked into your eyes and was reminded of him. You look exactly like your father. Tikey, I mean to change my ways, starting right now. I'm going to fill in the blanks and start telling you what I've kept to myself for far too long. I think sharing my past will be healthy for the both of us."

She placed both her arms around Tikey, pulling him closer to her while speaking softly in his ear. "Everyone needs to be aware of their history...it's what being a family is all about. Your daddy was tall, handsome--and like I said...you look just like him. Especially your wavy hair... which some colored folks would give their eyeteeth to have. I see it every day at the salon; it's why I stay so busy. Your complexion is smooth and chestnut in color...you got that from both your parents. But you can thank your daddy for that gorgeous smile of yours."

She hesitated momentarily, then smiled before moving forward. "Tikey, your daddy could charm a mink out of his winter coat during a snowstorm...with just his words. TaNellie, everything about you reeks of Frederick Douglass Purifoy. Son, you're a special person and even your name is special. It came to me during a dream and I don't think anyone else in the whole world has the same exact name as you; TaNellie Lafitte Purifoy. I didn't realize it at the time, but when I first left Nawlins, I was carrying you inside me. Your poor daddy didn't know he was about to be a father, and I fault myself for that. If he had known...it's no way he wouldn't have been a part of your life.

"There's no way to sugarcoat what I'm about to say, so I'll just let it all out. Some evil person in Nawlins put a hex on my whole family...including you. Son, I had to leave town in a hurry, with just the clothes on my back plus whatever I could stuff into my momma's old carpet bag. I didn't have the slightest idea where I was headed until the very last second. If I had stayed down south we would both be dead right now. We would have been killed in that awful fire which also took my sisters and brothers. It's sad to say...but neither one of us would be having this conversation right now. I thank God every day that we're all right, Tikey. There were a lot of good people who died on the day you were born. Always remember that they died...but coming to Cleveland is what saved us both. I know you're just a kid, even though you're tall for your age. I hope you're old enough to understand what I'm telling you?"

Tikey understood his mother's words, but they didn't explain why anyone would put a hex on people they didn't even know.

Although thinking about the past was painful...Bessie Mae left no stone unturned. She tried her best to recall everything. Giving her son a remedial course in history-- started with the family name. It was Goode...but was pronounced Güd. Tikey learned all about his aunts and uncles: their idiosyncrasies, personalities, and of course likes and dislikes. Bessie Mae spoke of her family... hoping to illustrate a relevancy in both their lives. Tikey was finally able to appreciate his relatives and better understand his mother's anxiety. Bessie had no family pictures, so Tikey formulated composites based on her stories and visualized them in his mind's eye. Silas and Elizabeth Goode, his grandparents, came to life based soley on Bessie's description. He howled with laughter upon hearing his grandfather's nickname for Bessie Mae, which was *six toe Joe*... because of small nodes on the sides of both her baby toes.

Frederick Douglass Purifoy, TaNellie's father, was a musician's musician. Even as a teen he was an excellent trumpet player who totally immersed himself within the musical culture of Nawlins. Drugs, drinking, gambling, and carousing were intricate parts of his musical education. Bessie Mae Goode lived with Frederick for about a year and assumed his name during their common-law relationship. Her youthful dreams and their shared aspirations for a future together never manifested. But their love for one another couldn't be denied...it seemed the timing just wasn't right. Leaving town when she did was best thing for their relationship. It allowed her time to grow and explore singular ambitions, thereby keeping deep feelings intact. Each would explore individual pursuits, and if the fates were kind, maybe they would reunite. It was Bessie Mae's reflections which colored her sadness today, causing feelings of melancholy. She was thankful for bringing Tikey up to speed about his relatives. The curse placed upon her family cut like a double-edged blade-- which was responsible for the good and bad times in her life.

TaNellie hugged his mother. "Thanks for sharing our family history, six toe Joe!" He smiled. "It sure is nice to know where I come from."

Bessie was proud of her son. He was becoming a man and she was growing as well, into a strong woman, coping with the loss of her entire family.

(22) Tears of joy...

Mattie's full-service gaming enterprise was finally open for business. The former three- story factory location had been gutted and given a complete interior makeover. Every floor catered to specific games of chance: slots, cards, roulette, and craps among them. Players from across the nation found their way to the small market town of Cleveland, Ohio for the opulent grand opening. An overwhelming number of patrons served as testimonial to the shared respect for Mattie Matt and Frank Leo. The black tie affair was by invitation only, and included more high rollers than you could shake a stick at. Something the principals looked upon as very encouraging for future business. The secluded location may as well have been on Broadway, considering the underworld buzz. Inside, the newest after-hours spot, was humming with activities as friends and associates stood in line to congratulate Mattie Matt and Frank Leo.

Rick Foy was an extremely good-looking high roller from Los Angeles and introduced himself to the pair. The sixty-year-old wore a black velvet patch over his left eye, which he had lost in a mishap many years ago. Professionally his friends just called him Dead-eye Rick, because of his craps and card-playing expertise. "Congratulations, gentlemen--this is truly a nice-looking joint. Frank, before I forget...Trip Stone sends his best."

Frankie smiled, recalling his friend. "How's that old cocksucker doing? I haven't seen him in a coon's age!"

"He's fine, Frank...just a little under the weather right now.

He's got to be in his eighties, you know." Mattie extended his hand to the stranger, saying, "Glad you could make it...I'm Mattie Matthews...so nice they named me twice."

"Good to meet you, Mattie...Rick Foy. Great place you've got here." After a few minutes of small talk, the tall man excused himself. He was anxious to find a craps table in need of his attention. "Nice meeting you both...see you around."

From the crowd came a familiar gruff voice. "Yo...Frankie Flowers...I want you to meet the wife!" It was an old racketeer buddy Frankie knew in New York, when he first got started.

"Little Angie Duca! *Minghia*...for Christ sakes, Mattie...these dago cocksuckers are coming outta the woodwork. Since when did you get married, ya bastard?"

"Who sez I wuz married? I just said meet the wife...this cute little dame is married to some stooge in the retail business! Christie...this is Frank Leo...and Mattie Matthews...both old chums of mine from way back when!"

The young blonde smiled, continuing to pop her chewing gum. "Nice to meet youse both... I'm sure."

Angie added, "This is a great place you got here, fellas...I should make out like a bandit with youse guys running the joint." Angie was a high stakes poker player, and was always accompanied by a dumb-acting blonde. In reality, the women were his shills: experienced decoys, and pretty shrewd ones at that. Christie's words, movements, and actions were all designed to keep Little Angie aware of everything around him, especially when he was gambling.

Little Angie waved to his friends. "So long, fellas...nice seeing youse again. Me and the wife are gonna try our luck at roulette... hope my credit's good!" When Christie and Little Angie departed, other well-wishers immediately replaced them. Mattie and Frankie felt like celebrities.

"Wow, Frankie! Can you believe this reception?"

"Mattie, if we can keep this spot going for at least a year, we'll make millions...maybe more!"

Inside, the venue looked like a pint-sized Las Vegas, the only difference being that it was in the Midwest. The inviting and lush accommodations spared no expense; even the restrooms were classy, each sporting attendants ready to assist with cologne, lotion, and towels. Lovely ladies in provocative clothing sold cigars and cigarettes while walking the venue. Mattie Matt was constantly circulating in every room like a proud peacock. He and Frankie continually made sure customers were happy while behaving themselves. Although illegal, this was an impressive joint. It was a real coup for the city of Cleveland. Mattie had pulled off something so huge it had never before been attempted. Those in attendance included high rollers from all over the East Coast. Sporting men, politicos, jazz musicians, and well-connected bigwigs were all caught up in the allure of the moment. Each guest rubbed elbows and spent money lavishly like it grew on trees.

"If only my momma and daddy could see me now," confided a smiling Mattie. He thanked Frankie for suggesting the move to Ohio all those years ago.

"Think nothing of it, Mattie. We're gonna need a fucking wheelbarrow to haul away all the cash."

"After your cut...my take's gonna be a heluva lot lighter, you old sombitch!"

"*Minghia*...Mattie...don't you start!"

Somewhere during the wee early morning hours, a telephone rang. A hushed voice spoke of grave concerns. "I want to be damn sure I'm right before moving ahead with the project. Hold your horses and stay put...I'll phone as soon as I'm sure I'm right." The mysterious caller hung up, vanishing into the night air as quickly as he materialized.

In the beautiful Ludlow area of Shaker Heights, Mattie Matt was unable to sleep. He was still relishing thoughts of a successful opening. Joy kissed his cheek and nestled into his arms. "I'm so very proud of you," she said. He nodded his appreciation but was still adamant about separating business from his personal life. Joy was a southern girl, happy just being part of his world, and never questioning what she deemed none of her concern. The less she knew about what he did, the better for everyone involved. The two had hit it off the very first day they met. Joy knew he was the one for her at the boarding house. In time their feelings grew into a love like no other. It was Mattie Matt who first popped the question about marriage. He trusted her and knew she felt the same. Perhaps knowing a wife can't be made to testify against her husband in a court of law helped to ease the proposal along. Mattie never doubted he would be with Joy for the rest of their lives.

On a humid and cloudy Friday in June, the two lovebirds headed for the Sands Hotel in Vegas to tie the knot. Although the hotel was segregated, Frankie Flowers was able to influence the rules on behalf of his friend. "Whoever heard of not allowing a bowlegged person into the Sands! Mattie, just consider this a token wedding gift from a family friend!" The honeymooners had a wonderful time and the two-carat flawless diamond Mattie presented to Joy was killer. Mr. and Mrs. Matthew Matthews—*if only his parents could see him now.* Upon returning home, Mr. and Mrs. Matthews took Mother Emma to a fine dining restaurant on Shaker Square to celebrate their wedding over an intimate dinner for three. Emma couldn't have been happier, adding: "Since this is the first day of the rest of your lives together, I'm going to continue praying until you're both blessed by a bundle full of Joy... or maybe even a little Mattie Matt."

Frankie gathered a group of associates...friends who happened to be high rollers. They were still hanging around town for the rumored high-stakes seven-card stud poker game. The anticipated jackpot could quite possibly reach $500,000. Some of the invited players had already paid their entrance fee and were champing at the bit for a chance to win the half million bucks. Just entering the tournament cost $25,000. The early birds included Little Angie Duca, Deadeye Rick, TaNellie, Raymond Paul, City Boy, Deuces-wild, and Sonny Wilcox--no relation to Short Stack. They bided their time until the complete field was chosen. Mattie, Frankie Flowers, and his boss, Denny D'Amilio, were alternates and put up twenty-five grand like everyone else. Alternate simply referred to those who replaced players opting out of the game for whatever reason.

There were three professional dealers and one floater, each with impeccable credentials. The three men and one woman had worked all over the world at popular casinos in cities where gambling was legal. Each player must adhere to international rules and play with specially designated cards and chips. Any player found cheating would be ejected from the competition and fined his winnings. Banned players meeting with mishaps once off the premises assumed personal responsibility. Any incidents were deemed acts of God. It went without saying that interpretations varied, dependent upon whom you asked.

Three tables each seated eight players who would fight it out until the last man...*winner take all.* The seven-card stud poker concept is simple. Once unwanted cards are discarded, the player with the best five-card poker hand wins. In actuality, however, players don't simply wait for cards to come to them. They use strategy, cunning, skill, deception, luck--all coupled with uncanny ability to remember what has occurred and pounce when necessary. Knowing when to hold or fold, stay and play is the grit often separating the best players.

Not all eyes were on the tournament; most folks entertained

themselves by playing the slots and other games. After all, it was their primary reason for attending such an establishment. A woman of about fifty was concentrating on the one-armed bandits. For more than two hours she played the same machine. When she felt the urge to use the restroom, she feared giving up her spot. She continued to look around the casino for a familiar face...anyone to sit at the slot until she returned. Unfortunately, help was not forthcoming. The middle-aged woman was somewhat antsy and squirmed in the seat, but continued playing. She quickened her pace and began to pull the slot's arm faster, as if on a quest. Meanwhile she tightened her sphincter and held her thighs together to keep from emptying her bladder. As she put quarter after quarter into the machine, her body began to gyrate. Against all odds, the woman stayed the course and kept playing. With just three coins left to her name, hope was fading fast. Before slipping her final quarter into the one- armed bandit...she used it to make the sign of the cross. After she deposited the quarter, the slots symbols spun frantically showing glimpses of cherries, lemons, oranges before finally landing on a row of stars. The woman hit the $25,000 jackpot! Elated, she sprang into action by doing jumping jacks for a small crowd of well-wishers. While she was escorted by security officers to the payout window, Moose, Mattie's trusted muscle bound guard, asked jokingly if she was responsible for peeing in the seat at the winning slot machine.

"Ohhh, no, young man...I would never do such an unladylike thing in public. I think the wetness you're referring to is merely tears of joy from winning the jackpot!"

(23) Flushed...

On this very same night, Mattie also hit the jackpot without playing a single game of chance. The casino was a vision he had carried with him during the lean years of the Depression and the free-wheeling racketeering days. Mattie Matt's business finally came to pass and was hailed as a tremendous success. In a forgiving world good things can even happen to bad people. When following your dreams, however, destiny can manifest in unimagined heights or depressing lows. Frankie Flowers had always backed his friend Mattie in every endeavor. They were joined at the hip and trusted each other with their lives. This current venture allowed them opportunities to spend quality time with loved ones and enjoy the fruits of their chosen profession. 1954 was a very good year indeed.

The long-awaited poker game was underway and things were moving along according to Hoyle, author of the definitive rule book on card games. Frankie experienced an uneasy feeling in the pit of his stomach concerning Little Angie Duca and his tall blonde shill, Christie. He decided to keep an eye on both of them...especially the dame. The longtime gangster knew every trick in the book and always trusted gut feelings, and today was no exception. If she was feeding information to Angie...he would surely catch them.

About an hour into the game, Frankie observed behaviors he considered suspect. Whenever Angie found himself in a position of being bluffed by a player, Christie did one of three things: either she lit a cigarette or had someone light it for her, or put a cigarette out in an ashtray. She often took a sip from her cocktail during crucial times…or announced going to the restroom or asked if Angie wanted a drink with or without ice. After Christie returned to her seat, Angie had either called the play, or gone all in, with an overwhelming raise. The result was a win in every situation. Frankie had a hunch, and walked over to Christie.

"Hey, Christie…why don't we have some champagne at the bar, and you can tell me a little bit about yourself."

Reluctantly the young woman went with him. "How long have you known Little Angie?"

"Just a few months, Frankie…not long at all."

"He's a sly old cocksucker, dating a good-looking doll like you…and married, no less."

"We're really not dating, Frankie…he's just a fun guy and I like being around him."

"Well, if you're not fucking him…are you at least a poker player? Do you guys have anything in common?"

"Not exactly…he just asked me to come along for the ride."

Frank sensed she was lying, and decided to put a little pressure on Christie. "I smell a rat, Christie…but I don't know if it's you, or the cocksucker you came with. Tell you what I'm gonna do…if you walk out of this joint right now, I'll have a car take you to Hopkins Airport. You can go back to wherever the fuck you came from. If you decide to stay, I'll assume you think I'm a fucking idiot…just a dumb dago who can't tell when someone is trying to fuck my best friend Mattie Matt. If that's the case, I'll have to consider cheating as a capital offense. So what's it going to be, toots!"

Without a second thought, she asked to be taken to the airport. "Good choice Christie… one more question: how much is Angie paying you to shill tonight?"

"He's giving me 20% of his winnings."

"Okay, Christie--here's what I want you to do, CAPISCI!"

After giving her instructions, they both walked back to the table. Christie walked over to Little Angie and took thirty G's in chips from his winnings, kissed him on the cheek, and left without saying a word. All eyes were on Angie as he lowered his head, shaking it from side to side. There must have been at least 150 G's in the pot. Frankie split the chips between those still seated at the table, and had security take Angie to his office.

"Frankie...please...give me a fucking break...it was Christie. That bitch is blackmailing me...I had to get a lotta dough, fast. C'mon, Frankie...how long you known me? *Minghia*...give me a fucking break, for crying out loud!" Frankie remained silent until they reached the office. Once behind closed doors, Angie cried like a baby.

"Angie, I've known you over forty years, and I always suspected you'd try and pull a stunt like this. Didn't you learn nothing in all the time you've known me? This is business, asshole... and where business is concerned, I got no friends...CAPISCI? So wipe your fucking eyes and admit what you did--it's your only hope."

"Okay...okay...I cheated, but I'll pay it all back. I swear on my children's lives!" Angie was rushed out of the building by security with his feet barely touching the floor. He was placed into the back seat of a black Lincoln sedan, accompanied by Frank's crew: Joey Cerito, Bocky Boo, and Chuckie Rundo.

Frank issued their marching orders. "Take this asshole to the airport and see to it he catches his flight, CAPISCI! I'm going back inside and finish Angie's hand. Maybe I'll get lucky... God knows he didn't!" Frankie poked his head inside the front window. "Hey, Ange...tell the Devil I said to go fuck himself!"

(24) Payback is a bitch...

‑‑

Drip...drop...splat...drip...drop...splat...drip...drop...splat...
drip...drop... splat. It was the incessant dripping that eventually woke him. He was cold and his head was pounding so hard it
was about to explode. When Mattie fully regained consciousness
he was concerned about what he might find. He prepared himself
for the worst, then slowly opened his eyes. He was faced with complete nothingness, and blinked several times just to make sure his
eyes were even open. Able to discern only darkness, he wondered
if he were blind. Mattie had been unconscious for what seemed
like an eternity. Of course there was no way to prove that asser-
tion. But for the moment, at least, he felt in control of his senses
and he desperately tried to gather his faculties.

It had been the most important day of his life. Some bits and
pieces were slowly finding their way back into his consciousness.
He recalled feeling light-headed after a few hands of poker. At
the time he thought it strange...but knew his resultant dizziness
wasn't due to alcohol. Mattie drank only club soda with a twist
of lime. It had been his preferred drink of choice for more than
twenty years. Even now he felt groggy, and considered the possibility of having been slipped a Mickey Finn. His vivid memories of little Angie Duca being unceremoniously tossed from the
big game after being suspected of cheating were resolute. Mattie
remembered Christie, his beautiful gum- chewing blonde shill,
cashing in thirty grand worth of chips before leaving the premises...with Frankie boy's blessings.

After Angie's forced exit, only three poker players remained in the game: TaNellie, Frankie Flowers, and newcomer Rick Foy, the one-eyed gambler from Los Angeles, who was vouched for by friend and racketeer Trip Stone. With Angie out of the picture, Ta-Nellie and Frankie represented Cleveland gamblers well, with their smart play and timely betting. Hundreds of thousands of dollars in chips were moving back and forth among the three players with no clear favorites. In time, however, even the hometown boys couldn't stave off a surging Rick Foy. His uncanny abilities and enviable luck overwhelmingly made him the shoo-in. Deadeye Rick was ultimately proven to be the best, and won Mattie's first seven-card stud tournament. A king's ransom of $486,125 befitted Foy's new status, since he won the jackpot with a royal flush. Mattie remembered asking Moose, the former Marine and friend, to walk him to his car. This was just minutes before Mattie dismissed security. Once inside his car, Mattie and Frankie drove off just minutes before things went completely blank for them both.

Mattie was now lying flat on his back with his arms and legs spreadeagled. He tried to sit, but was securely battened down like a hatch aboard ship. He was completely nude, and his wrists and ankles were lashed tightly to the hilts of long metal stakes driven deep into the mineral- hardened rich earth. He began shivering— partially due to the cold, but mainly because he feared for his life. Mattie was sore and had been bitten several times by vermin on his neck, arms, and legs. The annoying dripping persisted, reminding him of caves he explored as a young boy back in Mason, Tennessee.

He called out, "Help...help...help!" but the echoes of his pleas returned unabated. About ten feet away came a startling revelation.

"Ohhh, my fucking head!" Mattie focused in on the voice. "Frankie boy, is that you?"

"Yeah, Mattie! I'm staked to the ground like a fucking animal, and I can't move. Where the fuck are we?"

"Don't know, Frankie boy, but wherever it is ain't good. If it wasn't so cold, I'd say we died and went straight to hell!" Neither man had any inkling as to why they'd been all trussed up.

A match was struck, briefly illuminating a third party. Puffed cigarette smoke circled aloft, interspersing among stalactites before being absorbed by the dankness of the cavern. Glimpses of facial features appeared whenever the stranger took a drag off the cigarette. He was seated on a large flat rock. His youthful voice ordered both men to "Shut the fuck up! You gangster types are all alike. With gats, you got guts...but take away the guns and you're pussies. The whole lot of ya! I've been babysitting you two blowhards all night long. You ought to thank me for keeping those hungry-ass rats from eating you alive." He grumbled, "A couple of them already sampled your wares. I'll bet they can't wait for me to leave so's they can finish you bastards off. In case you're wondering where you are, my client has spared no expense in putting you guys up in the best cavern money can buy. This prime location is far removed from the city, and no matter how loud you scream...." He took another drag, letting the smoke slowly exit through his nostrils. "You'll never be seen or heard from again. They say only the good die young...that won't explain how two old farts like you wound up vanishing into thin air without a trace.

"Now, gentlemen—let's get down to brass tacks. You two took something from my client. Granted, it was a long time ago, but now you're both being held accountable. Just think of it as an eye for an eye and a tooth for a tooth. PAYMENT IS DUE RIGHT NOW!"

Frankie and Mattie had never been in this position before. Back in the day, it was always the other way around. "Let me get this straight!" said Frank. "Are you saying if we pay back what we took...you'll let us both go?"

"That's exactly what I'm saying. All my client wants is what you two owe him."

Mattie added, "Suppose you got the wrong guys. Suppose we didn't take anything from your client. Maybe somebody else did!"

The man shined his flashlight's beam directly into Mattie's eyes "Naaw...Mr. Matthew Matthews...so nice they named you twice. I've definitely got the right pair! It was you and Frankie what took from my client. I'll be getting a pretty penny when you deadbeats dish up what you owe."

Frank added, "Suppose we don't pay!"

"Well, in that case, I'll just leave you two badasses here for rat bait. Either way, I get paid! You bastards are worth just as much to me dead as you are alive...so your future, or lack of it, is all up to you! I just love this old cavern...I've been here many times. It's my favorite place to dump assholes like you. Especially when I really want to enjoy watching them die...CAPISCI, Frankie boy? Then after a couple of days of letting rats do whatever comes natural-ly, I'll mosey on back here and take a few Polaroid snapshots of what's left of my two favorite enforcers. Let me remind you both: it won't matter how loud you scream when those fucking rats start tearing away at your flesh. Nobody's gonna hear nothing...with the possible exception of you two! I wonder who's gonna scream the loudest. I'm putting my money on the flower man."

Frankie was fit to be tied...no pun intended. He wished he could lay his hands on the creep cracking wise. But it was totally out of the realm of possibility. "Who are you, ya cocksucker fuck? What perverted asshole sent you after us! Tell me his name, ya bastard! When I get my hands on you, ya blue-balled bastard, I'll fuck you both up. I'll tear out your client's heart and force feed it to you!"

The man took another long drag from his cigarette, calmly exhaling without a care in the world. "Temper, temper, Frankie boy. I'm gonna give you a clue...tough guy. How about the Big Apple during the Depression!"

"That could be anybody, you cocksucker!"

Mattie chimed in, "Hey man, how 'bout a better clue than that?"

Since the stranger held all the cards, he decided to deal another clue. "How does fifty grand suit ya?" After sharing the new clue, he settled in on the flat rock, awaiting their response.

Mattie was adamant. "I've never taken fifty grand at one time from anybody in my entire life! Especially not during the Depression...nobody had that kinda jack back then. You've got the wrong guys...I swear!"

The man responded to his captives, "Put on your thinking caps, fellas...you can do better than this. Maybe you guys split the dough...say twenty-five grand apiece...does it ring a bell now?" The man wanted to see the culprits stew in their own guilt-ridden juices.

"Take your time, boys...the longer you wait, the hungrier these rats are gonna be when I leave. So take your sweet-ass time...it's no skin off my nose. To bad you won't be able to say the same."

While they waited, the dripping continued...drip...drop...splat...drip...drop...splat...drip...drop...   splat...drip...drop...splat. It was driving them both crazy and starting to sound more like a countdown to an explosion. The man had them right where he wanted them. He knew it was just a matter of time before the hardened racketeers cracked.

Frank Leo and Mattie Matt revisited their past to a time when they worked for Bumpy Johnson and Lucky Luciano. Their memories were clear as an iced bottle of cream soda. Ironically, they had recently spoken about the incident. Perhaps this was all just a scam? They wondered how their former bosses found out about the deception. There was no way both Luciano and Queenie could have known about the pilfered money, unless they were tipped off. Even they couldn't remember who'd cashed in their policy slips. It took a while...but they finally figured out the mystery. Without prompting, they yelled out, "The CREOLE!" They had guessed right. The stranger's client was the deadbeat they had nearly beaten to death before putting him on a bus to Los Angeles.

Frankie was able to expose another twist to their fate. While playing cards at the tournament he remembered something oddly familiar about Rick Foy's voice and his demeanor. *"Okay, you cocksucker, remember what happened here today,"* whispered Frankie. *"I will..."* replied the Creole. Although Frankie didn't realize it then...the gambler and the Creole were one and the same. It explained the eye patch he wore, as well as snide comments he made concerning the loss of his eye... *"You should see the other guy...he got away with nary a scratch while pocketing all my scratch!"*

Frank's heart sank. "Mattie Matt," he sighed, "we're fucked. Payback is a bitch." There was still hope, however, a small glimmer of light. Neither friend had spent one red cent of the money. They were confident the Creole would offer the same deal they extended to him, and spare their lives. Mattie laid everything on the line...then hoped for the best.

"We have the cash now! We'll give it to you...all you have to do is set us free."

"Do you two assholes think I'm stupid? I may have been born at night—but it certainly wasn't last night. Fellas, here's how it's gonna be. First, tell me how to get the dough. I'll give it to my client. Once he's happy, I'll come back and turn you two deadbeats loose."

"How do we know you'll keep your promise? Why don't you let one of us go to get the cash?"

"Yeah...right...and you'll return with the goon squad. Naaw... I guess you'll just have to trust me on this one. Don't worry...if anything happens to me at the casino, you'll still be dead! Better start talking, boys...time's a-wasting, and those rats are still getting hungrier and hungrier!"

The two lifelong associates had no other choice. Mattie gave the man everything he wanted...the security code to the building, and the combination and location of the safe. Before he left, the stranger gathered a few armloads of sticks and assorted dead logs, and lit a large campfire, which he hoped would last until his return. The friends prayed and Mattie wondered to himself...*If only my momma and daddy could see me now!*

(25) The Kid... case file # 2064...

⎯⎯

Somewhere deep within the Bureau of Records are the patient files of former New York police psychiatrist: Dr. Eugene Jordan, M.D. This is a statement of Franklin Matthew Carpenter.

I swear the following is a true statement to the best of my knowledge. Ever since the shooting of Edward Patterson on April 1, 1945, was ruled justifiable homicide by Judge Willard McCann, my life has descended down a path of killing for hire. We lived in a small two-room flat in a New York tenement in the seediest part of town. It was just the three of us: my mother, my seventeen-year-old sister, and me. Like most single women her age, Mom had boyfriends. There was something about this new guy I didn't like. I can't explain why...something in my gut told me he was bad news. I was just sixteen years old when I first laid eyes on him, and still sixteen when I killed him exactly three months later.

My mother has always worked seven days a week for my entire life, without a break. She slaved when it rained or snowed. She worked while she was pregnant or when we were sick. She was never ahead of the game. My father, whom I never met, did send her money each month. Trying to make ends meet with two kids was tough enough. Often those Western Union moneygrams were spent before they were received. It was natural for Mom to seek companionship. In so doing she went for every line tossed her way, like crumbs to a bird. This latest guy had an evilness about him. He didn't have a pot to piss in or a window to throw it out. When Patterson moved in with us, things immediately went from bad to worse. He treated all of us as if we had leprosy. He called us white trash, and beat my mom and sister with a leather belt. With no real job, he performed menial tasks to earn money for beer and wine. When I first saw the son of a bitch hit my mother, I knew in my heart I would have to kill him. He started arguments for no reason just so's he could hit her. He was a cruel coward, and I'm not ashamed to say I often dreamed about blowing his fucking brains out. My mom said he didn't really mean to hurt her... but those black eyes told a different story. He never talked to or approached me. I think he knew one day I would turn his lights off for good. I can't say it any clearer...I was just biding my time.

After three months of us all living under the same roof, I came home early from school one day. I entered our flat to find my mother gagged and tightly bound to a chair...it was facing a corner. Patterson was sitting on the Murphy bed with my sister Monica. Her shredded clothing had been forcefully torn off her body. Her panties dangled around an ankle of one leg. He threatened to kill my mother with a revolver if Monica didn't do what he wanted. After she was complying, he put the gun on the nightstand beside the bed. He began raping her and was in the throes of an orgasm when I saw my chance. I had never held a gun before and used both hands, aiming directly at his head about a foot away. His reign of terror ended with one shot. The huge gun recoiled and sent my hands a foot into the air before settling back down. As the room filled with gun smoke, I remember thinking this was the last time he would ever hurt anyone again...I was relieved.

My sister was unhurt, but lost 30% of her hearing in the left ear because of the loud blast. She was screaming and hollering uncontrollably. Mom was bouncing up and down in the chair like a pogo stick, trying to free herself. I removed her blindfold and got a knife, and cut the tightly knotted rope. With her hands free, she squeezed and twisted life back into her wrists. She removed the gag and hugged us like crazy! She kept apologizing and smothering us with kisses. "Ohhh I'm so sorry... I'm sorry!" She said it over and over again. With all the ruckus and loud gunshot, someone called the police. When they arrived we were all huddled in a corner staring at Patterson's lifeless body. It's amazing how much blood people have inside them. After things settled down our home was full of cops, newspaper reporters and hordes of nosey neighbors.

The police officers told me how proud they were. "You showed 'em, kid...they ought to give you a goddamn medal!" "You killed him, kid...good for you" "You're a man now...you stepped up and saved your family." "You did what any man who loves his sister and mother would've done!" News cameras were pointed in our faces while flashbulbs popped all over the place. I was treated like a real-life hero. People donated money and clothing to us. State University of New York gave a full scholarship to all three of us. We were front page news and even had our pictures on the movie newsreels shown in theatres across the country.

The truth of the matter is that I had planned to kill Patterson from day one, and run away from home. His actions made things a lot simpler for me because our family remained intact. Since Patterson was killed, after committing a heinous act, I became the darling of both the public and the underworld. Secretly I was recruited by a NYC crime family and groomed as a hit man. It was all strictly hush-hush. I was finally hired and trained as an assassin. I was still just sixteen years old and was making good money tagging along with professional hit men. I learned the art of the ambush from those who killed for a living. After my first hit, I was able to move the family out of the dump we'd lived in all my life. I must admit I enjoyed the hunt. Setting up a take down became something I was very good at. I was sent all over to rub out rival gangland members, dirty politicians, and even judges on the take. Whatever was needed I did for a price. The cover was my youthful-looking face...and those in the business simply called me...the Kid.

When the law increased their efforts to solve the killings, I went underground. My family was completely unaware of my job. I begged my mother to sign a permission slip to join the Marines. President Eisenhower had been swept into office after promising to bring the troops home from Korea and the war was winding down. While in the Corps I really learned the business of killing... the Marine Corps way, from the ground up. I was trained in the use of the military's latest weapons and became an expert marksman with the .45 automatic, M-1 Garand rifle, Thompson machine gun, grenade launchers, 30 caliber machine guns, and the Browning Automatic Rifle or BAR for short. After graduating from boot camp at Parris Island I was once again lauded for being an exemplary Marine. I was among the top 10% of my platoon and was promoted to private first class. The Corps' mantra at the time was: the Marine Corps builds men. Since I was so young, I was completely mesmerized by the military bravado. In an indirect way it seemed I had found my calling. I was a master of weaponry and possessed the skill, determination, and willingness needed to utilize what I'd learned. In a word, I was a professional rifleman... a lean mean killing machine earning a whopping eighty-six dollars American, per month: Franklin Matthew Carpenter.

(26) Game...set...match

In the mid-1950s, other than the usual face-to-face or telephone conversations, the most preferred method of communication was via the mail. For as little as three cents, a person could send a letter anywhere in the world. TaNellie checked his mailbox regularly and was pleasantly surprised to find a picture postcard from the lovely señorita...Marta de LaCosta.

> *Dearest TaNellie... I'm in Havana, Cuba. Enjoying the sights alone. Will be leaving for Barcelona in seven days. Am staying at the Tropicana Hotel...the Monte Carlo of the Americas... would love to see you!*
> Signed...Marta
> con mucho cariños para ti...

TaNellie was extremely flattered after reading Marta's invitation to spend some time with her. He wondered how he could visit with all of the comings and goings on in his world. Perhaps a vacation with a beautiful woman was just what the doctor ordered. With passport in hand, he decided to accept the invitation, and immediately confirmed reservations on Pan-American World Airways. The flight departed Miami for Cuba on Thursday, just two days away. TaNellie followed up his booking with a call to the Tropicana Hotel, but Marta was unavailable. He left a short message with the front desk clerk. *Marta... looking forward to seeing you...Tee!*

During their recent telephone conversation, Marta had revealed her initial feelings about Tee. It was now time for him to look deep within and answer questions concerning his own feelings about her. Yes, she was beautiful...yes, she was fun to be around...and of course any man in possession of his faculties would be delighted to call her his woman. His answers raised even more questions. Would he expect her to share intimacy with others just to benefit him financially? Did he possess the ability or desire to build a monogamous relationship with Marta...or any other woman, for that matter? One based on true love? If answers to these questions were no...it would confirm that he was obviously just a pimp seeking an addition to his stable. If on the other hand--*en cambio*, in español--an affirmative answer meant a relationship between the two was entirely possible. To achieve those ends would entail compromises all along the way, with plenty of dumb luck thrown in for good measure. In other words, he would need to utilize the same methods that couples enjoying full loving and viable relationships found successful, where the only guarantee that comes with love is...anything is possible.

Unfortunately, most women who had ever spent time with Ta-Nellie had ultimately paid a high price for his affection. The first was Lola, the cougar, who tapped into his virtue when he was just thirteen years old. Once her feelings became entangled in their trysts...she demanded his attention, affection, and fidelity. Tee was only a youngster, but quickly learned to play the game and soon turned the tables with some demands of his own.

"Lola—if you love me like you say—I should expect more from you. I'm too young to have a girlfriend as old as you. I feel like you're trying to take advantage of the situation...and me." Those words coming from a boy still in puberty were a rude awakening. It shocked Lola Jenkins into assuming the only way to keep him was to pay for play. Soon Lola was lavishing the boy with clothing and money, as well as nice gifts. She even quit her job at Paramount Distillers just to be around him more often. Women at the shop were beginning to suspect her unsavory advances toward the boy. When her funds ran low, she began turning tricks full time...robbing Peter to pay Paul. At one point her self-esteem had been all but extinguished. Lola was so outdone by TaNellie that she threatened to tell his mother about the affair. Tee was not a happy camper.

"Help me to understand, Miss Jenkins, why you're going to tell my mother you raped me right under her very nose. You knew I was underage, yet you did it anyway. Will you also mention giving me the money you earned from sleeping with grown men? Boy, oh boy...Momma always said 'There's no fool like an old fool!' I guess she's right. Do you know what she'll do after she finishes kicking your ass? Call the police, that's what, and they'll put your sorry ass under the jail for rape!"

Lola was completely humiliated, and shamefully buried her face inside her hands. TaNellie delivered his coup de grâce. "Lola, the best thing you can do for me...is get the fuck out of my face!" Disillusioned, denigrated, and completely dejected, Lola ran away sobbing like a child. Months later, she hooked up with some chili pimp who whipped her ass regularly. After she lost what few good looks she had left, he literally kicked her to the curb. The last time TaNellie saw her, she was unrecognizable... living in the streets searching through garbage for food and turning tricks for small change.

Even if it were possible for TaNellie to separate personal life from his business, what self- respecting woman would ever put up with his shenanigans? What feeble excuse would he offer when finally asking her to walk the stroll? *Baby, I need you to do me a favor...I owe a lot of money to the mob and they've threatened to kill me if I don't pay the ten grand I owe them!'* It's the oldest and by far the dumbest trick in the pimp's player handbook. Yet women fall for the ruse because they love him, and of course the pimp loves them right back, or so they say. Tee knew he wasn't ready for commitment, and wanted to wait and see. He wondered how Marta felt.

Ana drove his white Caddy and dropped TaNellie off at Hopkins International Airport for his flight to Miami. She hugged him goodbye while he grabbed his things from the trunk. It was warm and sunny...a great day to travel. After arriving in Miami, TaNellie boarded Pan-Am for the last leg of the trip. Cuba was now just ninety miles away, and he looked forward to leisurely spending time walking the beaches, visiting cultural sites, and dining in enchanting Cuban restaurants. Marta's beauty rivaled exquisite orchids... white phalaenopsis blossoms, to be exact. Tee was intrigued by her looks, and rightfully or wrongly expected that "Que sera, sera...what will be will be."

"DAMAS Y CABALLEROS SUS ATENCIóNES, POR FAVOR...

"LADIES AND GENTLEMEN YOUR ATTENTION, PLEASE...

"WE WILL BE LANDING IN EL AEROPUERTO JOSÉ MARTI IN FIFTEEN MINUTES. THE TEMPERATURE IN HAVANA IS A BALMY EIGHTY-FIVE DEGREES. AS ALWAYS, WE THANK YOU FOR FLYING PAN-AMERICAN WORLD AIRWAYS, AND BE SAFE WHILE ENJOYING YOUR STAY IN CUBA."

The captain landed the aircraft smoothly, and while the plane was taxiing toward the gate, a female passenger sitting next to TaNellie asked, "Have you ever been to Cuba linda before?"

"No, señora, this is my very first time."

"Well, señor, if you want to enhance your experience...may I suggest you set aside some time and visit Trinidad as well? I think you'll find it quite exquisite."

"Muchas gracias, señora...I'll be sure and place it on my list of things to do."

She then added, "Its in the Sancti Spiritus province--not very far...just a little beyond Varadero's playas."

Before deplaning, he once again thanked the elegant-looking Cuban woman. He joined a line of passengers heading to the terminal, where he found a pay phone. This time, Marta did answer. "Hola!"

"Hello, Marta...I've just landed and I'll be checking into my room as soon as possible!"

"Sounds good, Tee...why don't we meet for cocktails in the lounge...say an hour from now, okay?"

Tee glanced at his watch. "Great, Marta...see you then!"

TaNellie arrived at the lounge first, after having dropped off his things in the room. He took a seat at a small table, watching swimmers frolic in the nice sized pool. The elevator light pinged as its doors opened onto the lobby floor. Marta was among the first to step off the small conveyance in a beige bikini top and navy and white polka dot sarong with leather sandals. Her dark-brown windswept hair was below the shoulder and gently danced across her face. Marta's blemish-free skin was the color of polished pecan shells. She spotted TaNellie immediately and walked up from behind and bent over, kissing him on the cheek.

"Hola... Tee!"

He stood up and held both her hands in his while looking into those expressive brown eyes. It was quite obvious he was very happy to see her again.

"Marta...Marta...Marta! You look marvelous, and I just love the richness of your tan. It's so smooth-looking! How've you been since last we met?"

She hugged his slim waist tightly. "I'm not causing any trouble, Tee...things here are just fine! I can't tell you how pleased I am you were able to come on such short notice. I almost didn't send the postcard for fear of what you might think. I must admit it was very presumptuous of me. Tee, I view it like this...the postcard only cost two cents...so I got my money's worth... right?"

TaNellie reached inside his pocket. "Marta... here's a quarter. Now the postcard didn't cost you anything. Let's get one thing straight, young lady...whatever happens while we're in Cuba... is my treat!"

She smiled provocatively...something she hadn't found cause to do in the presence of a man since who knows when. Marta was happy that the man she met at the Kentucky Derby had brought along his gentlemanly ways. A waiter welcomed them to the Tropicana.

"Señores, may I serve you something from the bar?"

"Gracias...si. The lady will have a dirty martini with extra olives, and I'd like a Cuba Libré, por favor."

Marta's smile widened. "Tee... I'm so proud you were able to remember my drink of choice...how delightful!"

Once again he glanced into her brown eyes. "Marta...I remembered everything about you! It's why I decided to come all the way to Cuba and see you in person. The telephone just doesn't do you justice!"

The waiter's name was Javier. He moved effortlessly past tables, balancing cocktails on his tray in one hand, while unfolding linens onto laps with the other. "Un dirty martini por la dama...y un Cuba Libré por el caballero. Disfrutar...enjoy!"

Javier vanished quickly like a cool tropical breeze. In the background, Nat King Cole was singing, entirely in Spanish, "Quizas, quizas, quizas."

"I just love this song," observed Marta, while swaying to its music. Tee had committed the word quizas to memory months ago.

"Yes...Nat King Cole is a great singer. I think the word means...perhaps? Marta was so impressed...she smiled to herself.

As was their custom, which started during the Derby, it was now time for a toast. With glasses nearly touching...Tee presented: "Marta, I'm honored you chose me to join you in Cuba. Whatever happens during our stay, know in your heart that you've touched mine deeply."

They sipped cocktails with arms entwined. "Tee...your toast...was it extemporaneous?"

"Yes it was, Marta...the words just seemed to flow by themselves. Why do you ask?"

She reached across the table and gently touched the back of his hand. "I loved it," she confessed. TaNellie told Marta about the woman he met aboard his flight. He shared her suggestion about visiting Trinidad. "Oh, Tee...can we? I've visited Cuba many times, but have yet to see Trinidad. How fitting for us to share such an experience for the first time together. We couldn't have planned this trip any better."

Javier returned and cleared away the glasses. "Con permiso, por favor. From the very first time I saw you...I knew you two were in love. Are you on your honeymoon?"

Tee and Marta looked at each other and smiled. "We've yet to consummate our vows... perhaps if you ask again tomorrow!"

Marta interrupted. "Oh, Tee...you're a real scamp. No, Javier...we're not married, nor are we in love." She looked into Tee's eyes. "Only time will tell. In the meantime, Javier...please bring us another round."

"Claro que si...absolutely, señora!"

"Marta, don't be upset-- I was just having a little fun with him. I must admit we would make a nice-looking couple."

"Looks aren't everything, Tee."

TaNellie asked a serious question. "Speaking of looks...what exactly is it you look for in a man?"

She hesitated before answering. "I'm really not sure, but I will say this...I'll recognize Mr. Right immediately."

"Just like Javier did...right?"

"Nooo...I'm sure he was just trying to earn tips."

"Well, if that's true," laughed Tee, "he won't get a red cent from me!"

The next morning they awoke--in separate rooms, of course. Tee rented a late-model white Cadillac convertible with red leather interior...some things would never change. After driving around the island, they stopped at a fresh fruit stand to pick out breakfast. They scrutinized the neatly stacked produce, buying cantelope, guava, papaya, avocado, coconut, plantain, freshly sliced pineapple, watermelon, and other ingredients for a salad.

They found a picturesque setting inundated with dunes of pristine white sand and lofty palms. Marta took out her Brownie automatic camera and took lots of photos. Dining on fresh fruit while overlooking the Caribbean turned a simple breakfast into a banquet fit for royalty. Tee had also purchased a bottle of coquito, a white creamy alcohol-laced drink made from coconuts, and some toasted confections called coco dulce. Together they spread a wide red-checked vinyl cloth onto a low mound, then flopped down right where they stood. The two began talking about everything under the sun. It was a fantastic opportunity to get to know one another better, something which had proved rather difficult in segregated Kentucky. The coquito was cool and refreshing, easing pre-conceived notions that either of them may have harbored. They agreed any topic was fair game, and Marta won the privilege of starting the ball rolling.

"Tee...how old were you the very first time you made love?"

TaNellie actually blushed openly upon hearing her question.

He settled down somewhat when his complexion slowly returned to normal. Tee spoke unabashedly about Lola Jenkins and shared their entire covetous experience. The episode with Lola may have been one of the motivating factors in TaNellie's entre into the world of flesh peddling. Even though Tee had already answered Marta's question, he continued his monologue.

"Marta, when I dropped out of Central State University, my mother was not amused. I wasn't aware of just how angry she was until she flat-out kicked me from her house. I could see the pained look of disappointment in her eyes and realized I had crossed the line. Before I went to college we were always together, come rain or shine. As I walked away with suitcase in hand, it dawned on me that I wasn't just broke...I had nowhere to stay. I walked all the way downtown before arriving at the Greyhound bus depot, where I pretended to be a passenger. I was hungry, sleepy, and tired as hell. After a week or so of dividing my time between both the Greyhound and Trailways bus terminals on Chester Avenue, I was unceremoniously tossed into the street by security guards. The bus station was where I first met Ana Whitmore. She was a 'killer diller'... that's a fine young broad. Ana was a beautiful blonde who ran away from home just to get away from her abusive parents. Together we walked the city streets throughout the night.

"After dusk, a variety of men began to stop us and hit on Ana for sexual favors. She was petite but had the heart of a lion. She turned a couple of tricks and instructed the Johns to pay me while I stood guard. That was the beginning of our friendship and we took full advantage by accommodating all comers. It all seemed so easy, and I was in my element--just like the rabbit in the briar patch. I can't imagine what might have happened without Ana. That was about six years ago, and I love her for what she did. We've been together ever since. If it weren't for Ana, I might not be sitting on this beautiful beach with you."

Marta had never given a second thought to ever meeting any-one in Tee's profession. Actually, even knowing a pimp was com-pletely out of the question. Yet, here she was sitting on a blanket in Cuba. Shooting the breeze with a gentleman of leisure, while enjoying the scenery and drinking potent coquitos. Even though Marta abhorred his profession, she felt an attraction toward him and wondered if he'd ever change. Her silent alarm, which pro-tected her heart from intruders, had sounded loud and clear. Prostitution loomed large...it was a dealbreaker she just couldn't ignore. Tee just didn't conform within the parameters she asso-ciated with pimp types. He was suave, educated, and extremely good-looking. He was probably the most handsome man she'd ever met. His clothes were the best money could buy. To humor her... Tee occasionally referred to garments as threads and used other specific terms for his hat, which was a lid or brim; a suit was a vine, while shoes were simply called kicks. His confident man-ner exuded class in every sense of the word. He moved within Marta's world as effortlessly as any jetsetter, albeit without the pomposity. There was something appealing, to be sure, about the man from Cleveland. Marta first noticed evidence of his charms at the Tropicana Hotel, on the faces of men and women alike. She had caught glimpses of his savoir-faire while dining at Pike's Peak Polo Club in Louisville. "Who is that good-looking man, and how can I strike up a conversation without appearing too curious?" It was a question she was certain crossed every woman's mind after seeing TaNellie for the first time. Marta was in no way an excep-tion...but the general rule.

Now it was Tee's turn to ask a question. He decided to build on the current theme. "Marta, when was the first time you ever had sex?"

She closed her eyes briefly, as if searching for the right words...then moved forward with her story. "I was in...what you

Americans call middle school. I'm a reasonably intelligent person who has always enjoyed reading. I never cheated, and completed my homework and classroom assignments in a timely manner. One day I was summoned to the head matron's office concerning a math test I'd taken earlier. The school's rather homely-looking matron was fortyish years old with a very prominent nose, reminding students of a bruja...or witch. We just called her Tacaña or Skinflint. After arriving at the office, I was immediately directed inside by the secretary. Skinflint was adamant that I had cheated, but offered no corroboration. The matron informed me I was in serious trouble and she was going to inform my parents."

"Did you cheat.?" asked Tee.

"Certainly not...she never mentioned an accuser, but demand-ed I strip bare. She wanted to make certain I wasn't hiding any crib notes or cheat sheets on my person. The matron got up from behind her desk and walked around it until facing me. I stood there for a while...my face was without affect. 'Strip down, young lady!' she said sternly while simultaneously stomping her heel hard against the wooden floor.

"I complied with her request and stripped down to my white cotton panties and training brassière. She was dressed mannish-ly—although wearing a white lace jabot. She was carrying her ever-present black leather riding crop. Skinflint used it to swat palms, knuckles, and backsides of misbehaving students...or even innocent children who happened to be in the wrong place at the wrong time.

"As she walked closer toward me, I began to tremble overtly and she raised her voice. 'We'll have none of that, young lady. I want you standing perfectly still, do you understand?' I nodded my head yes as she reiterated louder. 'Do you understand, young lady!' 'Yes!' I shouted. She circled a few more times and I remained perfectly still. While standing directly behind me, she positioned her riding crop under my brassière fasteners. Once again I complied by removing the garment, fearful of repercussions if I refused. The sound of her oxford heels on the hardwood floor was maddening. When I heard the office door being bolted, I was terrified beyond measure, as all sorts of crazy thoughts raced round my head.

"She kicked my brassière across the floor and walked over to me until we were inches apart. The matron smacked the crop hard against her gloved hand, then poked it down the front of my panties. The room was completely silent as she pulled the elastic band, extending it far as it would go, then letting it snap hard back into place. I assumed her actions were an order to remove my panties...which I promptly did. She glanced down at my saddle oxfords and used her crop to spread my legs apart. I can't remember what was going on in my mind. I just wanted my father to save me...but he never did. I closed my eyes as she fondled my private area using her crop as a middle finger. She was very gentle but deliberate and knew just where and how to touch me. As the minutes passed...I became aroused, and soon moaned with pleasure as she continued fingering me over and over and over again. I thought it ironic, experiencing my first orgasm at the hands of another. I felt ambivalent concerning my feelings...but couldn't deny the wonderment within me. She walked behind me again, and swatted my buttocks so hard that a huge red welt was raised. Its swell lasted the entire day, and each time I stroked it I became wet inside.

" 'Now get dressed, you wretched little snot, and report back to me next week at this very same time,' she said.

"I dressed and rushed back to my classes. I was completely ashamed and positive the students knew what had happened. The matron molested me once every week throughout middle school. I began to bemoan...yet somehow look forward to our office trysts. I found out much later in life I wasn't the only victim... which included both boys and girls."

Tee was appalled. "Marta...did you ever report the matron to school officials?"

"No, nunca...never...I was just too ashamed. I felt relieved and happy when she died years later. I have since tried to bury my pain with her...but it doesn't work. Ultimately I learned to cope by sneaking into my father's liquor cabinet and consuming martinis, which he made in bulk until desired. I continue the practice even now when I feel wronged or hurt. I don't think I'm an alcoholic, because I can go for weeks, even months, without a drink. Socially, when I'm out I do tend to drink one or two...maybe even three martinis during an hour span."

Tee was concerned about her. "Marta, how old were you when the molestation took place?"

"I had already reached puberty and like you, I was just thirteen years old."

Tee had just one more question. "Do you think a therapist might help you get a handle on what occurred when you were a child?"

"Quizas. Tee, I think you should know...you are the only person I've ever shared my story with. I want to thank you for listening to me. I must admit it does feel better having the experience outside of myself. Perhaps it would be a good idea to seek counseling...por si a caso... just in case."

For the first time, Tee appeared more concerned about someone else than himself. He was so serious that he offered to help monetarily to rid Marta of her demons. Their lives were so very similar, and gave them more in common than was first realized. While Tee didn't consider what happened to him at the hands of Lola a big deal, deep inside he wondered if he needed counseling as well. He would be sure to check it out when he found the time...

perhaps upon finishing Central State's liberal arts graduation requirements.

"My, my...where did the time fly!" The two had fallen asleep
on the red-checked spread while sprawled haphazardly near one
another. They were utterly surprised to find it was nearly time for
supper. They quickly folded the blanket and gathered their belongings, placing them inside the trunk of the caddy. The once-
full bottle of coquito was mostly drained of its contents, save an
inebriated fly who was caught unawares. It was tossed into the
trash bin along with the melon rinds and coco shells. Before
leaving, the friends stood motionless while embraced on sand
dunes anchored only by clinging toes. Swaying palms amid se-
rene breezes and exotic peaceful island whisperings bore witness
to the beginnings of a spiritual connection. This realization was
made possible through shared concerns, honest communication,
and a willingness to accept each other's foibles.

After arriving at the Tropicana, Tee parked the car. They made
impromptu plans on how to spend the remainder of their evening. The pair retired to their rooms to get ready. Afterwards they
met in the hotel lounge, where Marta decided they should visit a
club she enjoyed called Sabroso, which means tasty or delicious.
The club featured live music daily. The spacious dinner club was
packed, and tables were unavailable. Marta possessed an innate
ability for doing the impossible, and miraculously a table was provided for them. The waiter took their orders just in time. "Ladies
and gentlemen, la orquesta...Sonora Matancera!"

The famous band was affectionately known to their fans as
Café con leche...coffee with milk. Their newest member, recently
chosen to replace a former female singer, had struggled for fan
acceptance. She was Úrsula Hilaria Celia de la Caridad Cruz
Alfonso. Eventually she became known as Celia Cruz. The lights
dimmed and the music began with an exciting, albeit loud, timbale

and batá drums solo. When the drumming ceased, Celia shouted "Sugar!" in español at the top of her lungs: "AZÚCAR!" implying café Cubano was so strong it needed sugar just to be potable. Four trumpets from the brass section made their presence felt by joining in. Their enthusiastic energy level defied the audience to remain seated on their hands. Sounds emitting from orquesta de Habanera y la cantante were so exhilarating they captivated everyone. Celia's musical expertise was obvious with every rhythmic note flowing past her lips. Her stage presence alone endeared her to those in attendance. After nearly two hours of performing, there was no doubt she had been accepted wholeheartedly by the fans. Celia Cruz was now a full-fledged member of Café con leche… professionally known as Sonora Matancera.

"Marta…coming here was a great idea! I just love this music."

"That's not hard, Tee…I love it as well! You mark my words, the newest band member, Celia Cruz, is going to be a big deal one of these days!" Speaking of the singer, after the evening's performance she made her rounds among the audience and introduced herself in person. She felt the people's love and wanted to reciprocate. She eventually made her way to Marta and TaNellie.

"Gracias vienes, amigos! I hope you liked the show as much as I did singing."

Marta expressed her appreciation with,"AZÚCAR! Señora Cruz…me gusta! I'm Marta de LaCosta and this is a dear friend… Señor TaNellie."

"Es un placer, señores…I'm glad you enjoyed the show, and thanks for coming!" Celia moved on, shaking hands along the way while visiting every table. Her smile was infectious; it was a safe bet she never stopped smiling until she greeted every person at the club. Celia was a consummate professional.

"Ohh…Tee, I forgot to get her autograph."

"Not to worry, Marta…I'm sure she'll be happy if you buy an

album or two. Their music is exciting and upbeat, I'll have to get a couple albums as well."

Sabroso's musical entertainment was over and Tee paid the bill. The friends were now off to see the sights of Havana. It was dark out, and still very hot. They walked down Calle de Buena Vista where children were dancing to the sounds of street corner musicians, playing for pennies. Most were decent players, however, some were standouts. One such musician was a barefoot boy playing trompeta with such verve that his music tapped directly into the inner recesses of Tee's soul. Young lolas (teenage girls) devised impromptu dance steps mirroring his melodies. TaNellie placed a twenty in the boy's straw basket, which rested nearby. Soon other tourists followed suite with sizable donations of their own. The kid must have made $100 as a result of Tee's seed money. He also gave Marta a handful of bills to distribute among the girls. They were all very appreciative and responded with even more inspiring creations.

"Tee...what came over you? asked Marta.

He was puzzled by her question. "What do you mean, what came over me?"

"Why did you contribute over a hundred dollars to those kids?"

Tee was not often second-guessed, but answered anyway. "I thought the trumpet player was very good. His music touched me, and I wanted to reward him. Hopefully he'll continue playing and become a great musician someday."

Marta shrugged off his answer. "Actually I was referring to the girls...the boy's talents were obvious...but why the girls?"

Tee was still in a state of disbelief, but gave her question some thought. "It's a fair enough question, Marta. I did it because it was the right thing to do."

Marta countered, "You actually gave each girl the same amount as the boy. Do you feel they were as talented...or just young girls to be trifled with?"

Tee sensed the conversation was heading in the wrong direction. "It depends...they may not have been as talented as the boy, but I'm sure they were just as poor. I've seen plenty of poverty since being in Cuba. Some, I'd venture to say, was overlooked by you. Just because I'm a pimp riding around in a big ass shiny car doesn't mean I'm heartless. I wanted them to be recognized for seizing an opportunity...it's what carpe diem is all about. When given a chance seeds are allowed to mature and blossom. Show me talent without opportunity, and I'll show you unfulfilled promise. Those kids were dancing for sheer enjoyment. They weren't even thinking about tips, because they didn't set out jars or baskets. Marta, I was happy to contribute. Who knows...maybe one of them may just find herself dancing in Cuba's conservatory of music. If not, maybe this evening was their only chance to feel special. That's the reason I gave each of them the same amount of cash. Marta, what brought about all these questions?"

"Well, it just seems so out of character for someone who exploits women to also be concerned about them. After all, aren't you the one who routinely insists on taking the money your ladies earn?"

Marta had unwittingly crossed the line. "That's enough Marta...I think it's time to slow your roll. You're mixing apples with oranges. Why are you so upset about what I did? I don't remember seeing you reach into your purse. I wonder why such a strong advocate for women only gives lip service when she should be trying to help? Do you think any of those kids care where my money came from? Or perhaps maybe you think they should've given it back. Marta, money is a strange but necessary commodity. Some folks are completely miserable with it...while still others manage to find happiness without it! How can you stand there and criticize me for what I did? Just embrace what happened as something positive…poor families earning a little extra money to ease life's burdens. I don't know about a diplomat's family, but I have slept in the streets in the pouring rain. Shit, Marta…I've lived in bus terminals as recently as six years ago. I know exactly what it means to be poor, and I don't like staring at it in the faces of these innocent children!"

"My mother has always cautioned me…if you can't find anything nice to say about someone, then don't say anything at all. I didn't come to Cuba to be preached to! You certainly didn't seem worried where the money for this trip came from. Your outbursts are the height of hypocrisy! You need to check yourself, Marta, and start acting like a grown woman. If I remember correctly it was you who said, and I quote: 'Looks aren't everything Tee.' Marta, in your world, beauty may only be skin deep…but in mine, ugliness goes down to the bone."

Marta had opened a can of worms that couldn't be resealed. She truly liked Tee, but her obsession concerning his profession kept getting the better of her. Marta simply couldn't let it go. It was as though she intentionally tried to sabotage their chances of being together. Maybe she feared winding up hustling on some dark dead-end street like one of his prostitutes. Perhaps she didn't feel strong enough to resist his perceived charms, opting instead to end their relationship in a fit of righteous indignation. If her past were any indication of her fortitude, she really had nothing to fear…but fear. Marta had always been a tough little cookie who never hesitated to fight for what she truly wanted. Tee felt her past didn't cut any ice with him. Marta frowned upon his profession, but as for Tee, she'd failed miserably to prove she belonged in the same class with him.

Marta wanted desperately to make amends, but time was running out. Whatever she was planning needed to happen quickly, because he was fit to be tied. TaNellie hadn't uttered a single word to her while walking back to the car. They passed the same street corner where the talented trumpet player and young dancers were performing. When Tee and Marta walked by them, the boy raised his horn. Tee never noticed the boy or the girls. He was only seeing red. Marta returned the boy's wave and acknowledged the dancing girls. She stopped in the middle of the sidewalk and grabbed Tee by his hand.

"I owe you an apology, Tee. I don't know what happened. I picked a fight because I'm afraid of falling in love. There's no other way to explain what I did. I was willing to cut off my nose to spite my face. Can you ever forgive me? It will never happen again, I promise!"

TaNellie looked into her eyes for the last time. "Marta, we need some space."

In his mind he had already decided his course of action. *This woman must be crazy if she thinks I'm going to put up with her bullshit...I'm heading back to Cleveland on the next thing smoking. This gentleman of leisure is leaving the building...and he's closing the door behind him... I don't care if I ever see this BITCH again! As far as I'm concerned, it's...game...set...and match!"*

(27) Square business...

In the life, there are just two kinds of people in the world. There are the hustlers, who make a living by their wits, and the squares, who toil daily in traditional jobs. The goals for each sect are the same: receive remuneration by earning a living in areas of expertise. Most hustlers assume the world is filled with those who fear stepping out on faith. They argue that some hold fast to job security because of a lack of spirit. On the contrary side is the hustler point of view...nothing ventured means nothing is gained. True or not, they consider themselves hunters in a world where savvy dictates earning power. As a result they aggressively seek opportunities the old-fashioned way by grabbing hold of the elusive brass ring from an ever-revolving carousel.

The often-used phrase *easy come easy go* is a misnomer. It's usually applied to earning money by non-traditional means. Years of scrimping or saving is the standard approach used by the squares. In hustling, *easy come easy go* could not be further from the truth. If the real deal be told...it's probably easier to work a 9 to 5 than to assume the responsibility of risking life, limb and freedom on an *if come*. Take *the drag*, for instance--it's an old con game perpetrated on unsuspecting souls, bilking them of cash and valuables by dragging or pulling them into a variety of unscrupulous but well-thought-out schemes.

It was already dark outside and "Yockey Doc" was running late. Henry Sanford looked at his watch, deciding to give his friend a few more minutes. It was payday and Henry was looking forward to getting home and taking a bath before eating supper. After putting in long hours as a cement finisher, Henry's bib overalls were filled with cracked grey cement residue and needed to be cleaned thoroughly on a washboard. He had yet to remove his protective knee-pads or his work boots, which had already stiffened and were hurting his feet. Ann, God bless her, regularly used a cake of lye soap and washboard to clean the hard to get concrete grime from his work clothes. She always had them smelling fresh as a daisy before he left for work. He was employed by Honkin-Conklin Construction Company. The Cleveland-based firm had begun hiring Negroes for the skilled trades. Henry was among the first to be given a chance. A short and powerfully built man, he always gave a hard day's work for a fair day's wage. Any of his friends would have gladly traded places with him at the drop of a hat, just to be a member of the local building trades union.

A knuckle rapping against the passenger side window caught Henry by surprise...it was his friend. He unlocked the door, letting the man inside. "Sorry I'm late, Henry...just finished helping a partner of mine deliver two floor-model Motorola television sets to his house. You all set to go?"

"Yeah...just waitin' on you!"

"We got to go over on the other side of town...West Boulevard...it's just off the Shoreway. It'll take us about fifteen or twenty minutes to get there. How many sets you want, my man?"

"All I need is one, Yockey Doc...it's just me and my wife, Ann."

"Suit yourself, brother Henry. But I know these ofays will give you a great deal if you buy at least two. You know how them dagoes is...they always looking for a angle!"

Henry was a quiet man and not much of a talker, but nodded his head at Yockey Doc. Whenever driving, Henry always kept both hands on the steering wheel and his eyes on the road. When they arrived at the affluent-looking building, the parking lot was packed with luxury automobiles, and Henry was impressed.

"It looks like there's a lot of rich folks living in the building."

"Like I said, brother Henry...these dagoes don't mess around. They got plenty of connections and will fuck you up in a heartbeat if you ain't about square business. Brother Henry, you better go ahead an ante up some more dough so's you can get two sets while you got the chance."

"Naaw, Yockey...that's okay. If I change my mind later, I'll get in touch with you."

"Cool...just give me the scratch and I'll bring the TV back down to you. I'll get one of them guys upstairs to help me. Dagoes don't want strangers knowing what they be up to...so it's best you stay here."

Henry was uneasy about the situation, but didn't complain. "Don't take it personal, brother Henry...I had to prove myself before they let me peep the operation. Now you just stay put until I get back."

"Okay---I'll be right here waiting."

Yockey Doc added, "I'm gonna leave my spiral notebook in the car with you. It's loaded with important information and has the names of folks who want televisions. Oh yeah--don't you look inside, 'cause I don't wanna put anybody's business in the street. Be right back...and don't forget to stay put--these dagoes don't like strangers, let alone niggas!"

Henry tuned his radio to WJW...where Alan Freed, *the Moondog...* was spinning the tunes. He was a white deejay on the only white station in Cleveland to feature Negro rhythm and blues programming. A tired Henry closed his eyes just for a minute... he wanted to enjoy the music he'd been raised on. He was awakened two hours later by a flashlight shining its beam onto his face. A voice asked him to roll down the window.

"Let me see your driver's license?" Henry reached in his back pocket and pulled out his wallet. "What are you doing in this parking lot?"

Henry wiped the sleep from his eyes and cleared his throat. "I was just waiting for a friend of mine named Yockey Doc. He went to see somebody in the building...I just gave him a ride."

The man handed Henry back his license. "I've been watching you for a while, buddy...if your friend's not back by now, he's not coming back. You'd better move along and catch up with Yockey Doc tomorrow."

A nervous Henry put the standard shift in gear and carefully drove home via the Shoreway. He was still pissed at himself for being so foolish. He thought about what he was going to do to Yockey Doc...all of it bad. Henry looked inside the spiral note book the con man left behind. There was only one name inside: Henry. "That motherfucker!"

All Henry could think about was his missing money. He had given Yockey Doc $150 of his hard-earned cash for a television. "I'm fucking that black ass nigga up when I see him. He's toast... burnt toast." When he arrived home Henry shared what happened with Ann.

"You shouldn't be messing around with those kinds of people. They always lead to trouble...no sense in making life harder than it has to be." Henry had kept most of his pay, and Ann cautioned him not to do anything rash to Yockey Doc.. "I don't want you getting in trouble on account of that no-good hoodlum!" Henry kept a snub-nosed .38 in the house for protection. He carefully picked it up...but returned it to the dresser drawer. He'd decided to beat Yockey with a baseball bat.

"Why should I waste a bullet and catch a case for shooting his ass?" Henry carefully wrapped black friction tape around the handle of the Louisville slugger for a better grip. He was standing in the hall when he crouched into a batting stance and took a hard practice swing…nearly breaking one of Ann's favorite vases.

"I declare, Henry Sanford…you gonna break up this house long before you even see Yockey Doc! Now go put that bat in the trunk of your car before I use it on you!"

Henry smiled at his wife, even though he was still fuming inside. After he caught up with Yockey, he was going to beat the shit out of him and ask questions later. There was a silver lining and Henry counted his blessings. When Yockey Doc asked him to buy two television sets… he had been on the verge of saying yes, but frugality won out. Now at least, he was able to buy some groceries and pay the rent on their apartment…and maybe even buy Ann a little something nice.

Walking past Juanita's Restaurant without going inside was practically breaking the law, and it was almost impossible. So it was with a young lady who went inside the eatery, sat down, and found a white envelope lying on the floor beside her feet. The return address was: The Society for Savings Bank…in downtown Cleveland. The envelope was unsealed, so the woman sneaked a peek inside. She held it in her lap just below the counter and began to count the crisp twenties… totaling two thousand dollars. The woman was shocked and could hardly contain her elation.

"My God!"

Nita, the owner, overheard the comment while passing and stopped short. "What's the matter, honey?"

"I just found a lot of money and I don't know what to do!"

By this time a tall, smartly dressed white woman, obviously very well-to-do, eased her way into the conversation. She suggested they find an empty booth to discuss what should be done.

Juanita took a seat while she craned her neck, scanning the dining area. Before getting started, she asked to see the envelope and counted each bill. "Ladies…it's exactly two thousand dollars here. I know whoever lost it is sick right about now. If it were up to me...I'd wait for the rightful owner and return the money. If we're lucky, he might even give us a reward!"

The woman who first spotted the envelope gave her opinion. "I figured fate had something to do with me finding this money. You know what they say... 'Losers weepers and finders keepers.' I'm sorry for whoever lost it, but...I say we're in this together and should split the money evenly."

The well-dressed woman spoke up. "I dine here all the time...I think we should return it to the rightful owner. We can give the money to Juanita for safe keeping. Next week we'll all come back and divide the cash. Of course, it can only happen if the person does not return."

The youngest of the trio added, "Well, that's fine if there's a re-ward, but suppose we don't get anything for being honest...what then?" The white woman spoke up immediately.

"Without a reward, we're all just out of luck. That is unless we each put up a little good faith money. Say $500 from each of us. I can get mine from my bank right now. If everyone can do the same, we'll be in business!"

Juanita joined in, "I'll get mine from last night's sales receipts. What about you, honey?"

The younger woman seemed sad. "I've got twenty dollars to my name...but if someone will put up my end, I'll pay you back when we meet a week from today!"

Nita saved the day. "Okay...it sounds good to me. I'll put up your share."

Things were rolling along and the white woman added, "I'll get my money from the bank... and be back in a jiffy!" The young lady who found the cash held the envelope securely in her hand while ordering breakfast. Juanita quickly took a thousand in cash from her office safe and continued with her morning duties. She smiled and engaged the diners with her usual repartee. Both women waited patiently for the well-to-do lady to return with her share.

When she finally walked through the door, you could feel a collective sigh of relief from other women. Nita quickly finished what she was doing and headed directly for the booth along with the woman who initiated everything after finding the money. "Sorry it took so long...there was a long line at the bank. I got back as soon as I could...anyway, here's my good faith money... five hundred dollars exactly." She handed her money over to the proprietor. "Now, Juanita, if you'll put this money with your share...we can place the $1500 inside the bank envelope along with the $2000. Miss, what's your name again?"

"I'm Lajuanda, ma'am--and you?"

"Yes, Lajuanda...my name is Beth Peterson. Please hand your envelope to me and I'll seal it and give it back to Juanita to put in her safe until next week at 10:00 a.m. Does that meet with everyone's approval?"

They all agreed, and the woman handed the bank envelope back to Juanita. "Now if you could just put some Scotch tape across the flap and lock this in the safe, I'll be on my way. My thanks to everyone for being so nice--and I'll see you next week, ladies."

The white woman stood and shook both Lajuanda's and Nita's hand. "See you next week at 10:00 sharp. At which time we'll all share in our good fortune." The tall woman left, and Lajuanda finished her breakfast and soon followed.

"It was nice meeting you, Juanita...I don't know about you, but I hope nobody comes in looking for the money. Oh, well--see you next week!"

"I'll be here waiting and hoping things turn out the way they're supposed to. Bye-bye." Nita went back to work feeling pretty good about what had happened. If the person who lost the money did return...she'd give it to them in a heartbeat...it was just her nature.

The week crawled by and Juanita was looking forward to seeing both Lajuanda and Beth Peterson. About five after ten in walked a smiling Lajuanda. Nita walked over and gave her a big hug. "Well, honey...after Beth comes we can all celebrate, because nobody came for the envelope. Can I bring you some breakfast? It's on the house!"

"Yes please...thanks. Nita, I've already spent my share...and of course you can take what I owe you right off the top."

Lajuanda finished her breakfast at 10:45...but still no Beth. Juanita came over to the booth. "I wonder what's keeping Miss Peterson? I tell you what, Lajuanda...I'm going to get the envelope from the safe, and give you your money now. When Beth comes I'll take care of her then. Is that all right with you?"

"Yes, ma'am--it sure is...I can't wait!" Nita came back quickly and tossed the envelope to the younger woman. "Okay Lajuanda...do the honors." With a broad smile she removed the tape and tore open the envelope. Lajuanda's smile disappeared and her jaw dropped. Inside the envelope was neatly trimmed typing paper with $20's on the outside edges. Juanita was shocked. "Oh my God...we've been taken for a ride! Beth stole all the money...I'm sure that's the last time we'll ever see in here. I'll be goddamned!" Both women just stared at the envelope in disbelief. It was a tough pill for them to swallow. Just like that, Lajuanda's hopes went up in smoke and Nita was just too embarrassed to notify police.

(28) The Cavern...

He'd just started out on a very tedious road trip where obeying the speed limit to the letter was of paramount concern. The last thing he needed was to be pulled over by the state police. It was dusk when he switched on his headlights. His tired bloodshot eyes strained as they darted from one side of the highway to the other, eventually settling in on the road ahead... and he was good to go. Yesterday on his way to the cavern, he'd spotted a number of deer. Anyone who's ever seen the kind of damage they levy against cars and people knew his worries were well-founded. Frankie Flowers and Mattie Matthews accompanied him on his first trip. They were drugged, securely bound, and left bouncing about the trunk along with a sledgehammer, shovel, rope, long metal stakes, lantern, a full gallon of hi-test gasoline, and a worn spare tire. Under ideal circumstances it would take about two hours to reach his destination. An actual round trip was a shade less than four hours, providing everything went smoothly. He planned to open the safe in Mattie's club and remove exactly $50,000 to be returned to his client. Afterwards he would head back to the cavern and complete his task. Obviously he wasn't pleased about not being able to rest between trips. It began to rain--slowly at first, then it escalated quickly into an onslaught. *Damn, I sure don't need this shit right now!* His face was practically pressed up against the already clouded windshield. The stranger continually wiped his palm across the glass, attempting to clear away the haze. Squeaking wipers raced as if the blades would fly off the handle at any second. He cracked open his air vents in hopes of quickly clearing the windows...it worked. The stranger sat back into his seat trying to relax. He had never worked this hard to fulfill a contract, and questioned whether or not he was even in the right business. The driver couldn't wait to finish this job. It lacked excitement and sucked the green weenie. He just wanted to get back to the Big Apple.

After an hour or so, the rain ceased. When the roads appeared dry he decided to make up some time, finding comfort while listening to country music on his radio. The miles melted away and soon he pulled alongside the casino. He'd written down all the pertinent information supplied him by Mattie back at the cavern. As instructed, he turned off the alarm and went directly to Mattie's office. The floor safe was behind a sliding door and lived under a small metal file cabinet with tiny wheels. The cash was banded in $5000 increments. The stranger was careful to take just the right amount...he fancied himself a lover, not a thief. And besides, his client had insisted on receiving what was owed him...nothing more and nothing less. Before leaving he returned the file cabinet to its proper position and reset the burglar alarm. He drew his gun as he left the building and cautiously walked toward the rear of the structure. He looked around and in one motion unzipped his trousers, pulled out his thing, and took a long gratifying piss. "Uuu-whee!" Relieved, the stranger jumped into his car and headed for the drop. If the man had his way, the pair would have died once he received instructions on disarming the alarm and opening the safe. Of course, if the information didn't pan out he'd owe fifty grand by default...something which would've been terrible for business and his pockets. The stranger stopped at a pay phone and dropped a dime...then dialed a number. "Have prize—dropping it off." He glanced at his watch... almost midnight.

After completing the drop, he headed directly for the cavern. Traffic was a little heavier than expected, but he persevered. While driving, he thought about his mother and older sister Monica. He hadn't spoken with them in nearly three months and hadn't laid eyes on them in over a year. He was so proud that his mother and sister had completed graduation requirements at State University of New York, thanks to full scholarships awarded them following the death of his mother's former boyfriend. Darla received her degree in communications, while Monica got one in liberal arts. He felt like a proud parent, and wished he'd taken advantage of the same opportunity when offered the chance.

There was no need worrying about what might have been. He remained focused on the present. About an hour into the trip, traffic began to wind down. After two or three miles of slow going the automobiles ground to a complete halt. He had used the cavern before to dispose of assholes whom his clients wanted to see suffer before dying. Those rats could eat a man while his heart was still beating. He often took photos of the gory aftermath...presenting them to his bloodthirsty clients, who laughed like crazy at the final gruesome demise of one-time rivals. But those were different situations. His new client just wanted to scare Frankie and Mattie, because of the suffering he'd undergone when first coming in contact with the two gangsters. The driver feared for Mattie and Frank's safety and hoped the traffic would pick up. The hourglass was quickly running out of sand. He liked the two men...there was also something quite interesting about a tattoo Frankie Flowers wore on his forearm. It was of a red heart with the words "Darla and me...and baby makes three." Those words were made popular in a Depression-era song...*Mommy and me and baby makes three.* The word Darla caught his eye because it was his mother's name. Perhaps it was a just coincidence, but it was certainly strange seeing her name on Frankie's arm. *Could there be a connection? Probably not...the odds were too great.*

The traffic soon picked up...impatient gawkers passed the

bodies of two dead deer and an overturned oil tanker, which seeped fuel onto the highway. Emergency crews seemed to have the situation under control, and no one was seriously injured--except for the two deer, whose legs had begun to stiffen from rigor mortis. The stranger, whose friends just called him Kid, picked up the pace and arrived at the cavern over two hours late.

He parked out of sight and brought the kerosene lantern from the trunk inside the cave. The fire he made before leaving was completely burned out, but smoldering. He looked around and sensed rustling near his feet. "Hey, boys...daddy's home!" he shouted, his echo returning without reply. Holding his lantern high for increased light, he saw rats by the thousands covering the ground like carpet. They scurried in every direction, disappearing deep among the stalactites and stalagmites they called home. The Kid drew his gun and stepped lightly. While holding the lantern at arm's length he wondered why they hadn't responded to his humorous greeting? Maybe they were just tired of jokes.

A few steps more revealed an answer he regretted. Spread-eagled on the ground where he had left them was a horrifying sight that made the Kid's stomach churn. The faces of both men were entirely eaten away by rats. They were dead as doornails. From the look of things...hordes of hungry rats had attacked the men after the fire died down. Their facial features were nonexistent, and parts of the remaining flesh resembled cottage cheese. Most of the skin was completely stripped bare from the bones. The partially visible skulls resembled a scene from a horror film. But this was not fake...they had been living, breathing human beings. The Kid could only imagine the pleading and woeful screams of the two partners in crime. Tormented by rats, the men had finally succumbed to agonizingly painful deaths...one bite at a time. Being eaten alive had to be the worst way for any human being to die. It was a case of the hunter becoming the prey. Just imagining such a death gave the Kid goosebumps and made him cringe in disgust. He wouldn't have wished this kind of death on his worst enemy. He tried to steady the lantern while closely inspecting both bodies. Their bindings were still intact, indicating a complete lack of resistance from the men against ravenous rodents. Once again, the Kid noticed Frankie's tattoo. He knelt down for a better look. The hit man remembered similarities between himself and Frankie Flowers. They were 5'9", with chiseled features, solid build, and the same hairline. The Kid also had a penchant for nice clothes. He vaguely recalled Darla's comments about favoring his dad. The Kid quickly followed his regular routine after a hit. He said a prayer over the deceased while reminding himself it wasn't personal...just business.

Suddenly there was a large shadowy bearlike figure at the entrance to the cave. The Kid reacted quickly by blindly firing his weapon at the figure until it was empty. After the noise and staccato bursts of light ceased, there was complete silence. His ears were ringing as he waved his hand back and forth clearing away the smoke and picking up his lantern. A large colored man slowly rose from off the deck with a .45 Colt automatic pistol pointing directly in the Kid's face. He didn't recognize the man, but the gun was the exact same model as his...a military issued .45 caliber M1911 Colt automatic.

"You almost killed me, motherfucker!" shouted the man.

"Sssorry...I was shooting at a bear."

"Hold that light steady and tell me what the hell's going on here."

"There's nothing to tell...I was exploring this cave and came across a couple of dead bodies."

The negro spoke knowingly. "They wouldn't belong to Frankie Flowers and Mattie Matt-- would they, motherfucker?"

"Who's asking?"

With his gun still targeting the space between the Kid's eyes, the man pulled back the gun's slide, chambering a round. "Colt .45's asking, motherfucker! Now answer the goddamn question!"

"I don't know...like I said, I was just...."

"Listen, motherfucker! I followed your ass here all the way from Mattie's joint. Unless I get some answers fast, I'll put your young ass to sleep right here, right now! If that's what you want, fine...or you can tell me what the fuck's going on!"

The Kid decided to relent and buy some time by giving the man bits and pieces of information.

The man gestured with his gun. "Kick that .45 over here!"

The Kid did as instructed and carefully watched the negro as he stooped to pick up the piece and put it into his belt. "What the hell is a young boy like you doing with a fine gat like this?"

"I'm not a boy...and I got it while I was in the Marines." The Kid dealt a question of his own. "How'd you get yours?"

"The same goddamn way, motherfucker in the *Crotch*! Boy do you even know what terms like the *Crotch* or the *Suck* means to a jarhead?"

"You may be holding the gun...but I don't appreciate being called boy. I'm sure you can relate to that...BOY!"

"Point well taken. Now answer my goddamn question! What does the phrase *the Crotch* or...*the Suck* mean to a Marine?"

"They are terms of endearmeant we jarheads lovingly call our Corps. It's befitting because it's based on all of the godforsaken places they send us and all the awful things we do once we get there!"

The big man responded, "Semper Fidelis [always faithful], motherfucker! Now last question...it's a two-parter. How come the alarm didn't go off when you left the club, and what the hell were you carrying when you came out?"

The Kid was in a pickle and didn't know quite how to respond, so he told the truth. "I was carrying some money that Mattie and Frankie owed my client. I'm sure you saw me drop it off when I left Mattie's. After that, I came directly back here. I was going to let them loose, but I got back too late."

"You expect me to believe that bullshit?"

"Look…devil dog…I don't give a shit if you believe me or not. I'm only interested in knowing where we go from here."

The Negro contemplated another question. "How much cash did you drop off to your client?"

"I turned in fifty grand exactly."

"Just fifty grand, huh? I know for a fact there was over two million clams inside the safe… and you only took fifty grand?"

"That right…my client only wanted what was stolen from him, so that's what I took."

"I assume your client is happy as a motherfucker now. How about you, young fella… how you feel? Shit…for that matter, how do we both feel about all the money still lying in that safe?"

"I don't feel anything," responded the Kid.

"Don't you want to do something positive with your life? Two million bucks could buy a lot of happiness. Listen, young fella--sometimes not taking advantage of an opportunity is a crime. Especially when it's in a nice colorful bow all wrapped up for the taking! This is one of those opportunities--a chance of a lifetime!" Although the Kid wasn't a thief, he was a pragmatist and carefully weighed the pros and cons of Moose's idea.

"You're right, Marine! We'll never have to put our lives on the line again!"

"Fucking 'A', Kid!"

"Not for God, country, or anyone else. We've been there, done that. Only warriors care about other warriors. We are the fucking warriors who stood up, signed up, trained up, and showed up in the shit holes of the world! That dough is ours…now let's go get paid up!"

"Here's the marching orders, young fella--we'll both drive back to the club and just take a million in cash to split between us. Since the club's only open from Thursday to Sunday, we've got a couple of days without nary a soul even around the joint. Can you imagine having a half million apiece? We could get out of this life and become legitimate. What do you say to that, young fella?"

"Well--you're right about one thing, man...there's still a ton of dough left in the safe. I remember thinking when I took the fifty grand...*I've never been around so much money in my life!*"

"Yeah, young fella--all we'd have to do is walk in and walk out. It's as easy as tossing a grenade...one...two...three...BOOM! Let's do this Marine... *let's go get some!*"

"Semper Fi...man! You've got yourself a deal!"

"What's your name, young fella?"

"My name is Frank...but I like the Kid...what about you?"

"My real name is Clarence, which I hate, so everybody calls me Moose because of my size."

"Man...I woulda thought it was because of your looks!" The large man laughed. "You a funny little motherfucker, ain't you!"

Then he returned the .45 to the Kid. "You almost killed me with that pea shooter, motherfucker."

"I've never missed what I was aiming at in my life. If I'd been trying to kill you...you'd be in Hell right now. Like I said before--I was shooting at a bear when your big ass got in the way!"

"Yeah—right, Kid...whatever you say."

"Okay, I'll bet half the cash there's a dead bear in the cave's entrance!"

They went to the opening, and sure as shootin' a large black bear with its tongue hanging limply had bought the farm. "Well I'll be goddamed if you didn't kill that motherfucker! No shit... this bear is dead as a motherfucker!"

When Moose realized what had happened, he began to break

out in a cold sweat even though the cavern was freezing inside. "You're an expert marksman...the Corps taught you well. Thanks, Marine!" Moose smiled. "You know I was just kidding about my share of the million."

They both laughed while Moose gave the Kid a little insight. "Part of my job at Mattie's is to watch over the place after dark. Sooner or later, someone's gonna come around to open the joint. Let's take it down this evening. We'll cop a million and leave everything else intact. Then whoever opens the club will have to assume everything's hunky-dory, because nothing's out of whack. This is gonna be a huge score, Kid. The serial numbers aren't registered, because it's all used money. It's also in small denominations, so it won't raise any suspicions when it's spent. We've got to be careful, though...don't spend lump sums on major purchases. Other than that, we'll be just fine. This is dream come true, Kid."

The Kid's eyes expressed his feelings. "I agree...I've been wanting to walk the straight and narrow for a long time, and now's our chance. Moose--I'm with you a hundred percent." The veteran extended his massive hand to the younger vet. "Semper Fi, Kid. Now let's get the hell out of this motherfucking cave!"

They decided to carry out the plan at 1700 hours (5:00 p.m.) while it was still light outside. Taking down the place in broad daylight would allay any suspicions. Moose would stay in his car and perform his regular security duties while the Kid went inside and grabbed the prize. He parked a block away and walked to Mattie's, carrying two large zippered gym bags. The desolate area was deserted except for a few stray cats and dogs. He passed by Moose's car and went directly into the club. In less than fifteen minutes, it was over. The Kid came out of the building with a shit-eating grin on his face. Again he walked past Moose's car and lifted the already unlocked trunk, hesitating momentarily to toss a gym bag inside. He continued walking until he disappeared from view. Moose scrambled from his car to check the bag...everything was copacetic. With his heart racing, he drove to a predetermined location, where he stashed his gym bag. Moose returned to his worksite by 7:00 p.m., the normal start time for his shift. He leaned back in his seat and popped open an ice-cold bottle of Carling's Black Label beer and turned on the baseball game. The Indians had clinched the pennant and were World Series-bound.

Meanwhile, the Kid stopped by the location where he'd made the drop and retrieved his payment, which was waiting in the usual hiding place. He drove back to New York City and never returned to Cleveland. His chance encounter with Moose changed his life. It was almost an afterthought, but the Kid decided to take his mother and sister out for dinner at a restaurant in the Williamsburg section of Brooklyn. The popular eatery had been around for over sixty years and was called Peter Luger Steak House.

"Mom, I figured you'd enjoy being served for a change--and Monica, don't you worry about having to wash the dishes either!"

Not surprisingly, they ordered the famous Porterhouse Steak for four with all the trimmings. Having survived the Depression, nothing was as satisfying as a big juicy medium rare steak. The Kid was as content as could be with his family. He hadn't seen them in over a year. With all the happenings occurring during the week, he counted his lucky stars to still have the two of them in his life.

"Mom, I never asked you this before...but did you and my father ever get married?"

She smiled. "Yes we did, son. One weekend I took off from the restaurant and we hightailed it to Reno, Nevada. We took our vows in a gambling parlor called the Last Chance Chapel. Right afterwards, we went next door and got a couple of tattoos. I must have been one of the first women to do such an onerous thing. But I said..what the heck...we loved each other!"

"What kind of tattoo, Mom?" She motioned with her hand. "It's right in the small of my back. It says 'Frankie and me and baby makes three.' His was different and read... 'Darla and me and baby makes three.' Frankie-boy, you weren't around yet, and baby referred to your sister, Monica. Your father was a racketeer, but he always treated me like a lady. Much better than any man before or since. He made me feel special, and he respected me. He always said there wasn't anything I couldn't do. Frank encouraged me to hold my head up...saying that's the only way to bask in the sunshine. Whenever I felt less than other girls, he quoted Shakespeare to me. 'Self adoration is no less vile a sin as self neglecting.' I believed him...and began to take care of myself healthwise, as well as learning to apply makeup and wear my clothes with pride. After fifteen years, we lost touch. But I've often wondered whatever happened to him. Sooo, Frankie-boy... why all the questions!"

"No particular reason, Mom, I was just wondering about our history...is all. I wish I'd gotten to know him and see the tattoo for myself. Maybe I'll get the chance one day?"

The Kid's wistful look revealed his inner turmoil as he lovingly placed his arms around both his mother and sister. "Well," he sighed, "we'll always have each other." They held their glasses high and the Kid offered up a toast. "To Frankie Flowers, wherever you are! This toast has nothing to do with business and everything to do with family: 'Darla...Me...and Monica makes three!' Frankie Boy, this wasn't business... it was strictly personal!"

They drank wine and consumed the largest, best-tasting Porterhouse ever. In her mind's eye, Darla could still see the ever-dapper Frankie Flowers. His voice seemed to resonate whenever he entered Blossom restaurant. "Hiya, toots!" The Kid was finally able to put his past behind him and concentrate fully on the future. At long last, he accepted the scholarship he received from

State University of New York, and enrolled in SUNY at Old Westbury...majoring in pre-law. "Who'd've thunk it!"

Moose continued reporting for work every day until Frankie's crew informed him they were closing the club and he was relieved of his services. He knew it would have been impossible for anyone in the crew to know exactly how much cash was in the floor safe. Joey Cerito gave him $500 in severance pay and told him to get lost. So much for honor among thieves. Moose was never asked anything concerning missing funds or the missing men. Clarence "Moose" Higgins, former corporal in the Marines and Korean war veteran, kept his information to himself. He was never again plagued by monetary woes, and flew the American flag outside his home regularly. On major holidays like the 4th of July, Memorial Day, Veterans Day, and November 10th, the Marine Corps Birthday, he felt an extra surge of pride. He never saw the Kid again, which was probably a good thing. The Corps had instilled in them both pride, discipline, and the good sense to opt for maximum utilization of available resources...something he and the Kid took full advantage of in that dank, dark, cold cavern where they acted on an impulse and began putting their lives back on track. Their circumstances were quite similar to those of Mattie Matt and Frankie Flowers back at the Harvard Hotel on Delancy street. The two friends buried a dead dog they found alongside the road to conceal their charade. When Moose and the Kid were faced with the same dilemma, which had perplexed their gangster counterparts...they decided just to let sleeping dogs lie.

(29) Missing persons...

J oy Hensen had not spoken with or seen her husband in days, and was understandably worried sick. She never intruded in his business dealings, but was well aware of the lifestyle he'd chosen. Going to the police and reporting him as a missing person was the last thing on her mind. She did retain a private investigator from a prestigious firm to help find her husband. Being incommunicado was totally out of character for Mattie, who talked with his wife two or three times a day. Logically she had hoped for the best, but somewhere in her heart of hearts she knew something was terribly wrong. Joy visited her old boarding house to inform Miss Emma of the situation and to be around friends. The older woman was saddened to hear the news and immediately asked Jesus, her source of all blessings, to "Please return Mattie home safely into his wife's arms."

Miss Emma insisted Joy Hensen stay for dinner, noting the change of scenery would help her cope. "Miss Hensen...we're having baby beef liver smothered in onions with mashed pota-toes, gravy, cornbread, and some ice-cold lemonade for supper. You've got to stay...it's your Mattie's favorite dish!"

Miss Emma wanted Joy to be among friends--folks who were deeply concerned about Mattie's well-being. So far, Joy Hensen had struggled all alone with the disappearance. Now she felt an immediate sense of relief. Miss Emma was absolutely right to in-clude their friends into the circle. Joy was no longer alone. During supper she met Miss Emma's newest roomer.

"Joy, I'd like to introduce you to Mr. Rick Foy...he's a very nice man and has been with us for a couple of weeks now."

The tall man stood and graciously extended his hand. "I can't tell you how sorry I am to hear about your husband's disappearance. I hope everything works out well for both you and your husband."

"Thank you for your kind words, Mr. Foy. I'm certainly praying for a blessed conclusion."

Miss Emma allowed Joy to sit in her former seat between Lurline Smith and Mr. Roebuck. "Sit down right here, child." She lovingly patted Joy's shoulders. "Now isn't this better? It seems just like old times, huh?" Joy searched her purse and found some tissue to dab her reddened eyes...this was where she had met Mattie.

Miss Emma hadn't lost her touch as far as cooking was concerned. The meal she prepared was scrumptious, and the lemonade hit the spot...as usual. Joy recalled the memorable moment when she first laid eyes on Mattie at the dining room table. "He was originally from a small town in the South...but had big-city swagger. I just loved how he dressed, and everything about him shouted New York City! By morning I knew we were meant for each other."

A tenant added a little levity. "That's not all you knew, Miss Hensen! I couldn't get to sleep to save my soul. Things was real noisy 'round here that night."

"Now, Mr. Roebuck—let's not give Mr. Foy the wrong impression about our little family, even though there is some truth to what you're saying."

Miss Emma looked up from her plate, glancing sheepishly over at Joy with a huge smile on her face. "I love him so much, Miss Emma...even though we've been married only a short while. I don't know what I would do without Mattie...he's my rock of Gilbraltar!"

Mr. Blair cleared his throat and pushed his empty plate aside. "I'd like to make a special announcement to the roomers who were living here when Mattie Matthews first moved into the boarding house. As most of you already know, I'm an insurance representative for Mammoth Life Insurance Company. Mattie loved his fellow roomers and took out a sizable whole life insurance policy on himself. I think you should know he made us all beneficiaries in the event of his death. Of course Joy, his wife, was given the lion's share of the policy's benefits. Miss Emma, along with Miss Lurline Smith, Mr. Ichabod Roebuck, and myself...Hollingsworth G. Blair III...are all listed in the document and are entitled to ten thousand dollars upon his demise.

"God forbid he should die at this time. I'm sure we all pray he lives to be a hundred. I want you to know I wrestled with sharing this information. When we drafted his policy, he asked me to divulge its contents only when the timing was right. Mattie's the salt of the earth, and considers us his family. His parents died years ago, and he has no living relatives. Since none of us know what tomorrow may bring, I felt compelled to apprise everyone of his thoughtfulness at this time. He is a generous person, and I'm sure he's going to be okay."

"Lord have mercy." Miss Emma's response summed up the feeling of those seated around the table. "I surely trust he's all right... 'cause none of us want his bequest under these circumstances. We just hope and pray he's all right."

Mr. Foy had remained silent until now. He requested permission to share his opinion with the group. "I haven't had the opportunity to sit around the dinner table with such nice folks in a long time. I'm sure Mattie was a welcome addition to your rooming house. In the short time since I've lived here, I've experienced the same sense of belonging I'm sure Mattie must have felt. I wish I could change things...but I want you all to know...God works in mysterious ways. If for some reason Mattie doesn't find his way back home, I'm sure he would want you to put the legacy he has bequeathed you to good use. One way is by generously using it where it will do the most good. Now if you'll please excuse me, Miss Emma, I'm going to my room and do a little reading. Having just one eye means it takes me twice as long to read the Bible as most folks. Thanks for hearing me out, family--and good night, everyone."

"Good night, Mr. Foy."

Rick lay down on his bed...which ironically was the same one Mattie had used. The gambler thought about the occurrences of the last couple of weeks. *How could I have told the other roomers what I really know about Joy's husband? God knows I didn't want either Frankie Flowers or Mattie Matt dead. If I had gone to Frankie and Mattie in person and asked for my fifty grand...they might have killed me. That's what Frankie promised to do if he ever saw my face again...and I believed him. That's why I contacted the Kid to scare the bejesus out of them and get my cash. Even after the terrible ass-whipping they gave me and the loss of my eye, I never wanted them dead. I just wanted my money back. Hell...I even gave the Kid ten grand just so's there wouldn't be any problems. I'm going to match whatever the insurance company gives Joy... hopefully it'll make things a lot easier for her. She's a square broad and should have never gotten caught up in my beef with her old man. I'll have one of my partners assume the identity of a legit businessman and get the money to her. I'll figure out some kind of ruse so she won't suspect it's from me. I really like this town a lot... maybe I'll hang around for a while until I decide how to maximize my winnings. Cleveland's been real good to me and I can't help but feel it's not finished with being generous.*

(30) Whiplash...

William "Whiplash" Harris always had at least ten different insurance scams going on at any given time. It was something he was really good at doing, and it kept him in the chips during the lean times. He'd received out-of-court cash settlements for mishaps including everything from slipping on banana peels and spilled liquids in supermarkets to tripping over unattended mops and buckets. Feigned injuries after being bumped by cars in parking lots were among his favorite ruses. Falling on patches of ice, snow, unsafe sidewalks, and chuckholes were historically tried and true money makers. You name it, and Willie had done it. Whiplash's list of *accidentally on purpose* misrepresentations went on and on and on. His real claim to fame, however, was an Annual Hustler's Holiday. Once a year he sponsored a gala affair at the Majestic Hotel on East Fifty-Fifth Street in the Roaring Third district of Cleveland. Hustlers and players visited the unique assemblage en masse and came from all across America and Canada. Most attendees prepared well in advance of the event in order to purchase custom-made clothing, alligator shoes, and exotic furs all designed to best exemplify the player lifestyle. There is nothing sharper than a well-dressed pimp in all his regalia strutting a *mean kimble* (unique gait) to match his *pimp until I die braggadocio.* As the hustlers and pimps in the life say, *"Game recognizes game."*

Whiplash considered himself an impresario of the highest order, and never missed an opportunity to make a little extra pocket change by sanctioning a litany of diversionary sideshows during his holiday event. Included in these contests were: best pimp of the year, most popular wench, hoe turnout lines, pimp daddy dozens, best-dressed player, best-dressed wench, and best custom ride...just to name a few. Contestants took part in an assortment of activities for prestigious titles, huge gold-colored trophies, and cash money prizes. The ultimate honor in this series of challenges was being selected as the best all-around player/hustler in America. Events were open to all, and entry fees ranged from $500 to $1500 to guarantee a spot in specific categories. Winners enjoyed bragging rights for a full year...at the end of which, competition started in earnest all over again. This year featured Redd Foxx as host and master of ceremonies. Local doo-wop singing groups including the mighty El Deons, the impeccable Sahibs, and the world-famous Hesitations...all would be on hand to provide the guests with rhythm and blues entertainment.

TaNellie had attended the functions before and has always enjoyed hobnobbing with business associates. Although he had never shown an interest in participating; lately he'd been composing intricate rhymes and honing his verbal skills with the help of close friends. They often relaxed after a long night by reciting timeless classic rhymes among themselves. The 'Signifying Monkey' and the blue version of 'Little Tommy Tucker...the bad motherfucker...' were the most popular. TaNellie even incorporated himself into some creative limericks. His short poetic verses spoke of daily pimping activities while he embellished his own pimping prowess. At the Hustler's Holiday Gala, these vocal competitions fell under the category of... *pimp daddy dozens.* TaNellie paid his entry fee in advance with high aspirations of winning this year's title. The *dozens* were a time- honored art of communicating insults about a competitor's mother in a stylish manner using colloquial expressions integrated with gritty street vulgarisms. A key to winning this coveted title was an ability to recall one's vast repertoire of momma insults while simultaneously displaying a unique brand of unequaled showmanship.

Tee's mother often spoke about his gift of gab, which was inherited from his father, who loved playing the *dozens* down in New Orleans. Players used one-upmanship to gain tactical advantages, just as with university and rival political party debaters. The *dozens* had been around since the days of Reconstruction, and elevated sharp-tongued devotees into respectful celebrity status. The object was to use rhymed words, while bombarding and slandering a player's mother in the most vile and explicit ways. Battles, as they were often called, might last just a few minutes or many hours. Whoever was left standing when the smoke cleared was usually declared the winner. Players were disqualified after repeating a rhyme or failing to answer an opponent's verse. The action began with deliberate sparring—it was a feeling-out process similar to the early stages of combat in a prize fight. Soon it escalated into a fierce *in your face* competition with the warriors so close they literally sprayed spittle on each other. Style, delivery, and speed were marked advantages, worth their weights in gold. Side bets abounded during these battles, and enthusiastic followers rooted their champions onward. With crowds of onlookers egging them on, players landed verbal jabs with the ferocity of heavyweight champions seeking to silence opponents with a knockout blow. Combatants were constantly revolving around each other as if tethered by leather bindings, while hurling despicable barbs to the delight of spectators. Under normal circumstances, were it not for rules of engagement, these insults could have surely resulted in fistfights or even worse.

During the Hustler's Holiday Gala, each contestant was given eight seconds to respond to a verse. Judges rated each contestant and compared scorecards after the competition was over. As the raucous audience champed at the bit for the contest to begin, a nervous TaNellie glanced over at his girls, giving them a thumbs up. They were dressed to the nines and seated in the front row. Tee was number five among twelve pairs of contestants. Outwardly he looked cool as a cucumber, and knew his performance would have a direct affect on his girls. If he did well, his ladies would also reap the benefit of his performance in the form of status and accolades high above the other ladies. Tee's eyes were fixed while steering a stick of gum into his mouth one bite at a time. He studied his opponent slowly and carefully. When the jousting began, he wanted his pipes to be fresh and moist. Comedian Red Foxx gave his blessings to each of the contestants just before the rumble started.

"I want to give y'all a word of advice...WIN!" he challenged. "Ain't nobody gonna care who came in second place. This is a war! The *dozens* is just another word for smash mouth football...so take no prisoners! I want you to pulverize the bastard standing in front of you! He's keeping you from your goal. Now let's go out there and kick some ass and show those hustler motherfuckers in the audience how to play some...dozens!"

The crowd began to chant, "DOZENS...DOZENS...DOZENS...DOZENS!"

Two contestants kimbled toward center stage and were given their mics. "Testing...1...2...3." Everything was perfect and ready to go.

Redd Foxx calmly lit a cigarette, slowly taking in a few long drags before getting underway. "Ladies and Gentlemen...I'm Redd Foxx." The audience rose to their feet and gave the popular comedian an enthusiastic round of applause. "How many of you niggas out there in the audience have ever played the dozens!" Practically the whole crowd stood while hooting and hollering. "Well...that's just what I expected. You're in for a treat this evening. Since you already know the rules, I won't waste your time with explanations." Redd beckoned the players closer. "This good-looking fellow on my left is Moe Bowie from Chicago, Illinois and his opponent is Jimmy Hamm from Long Island, New York."

Once again the crowd chanted, "DOZENS...DOZENS...DOZENS...DOZENS!"

"Okay, men—it's time to get it on...now shake hands and come out slinging insults!"

The battle was underway and Moe Bowie was first. "I saw ten toes up...I saw ten toes down...I saw a little black bootie going round and round. I saw bright red lips...just as big as you please...your mom was giving head right there on her knees. She sucked...then gargled with some Listerine...but her breath still smelled like...an army latrine. Her eyes were closed, so she didn't see me...but what she didn't know...she was gargling with pee! She gagged for a minute...I thought she was dead...but the bitch kept on sucking all over the bed!"

Jimmy Hamm fired back, "I screwed your mammy on top of a stove, the more she yelled the deeper I drove. When all of a sudden she said something strange: 'Hold on to me Jimmy...I'm too old to ride the range!'"

Moe wasted little time. "I finally gave your momma's pussy a try...you know how that bitch always lie...her poontang was hot, to my surprise...but I just couldn't stand them motherfucker's flies!"

The adversaries went toe to toe for twenty minutes or so before Morrie was able to best his opponent, who failed to answer an offering. "Way to go, Moe!"

When it was time for TaNellie to do battle, his stable stood and cheered like crazy. After shaking hands, the two opponents came out with guns blazing. Tee let go with a solid barrage, setting the tone early. "I fucked your momma in a sack of flour...the bitch was shittin' pancakes in half an hour!"

His opponent knew his craft well, and his response was swift. "I screwed your momma on a red-hot heater! I said slow down bitch, you made me burn my peter!"

Onlookers awaited the answer. "I screwed yo' momma between two logs...she had one pup and two bulldogs!"

The sizable crowd began choosing sides. "Let's go, Tee!" "C'mon Honey boy...get 'em!"

Tee staggered momentarily. "Ooohhh no you didn't! I screwed your old lady like an alarm clock...she say keep working daddy, cause I love your cock!"

"I hate to talk about your momma, she's a sweet old soul—but her breath smells like a spoiled asshole!"

"Ooowheee! That's bad," came a response from the crowd.

"I wanna talk about your momma...cause you don't know how...but the bitch got titties like a Guernsey cow!"

The players' vituperative physical antics and posturing had to be seen to be appreciated. In a very real sense, they were just as important as word choices. "I don't play the dozens...I play the Cisco Kid...I fucked your old lady before your daddy did!"

"Yo'momma's like an old pussy cat...handing out booty from the front and back. Her titties move 'round like windshield wipers...her crack's so wide she wear two pair-a diapers!"

"Ohhh noooo--he scorched your ass, man!"

After the judges decided a contestant's fate, the vanquished player slowly slunk away licking wounds, hopeful that next year would hold the sweet promise of victory. Size didn't matter when fighting with words, and even timid souls could be fierce competitors while playing the dozens.

Once all was said and done, a proud TaNellie strode to center stage to pick up his gold- colored trophy and $3000 in cash. To make it appear as though the winnings were much more substantial, Whiplash placed a few crisp hundred-dollar bills atop a stack of five-dollar notes. Redd Foxx shook the winner's hand, then addressed the crowd.

"Do you folks want to hear TaNellie's winning rhyme once more!"

The crowd went crazy, once again standing and stomping their feet while cheering their butts off. "TaNellie...TaNellie... TaNellie!"

The pimp took the mic and proceeded to spit the words that put him over the top. "Your momma pulled me into a telephone booth. She wanted to screw just to sap my youth. She took me on the deluxe tour and her snatch was hot like soup du jour. Her hair was nappy, with no bounce or curl...that's when she say...'I'm a working girl!' Now I never minded sampling her wares. But paying for some pussy is strictly for squares! So I screwed her hard and busted my nut! You talk plenty shit for an old poop butt! She said 'I don't give a damn about what you say, I'm only here because I'm off today. So check yourself and don't give me no lip. Just finish what we started and after my thrills, I'll give you what you want...'cause I always pay my bills!'"

Everyone jumped from their seats and rolled with laughter, giving Tee another standing ovation, much louder than before. He was a happy camper. The warm display from people he didn't know was a fitting end to the contest. Redd Foxx raised Tee's arm in victory. "Ladies and gentlemen...our *Pimp Daddy Dozens* champion...TaNellie!" The crowd stood and applauded all of the contestants who participated in a great show. Red Foxx approached Tee.

"TaNellie...I know you're tired...that was a great battle. Is there anything you'd like to say to the folks?"

Ana stood and exhorted the rest of Tee's girls to follow her example. "Speech.... Speech.... Speech!" Soon the entire audience joined in: "Speech...Speech!" A relaxed TaNellie took the mic from

Redd Foxx like a seasoned professional, obviously happy with the results of his hard-fought win. His adversary was good, real good--but just ran out of rhymes when it mattered most. Tee hadn't given any thought as to what he wanted to say, and his comments were strictly off the cuff.

"Ladies and gentlemen, here's a small glimpse of how I make my way in a world full of pimps, players, and working girls: *First I check my snow Janes by counting all their money. They've never been short because I file a report. I double check them wenches just the same, 'cause lying is the nature of the pimping game. After a short rest I'm down for the test to eliminate stress and insure my success. I set all my traps, then go shoot some craps, and win enough money to make every day sunny. I cop me a squat before going to bed when I spot the silhouette of a drowning head. When I jumped into the pool he was almost dead. I put him on the deck, just as quick as you please, all of a sudden he started to sneeze. I said bless you my man, but can't you cover your nose. He said ain't you TaNellie, the Prince of the hoes? I nodded my head saying, yeah I suppose. But what do you know about chasing hoes? I dried him off by setting my winnings ablaze. The cash was piled high and it burned for days. He took a swig of rum to soothe his spirit and offered me some but I never go near it. The dude sneezed again and to my amaze, he rapped about the game but I still wasn't fazed. So I pulled his coat about the nature of the beast. It's like a roll of the dice, it's either famine or feast. Sometimes it's bad, and sometimes it's good, but a boss player always pimps like he should. The moral of this story wasn't hard to figure. Keep your hoes in line and your finger on the trigger!"* TaNellie hesitated and glanced at the prize money still clutched in his hand. He adjusted his clothing, making sure they fit, and after a moment he continued to spit. *"A day after I gave my helpful hint, I slid by the bank to pay my rent. I put on some threads and combed my do. Then picked up the phone and started talkin' to you. I hopped into the Caddy and the wenches said 'morning daddy'. They were acting sort of giddy so I drove into the city. The Johns get saditty [full of themselves] when they see a little tittie...tossing cash into the back, of my brand new Cadillac. My girls are so pretty...it's the Johns I pity 'cause they just don't know the deal. It may seem funny, but he who spends the money, is the dumbest hoe...for real! I gunned the engine like I was flying a plane--it's the only thing I can't explain. I split the scene in that flying machine, and two days later I was still counting green. Now if you don't believe this story is true, go talk to the blind man because he saw it too!"*

TaNellie was always promoting himself and his girls. But he could turn at the drop of a feather... and show a side of himself that the public seldom saw: that part of him which is not to be fucked with...a lesson many in his seraglio knew all too well. TaNellie was successful in the world's oldest profession because he was immune to bullshit. He'd heard it all before, and had even dished some himself. So it stood to reason he was always skeptical and forever on alert...it was just the cost of doing business.

Tee was indeed the winner of the 1954 *Pimp Daddy Dozens* competition...*a newly crowned world champion.* His impromptu rhymes were enough to put him over the top with his new-found fans. Next year he promised to return with a vengeance...and even better limericks than before. He had to prove his victory was no fluke, and he was up to the task. With his reputation at stake, Tee refused to rest on his laurels...it's not how the dozens are played.

(31) Ted August...

Ishmael Silverman had successfully eluded authorities, but the indictment against him remained. He disappeared into thin air once he decided to avoid prosecution all together. Everything seemed to fall right into place for the beleaguered Silverman. He assumed the moniker Ted August, a name he considered less descriptive than his own. *"My name is August...like the month!"* His first order of business was to secure all of the assets that were still under his control. He had over a million dollars in a numbered Swiss account. This would allow him to maintain his lifestyle no matter where he decided to relocate. His gold coin collections, along with his precious gems, were placed into safety deposit boxes at banks where he'd opened checking and savings accounts. Ishmael's car was sold and replaced with a new one, which was purchased on an installment plan, in spite of his feelings concerning interest payments. It was his way of establishing a credit line and business record under his new identity. Ted August enrolled in the YMCA and began a daily regimen of running, to increase his stamina and lose some weight. Ultimately the newly minted runner was able to complete his first marathon at the age of sixty years old--a feat which instilled in him a belief that there was nothing he couldn't accomplish. With the passage of time, the name Ted August became rather noteworthy, and fit him like a comfortable pair of shoes. His transition was nearly complete. August was now in possession of a new driver's license, passport, and social security card. For all intents and purposes he was now a law- abiding citizen. He had at long last fallen between the fissures of American society. The yoke of anxiety was no longer an issue for Ted August.

With untethered freedom, August was able to pursue a career he'd longed for since he was a boy: to be in the moving picture business. He'd been an avid moviegoer, practically living in theatres while viewing his favorite films over and over. In most theaters, an adult fare was just 15 cents, while children were admitted for a dime. As with rollerskating rinks, one could spend endless hours immersed in a weekend fantasy world limited only by imagination. As a young boy, for Ishmael Silverman, nothing compared with spending an afternoon eating popcorn in a darkened movie house and being frightened by the likes of Boris Karloff or Bela Lugosi. Their horror films, along with a Little Rascals or Three Stooges fifteen-minute short reel, tossed in for good measure, was what being a kid was all about.

August started his path on the ladder of movie-making success at the bottom. He learned all he could about a business that seemed both familiar and intriguing at the same time. Everything--from exhibiting movies to making them-was his ultimate goal. His was a journey he would come to love, and it would love him right back. He took college courses in business and attended seminars hosted by studio executives. Ted read books authored by studio executives...along with every edition of *Variety* magazine he could get his hands on. Even lesser-known movie trade magazines were read from cover to cover.

The novice film maker's first attempts at making features were promising, though a bit too dark and grainy. The story lines of his ten-minute shorts, however, were quite interesting and well-received. August worked tirelessly developing his expertise, while at the same time, gaining invaluable industry knowledge. Ted August was paying his proverbial dues. After a while he stepped up in cinematic class and began producing "B" movie Westerns. In due time he found his niche and began to scout and sign unknown actors, developing them into popular stars in the mold of mainstay actors like: William Boyd, Spring Byington, George "Gabby" Hayes, Gloria Grahame, Franklin Pangborn, Gilbert Roland, Rory Calhoun, James Gleason, and Randolph Scott.

August knew a good thing when he saw one, and worked diligently like a man possessed, learning the ins and outs of the business while developing lasting relationships with those he came in contact with. He had discovered a talent he was completely unaware of. Soon he was writing scripts and screenplays, and pitching them to major studios. For the first time in his life, he was doing what he truly loved. If the truth be known, this was something he would have done for free. Well maybe not free...but you get the picture.

Ted had all but forgotten his past when he happened upon someone he never expected to see standing in line at a Cleveland Trust Bank. While waiting for a rather slow moving teller he turned around to ask the gentleman behind him a question. "Sir, is your last name Purifoy?"

The man responded in the affirmative, but was oblivious with to whom he was speaking. "My name is Ted August." Before continuing, he lowered his voice. "Tike-allah...its me." Then he reached into his pocket and gave the man a peppermint. He extended his hand and repeated his name. "I'm Ted August...how are you and Bessie doing? It's been years...you were just a little boy when I saw you last. Now you've grown into a fine looking young man."

TaNellie was shocked to see Silverman but pleasantly surprised. "How are things going, Mr. Sil...."

The older man stopped him. It's August...like the month!"

"Yes, of course...Ted August. Mother is going to die when she sees you. Say…if you're available…I'd love to have you attend my graduation from Central State. I'm sure I can get you a ticket. You can reconnect with my mother then. Why don't we walk to your car so I can give you all the details? Boy, it's good to see you. We were so worried, with all of the rumors swirling around. I won't mention anything to my mother…it will be a real treat for her to see you again."

"I'd love to see her as well…I think about you guys often."

The two traded contact information and promised to see one another at the university's commencement.

(32) Sister Hard Leg...

Sooner or later it was bound to happen. Some unknown John... drank from the well once too often and went berserk after discovering he'd been seduced by smoke and mirrors. Early one Sunday morning, just a few doors past Juanita's restaurant, lay a dumped lifeless corpse of a prostitute known simply as "Sister Hard Leg." The Asian beauty was about twenty years old and had worked nearly two years in a closely knit neighborhood surrounding 30th Street on Payne Avenue. There is a Latin axiom considered the quintessential rule governing all business transactions: *caveat emptor*, meaning *let the buyer beware*. Unfortunately, Sister Hard Leg carried some baggage that didn't quite conform to most tricks' expectations. Sister had a rather large prick.

If the exotic-looking wenches walking the stroll in the Chinese section of town were to be believed, Sister Hard Leg had been dating an ofay for months. The middle-aged trick always showed up every Saturday evening at precisely ten o'clock, rain or shine. Timetables at the Terminal Tower railroad station could be set based solely upon his prompt arrival. The lovelorn ofay even proposed to Sister Hard Leg. Once he went so far as to beg for the prostitute's hand in marriage by presenting Sister with a two-carat diamond ring. Even though his offers were never accepted, the pair continued dating every Saturday night like clockwork. Whenever he arrived, Sister Hard Leg escorted him into a darkened alleyway next to an Asian supermarket and Chinese laundry. There she proceeded, as if on a mission, to relieve him of his *load* and his *money*. Sister Hard Leg took pride in the job at hand and always received a crisp fifty-dollar bill.

One must keep in mind that the going rate for fellatio during 1954 was five dollars. After their business was concluded, they continued passionately busting slobs (kissing) while the John professed his undying love for her.

After finding the body lying outside the doorway of the Hawthorne building, detectives noticed that Sister held an old wadded fifty-dollar bill in her fist. The decedent wasn't wearing underwear, and Sister's genitalia was exposed. Even though most prostitutes don't wear panties... this served as a red flag to the police. There's no way a male posing as a woman would not wear panties to cover up his business. Some believed a sexual encounter occurred at the time of the murder. Questions still remained: where were the panties? It was obvious the Asian had been killed somewhere else before being dumped off in TaNellie's haunt. Rumors persisted, some claiming once the trick realized she was a he... the John went crazy and beat the Asian to death. City medical examiners estimated the killing took place between the hours of 10:00 p.m. and 1:00 a.m. The victim had been hit multiple times about the head, shoulders, and arms with a blunt object. Since the ofay was a regular, he was considered a prime suspect. That is...until he returned the following Saturday with a pocket full of crisp fifty-dollar bills, looking for Sister Hard Leg. The murder was never reported in the news media and the general public was completely unaware of what happened. The ofay was wrought with emotion after being informed about Sister Hard Leg's death, which led authorities to assume he wasn't sophisticated enough to have planned such a murder. Additionally, the man's perceived grief was deemed sincere and he wasn't held by detectives.

With the release of the prime suspect, the rumor mill continued unabated. Amateur sleuths contended that the killer was a vice cop. As of today, not a soul has stepped forward to officially present those assertions. It seemed everyone talked a good game, but when it really mattered, most abided by the no snitching rule. Ta-Nellie remembered the young Asian seeking his protection when coming to Ohio. Tee politely declined the request, admitting, "I only deal with white wenches." Sister's death gnawed at Tee's humanity, and he wondered if he could somehow have saved the boy. This was a question he would never be able to answer. He cast the mishap into the inner recesses of his mind with similar stories. It was his way to cope and move forward with life. He summed it up this way: "When Sister Hard Leg was all decked out, it was hard to believe he wasn't the genuine article." Unfortunately, someone could tell...and by all appearances, he wasn't amused. The murder of Sister Hard Leg, like so many others among prostitutes, was simply charged to the life...and stamped payment due upon receipt of the murderer.

All roads may lead to Rome, but to truly understand Sister Hard Leg's fate, we need only amble down the path less traveled by a disillusioned eighteen-year-old living in Chinatown who purchased a *New York Daily News* on December 1, 1952. Its bold headlines helped to thwart her suicide: "EX-GI BECOMES BLONDE BEAUTY."

The boy read the story over and over again. He felt the article was describing him perfectly because it summed up his own feelings so accurately. The article gave the Asian hope for his future. George William Jorgenson, Jr. who morphed into Christine Jorgenson, became the boy's hero. NYC radio host Barry Gray once asked Christine during a broadcast if jokes about the operation saddened her. Barry quickly gave her an example of one of the jokes circulating town. "Jorgenson went abroad and returned a broad!" Christine tolerated the jokes and added she was happy to shine a light on the subject, which affected thousands.

Christine Jorgenson, who by now was a famous celebrity and national treasure, treated himself with the female hormone ethinyl estradiol before going to Denmark for sex reassignment surgery. His surgery gave hope to others contemplating suicide. It was a welcome alternative to living a life of misery, suppressing who they really were.

The young Chinese boy was slight of build and was on the verge of taking his life when he read the article. He had reached his wits' end, assuming that a mistake of gender during birth had perpetrated a cruel hoax on him. Inwardly he felt like a woman, and jumped at the opportunity of a lifetime to right a perceived wrong. He decided to save every penny he earned in a concerted effort to obtain the same surgery as Christine Jorgenson.

The diligent young man researched reassignment surgery at local libraries, consuming clinical and university studies and related medical articles, as well as in-depth interviews given by expert doctors in the field. He began with the first known operations, which had been performed by two German doctors in the late 1920s and early 1930s. The eighteen-year-old was elated at finding his new sense of purpose. Seeking approval, he shared his new-found knowledge with his parents. His father laid down the law and forbade him to alter his divinely conceived body in any form whatsoever. An argument ensued, and during the spring of 1952 an undaunted young boy moved to Cleveland, where he'd once visited relatives. Soon he found work at a meat processing plant and augmented his earnings by dressing up in drag and moonlighting as a prostitute. Time was of the essence and he wanted to raise the money for an operation as quickly as possible by giving one blow job at a time.

In a morbid twist of fate, Sister Hard Leg worked night and day for nearly two years, finally raising the required amount of cash needed for the reassignment surgery. Just days after receiving an affirmative answer from an inquiry requesting the operation, Sister was murdered. The probate court, pursuant to the laws of the state of Ohio, ordered all monetary funds and personal effects, along with any written Chinese correspondence be returned to Sister's heartbroken parents in New York.

(33) The ghost rider...

Juanita's restaurant seemed as good a place as any for TaNellie to prepare for his final exams. Tee could see the light at the end of the tunnel. He was so psyched that he carried his books with him constantly, opening them wherever he happened to be. Once he tuned out all the distractions, he promptly proceeded with his required reading. He loved political science and was doing quite well in the course. An "A" in class would raise his accumulated grade point average well above 3.5. He was proud of himself and wondered why he had ever dropped out in the first place. We all do things we regret, and TaNellie was no different.

Commuting to Xenia from Cleveland and staying over for both Tuesday and Thursday classes kept him away from his pimping responsibilities. Ana handled things admirably and Tee's cash flow remained consistent during the quarter. Since he was five years older than most of his classmates he was looked upon as a mentor of sorts and was referred to as the "ghost rider." It was a perfect nickname because he always disappeared after Thursday's classes only to return bright and early Tuesday morning. TaNellie hadn't spoken with his mother since he dropped out of Central State. She was kept completely in the dark about his return to school. TaNellie couldn't wait to see her reaction in person after presenting Bessie with a guest ticket to his graduation ceremony. He'd requested three tickets, hoping to include Marta de LaCosta...but it seemed unlikely he would ask her to attend, after their recent fiasco in Cuba.

Juanita, the restaurant owner, greeted him in the booth. "Hey, Tee...I see you've been hitting those books really hard lately."

"Yeah, Nita...I'll be graduating soon and I want to make sure my grades are good as possible...I can't wait!"

"Tee, I'm so proud of what you're doing. Most folks I know would have just given up...but you were different. The way you returned to school...." Nita was at a loss for words. "Well, I want you to know you've been an inspiration to me, and a lot of folks around here. We're all pulling for you! On the surface you're a hustler... but there's more to you than meets the eye. You've shown what can be done when you set your mind to something. The degree will give you a lot more options, and I'm sure you'll take advantage of them. After all, you excel in whatever you do."

"Thanks, Nita. I'm not sure where all this will lead, but I'm going along for the ride and I always make the most of my opportunities...we'll see!"

"You ain't never lied, Tee...let me get back to work, baby! I'll talk with you a little later-- enjoy your meal!"

"Without a doubt!"

Rick Foy, who had won the jackpot at Mattie's place, was sitting at the counter. Once Nita left, he came over and sat down across from TaNellie. "Hey, Youngblood...I didn't recognize you without the fez. I see you got your face buried deep inside them books...what's up, man!"

Tee looked up, smiling. "Hey Rick...I'm surprised you're still in town. After the killing you made at the poker table, I figured you'd be long gone by now."

"Sho you right. There was something about being in this town that made me want to stay. I don't know why, but I decided to keep put for a while and see what was happening here."

"That's great! Cleveland gets a bad rap, but it's really a nice place. Hey, Rick...since you're here, why don't you come to my college graduation? I'd love to have your support...plus I got an extra ticket. I'd hate to see it go to waste...whatcha say?"

"I'd love to share your special day, Youngblood."

Tee was pleased, and dog-eared the page of his textbook. "Here, Rick--I've been using this ticket as a bookmark. It's yours... I'll see you at graduation."

Rick shook Tee's hand. "I'm proud of you, Youngblood. I dropped out of school years ago when I was just a teenager. None of my family ever graduated high school, not to mention college. This is huge, Youngblood...I'm certain your folks will be excited. See you in Xenia!"

Up until now, Tee hadn't realized the effect his graduation was having on those around him...it was as though they were all getting a sheepskin. Even Ana and the girls showed their pride and called him endearing names like *professor, bookworm,* and *too smart*...which he enjoyed immensely.

TaNellie left the restaurant only to find a police car parked right out front. The officer beckoned him over...it was Captain Dale Murphy, who had helped bring him into the world. TaNellie smiled and bent his tall frame to face the captain.

"Hello, son...I hope all is well?"

"Everything is fine, Captain." Tee raised his books. "As you can see, I'm hard at work trying to pass my exams. I'll get my degree from Central State after I ace my tests. What can I do for you, Captain?"

"Nothing...nothing except take care of business on your tests. TaNellie, I just want to pull your coat to a couple of things. I hope what I have to say makes you feel better."

"Give it to me, Captain Murphy...what's up?"

"Well, we were able to solve the murders of both Perry Wilcox, aka Short Stack; and Craig Chen, aka Sister Hard Leg."

"Wow...that's great news...tell me more!"

"In the Wilcox case we found a piece of discarded gum in the ashtray of his car. At first it looked like any other piece of chewed gum, but it had a strange protrusion on it that looked like a piece of spaghetti about an eighth of an inch long. We questioned Short Stack's woman, who claimed she had never been in his 1949 Plymouth. She said he had just purchased it and she wasn't allowed to even ride in it. We had a dentist examine her teeth and found a cavity in one of the bicuspids. It fit perfectly with the protrusion in the discarded piece of gum. The female suspect later confessed to the crime. She opted not to chance a court appearance and have the book thrown at her for first degree murder. In the Chen case...there was a diary written in Chinese in which the young boy spoke of a client who wanted to marry him. He said the man didn't want him to have an operation. He wanted him to keep his penis right where it was. The man became angry during an argument and killed the young prostitute. It was the same man we first suspected...he spilled the beans. It seems he killed out of selfishness. He wanted to have his cake--or should I say cock?--and eat it too!"

"What a world!" replied TaNellie.

(34) The graduation...

When graduation day arrived, Tee was totally surprised to see his whole stable in attendance even though he had been given only three tickets. He was afraid to ask how they were able to get in without tickets. The weather was perfect, and the campus was packed with people.

Tee's mother couldn't have been happier. "Tikey, I'm so proud of you. I prayed for this moment. You are the first person in our family to graduate from college."

TaNellie recognized the bare-faced Mr. Silverman, who had lost a ton of weight. He was still a fugitive from the law, but no one would ever have recognized this good-looking man with the svelte body. The massive weight loss was the perfect disguise, making him look like a forty-year- old man. Even after seeing Silverman, aka Ted August, at the bank, Tee was unaware of who he was. It was the wrapped peppermint that told the tale. On Tee's special day, Ted August presented him with Silver Certificates.

"Tike-alah! These bills are for your new collection. They are worth more than regular bills because they're backed by silver bullion." Silverman couldn't help giving Tee the sales pitch. "Try and get as many as possible, because silver is going up in value, you mark my words. Consider these bills a graduation gift to my favorite gentile!" Tee showed the former Mr. Silverman some love by giving him a warm hug.

He took August over to see Bessie Mae, who was literally shocked at his transformation. "Are you still in hiding, Mr. Sil...."

"My name is Ted August, Bessie, just like the month. So call me August...and I'm sure all will be fine. Tikey told me about the graduation days ago when we ran into one another in the bank. I wouldn't have missed this for the world. I knew I would see you both sooner or later. I'm just happy I get to congratulate you and your boy. I know you had a rough go of it...but I knew you'd get the job done. It reminds me of the coffee stain on my shirt. After you removed it, I knew nothing was impossible for you. It was so nice seeing you, Bessie Mae...I've got to get back on the road. Be well, and God bless you both!"

With that, the fortyish Ted August gave them a hug and walked over to a black Chrysler Imperial. They never saw or heard from him again.

Bessie Mae had used tough love on her son...and he finally saw the light. Tee realized why she didn't want him staying at her house. Living under her roof after dropping out of college would have hampered his ability in becoming a man. Graduating from the university was something Tee had to do for himself, because his mother couldn't do it for him. This was a giant step in becoming a well-rounded adult who finished what he started. He had reached for the brass ring and would soon have it in his possession. Bessie Mae had longed for this moment ever since he was born, and was so happy to be a part of the festivities. Tee spotted Rick Foy sitting alone near the stage, and brought him over to meet Bessie Mae.

"Mother, before I forget...here's another friend I'd like you to meet: Mr. Rick Foy."

Bessie Mae was still wiping her tears when she turned around. Her knees weakened and she almost fainted. Bessie Mae Purifoy was speechless and her tears began falling all over again. "Will wonders ever cease...it's Frederick Douglass Purifoy, as I live and breathe." They embraced for what seemed like forever. Tee was puzzled by it all and didn't know what to think. Bessie grabbed her son by the hand. "Tikey...I'd like to introduce you to a friend of mine. This is your father, Frederick Purifoy. Son, how did you arrange to get him to come to your graduation?"

"Mother what are you talking about? Father...arrange...what's going on here?"

"Son, I haven't seen Slim--or Rick, as you just called him--since I left New Orleans to come to Cleveland. I was beginning to think we'd never see each other again. Tikey, this is one of the best days of my life." Bessie stood back from the men she loved more than anything, admiring the view. "We're finally together and occupying in the same space." Their resemblances were remarkable, except Tee was just a little on the heavier side. "Slim...other than the eye patch, you haven't changed at all."

"Bessie Mae...my love for you hasn't changed either...I've never stopped loving you. I didn't doubt for a second I would see you again. Something told me to stay in Cleveland."

Bessie smiled while giving him a hug. "Well, now you know why!"

"TaNellie and me were just talking the other day about my feelings concerning Cleveland."

"Mother, are you saying Rick Foy, the gambler, is my biological father?"

Tee burst into nervous laughter, as if expecting to wake from a dream. "Hallelujah...when I first met him I felt a kinship...something I couldn't explain, so I let it alone. This is unbelievable...simply too good to be true. Mother, I've always had questions about my dad and wondered why he wasn't in our lives."

"Tikey, I was never able to tell Slim he had a son, because of the hex. I'm so glad all of that is over now. You and your dad can finally get to know each other."

Rick was puzzled. "What hex, Bessie Mae?"

It took her most of the day, and all of the night, but she managed to explain everything. Rick helped shed some light about once having met Irene Hightower, the woman responsible for the hex. According to Rick, he met her at a club in New Orleans. She became highly incensed after he mentioned that Bessie Mae Purifoy, the love of his life, attended Saint James AME Church. He recalled Irene Hightower marrying a widower who ministered at the same church.

But for the moment, today belonged to TaNellie and the other Central State graduates assembled together in Xenia, Ohio. After the name of each graduate had been announced over the public address system, there came a loud cheer. Hundreds of mortarboards were simultaneously tossed high into the air. For the 212 students, this celebration was just the start of a new beginning.

Not surprisingly, TaNellie could be whatever he desired. With a degree under his belt, he was sure all things were possible. With his options as vast as the universe, he thought about his larger-than-life persona as a hustler. In the Negro world of the 1950s, wavy hair and light skin were viewed as positive attributes. The opposite was true of kinky hair and dark skin. TaNellie, whose good looks reminded some of a young Duke Ellington, knew looks weren't everything. Unlike some associates, who felt forced into the fast life, TaNellie never had those concerns. Granted, he'd been homeless when he and Ana were saved by the life. But he realized that even his mother was able to overcome obstacles on her way to becoming a rich woman. Being homeless and hungry had never been used as a crutch. Those days were in the past. Bessie Mae's talent for doing hair turned her modest skills into a lucrative profession where maids, cooks, seamstresses, teachers, and other working class women had one thing in common. In spite of their status, they wanted to look and feel glamorous. Bessie Mae had successfully tapped into their desire and allowed them to step out of society's shadows with a flick of her hot comb.

TaNellie's rough times helped to make him the man he was now. The lack of employment, racism, or prison was never a factor when choosing to be a pimp. The profession wasn't easy, but it suited his style, and he grew to love the skin game. He was a procurer of women, furnishing a commodity men have sought since time immemorial.

He realized women were often forced into becoming hookers by a variety of methods, including drugs and even rape. On the other hand, some girls were attracted by a pimp's notoriety. It wasn't unusual for a wench to buy her way into a stable with a large sum of cash. In the life, the more popular a pimp, the more esteemed were his girls. It was like being a general in an army of ladies...and the pimp was totally in command. Surely every stable had a woman who might be smarter than the pimp, but she acquiesces to his position. Delegating authority was what helped TaNellie maintain his standing. He did this by allowing his girls the freedom to make decisions on their own as independent contractors.

The game is a simple enough concept, one in which everyone involved pays the price for a perceived benefit. Quid pro quo is something old-school hustlers refer to as...the chicken farm... pie in the sky...or, by and by, as the ministers often say. TaNellie realized being a nice guy was something the squares loved, but that could never cut the mustard on the street. Prostitution supplied Tee with the things he wanted, and they were flaunted in a most audacious and unapologetic way.

A boss pimp, the one other pimps look up to, tries to keep light years ahead of the game's most intelligent hustlers and smartest women. The life is a perpetual chess match, and any pimp worth his salt knows the mind is where the game is won or lost. Thinking ahead makes everything else possible within this vicious cycle. It all begins with a desire for control. Sitting atop this system is the pimp. His wench turns the John's sexual craving into a commodity. She treats him like a trick, charging for his every whim. TaNellie treated whores precisely like they treated Johns. To the pimp, she is just another trick being charged for services rendered. The whole procedure takes one-upmanship to a higher level. Pimping is a never-ending battle where the spoils go to the victor.

How long could Tee realistically play the skin game before his fortunes changed? It's something every gambler knows is bound to happen sooner or later. In his heart, Tee wondered if he still had the desire to continue living on the edge. Because of all he had witnessed, and with tons of secured cash, there was just nothing else to prove. He'd reached the pinnacle of success. Why continue tossing the dice, just to crap out. Should he use his degree to pursue other avenues? It was decision time for TaNellie...and the stickman was waiting.

(35) The more things change...

Baseball season ended with a thud, to the dismay of tribe fans everywhere. The 1954 World Series was history. The Cleveland Indians, a team with the year's best record in baseball, was swept in four games by the New York Giants. Former Negro League player Willie Mays sealed the Indians' fate after making a terrific running "back to the plate" catch of a hard-hit game- saving fly ball off tribe first baseman Vic Wertz.

"WAIT TILL NEXT YEAR!" Soon the clarion call among dejected fans was heard. "YOU'LL BE SORRY... JUST WAIT TILL NEXT YEAR...YOU'LL SEE!"

Miles away from Cleveland, socialite Simone Michaels had been spending quality time with an intimate associate ever since her recent divorce from Bradford Michaels. Her former husband, so the story went, wasn't considered culpable in any way and was able to provide proof she had been involved in numerous extramarital affairs while married to him. He gladly parted ways with Simone, along with nearly a fourth of his tobacco fortune just to rid her from his life. It was common knowledge that he had been trying to get out of their relationship for a number of years. Her most recent indiscretions served as an excuse to obtain what he'd always wanted: freedom. Just as soon as the divorce became final, Bradford quickly married the love of his life. Miss Viola Darden was the beautiful and vivacious Negro entrepreneur who owned the very popular eatery called Viola's. Ahead of the times, Viola's was the only integrated restaurant in Kentucky. Its claim to fame was the finest selection of southern-style cuisine south of the Mason/Dixon line, featuring a sweet tea to die for.

Simone had gone up to the master bedroom to remove a few loose hanging threads from her new slate-grey custom-tailored men's suit. She stared into a full-length mirror and fluffed up the white lace jabot around her neck. Simone made certain her hair bun was perfectly situated just the way she liked—mere inches above the nape of her neck, and without any loose strands. Once pleased with her appearance, she marched smartly down the stairs as her delicate gloved fingers danced along the banister. Marta de LaCosta was just as she had left her, standing nude in the middle of an air-conditioned living room, clutching a black leather riding crop between her teeth. Simone circled the young woman several times, scrutinizing every inch of her perfectly formed body with a keen eye. Suddenly she stopped on a dime and faced the girl.

"How dare you eyeball me, you wretched little snot!"

She removed the crop from Marta's mouth, then firmly squeezed both her cheeks together, using her right hand. She applied still more pressure until Marta's lips puckered like a tight anus. "Your filthy mouth appears as though it's full of shit, you turd licker. If you obey as you're told, you may remind me later to prepare a can of your favorite cat food. You'd better not forget my little pussy...or there'll be hell to pay!"

The unknown becomes obvious when you learn to read between the lines. It's a useful skill when refined—one that differentiates salaciousness from the obscene.

Epilogue...

The savvy Sundance audience leaped to their feet. TaNellie, the movie, was given an unprecedented sustained standing ovation which lasted well into the credits. A much older Darla Carpenter was completely overwhelmed and shedding real tears. She was thrilled that her book was well-received and had been made into a movie. She felt so out of place seated with such an illustrious array of famous movie stars, each of whom had played their roles expertly, helping to bring the characters to life. *What an honor*, she thought, one that exceeded her wildest imaginings. Not in a hundred years had she expected such an outpouring of support accompanying her debut novel. It was a tribute to her fortitude and spirit, which had been called upon to complete the arduous task of writing a tale so near and dear to her heart.

The movie reminded her of all the hard times she had spent struggling just to make ends meet. Darla regularly fed her family pinto beans and restaurant discards, while trying to keep a roof over their heads, that was more than a notion. She even taught her kids how to soften the Sears catalog's coarse pages...and use them as toilet paper. Darla was fortunate, having found a job at Blossom's Restaurant and meeting the ever-dapper Frank Leo. On many occasions he helped ease the hardships of tenement living, under whose leaky roof she raised her children as best she could. Darla was a lot younger back then. But now she was a lot wiser, thanks to scores of rediscovered annotated letters sent her by Frankie Flowers. His insightful knowledge of the rackets, along with her own imagination and intuition, helped her pen *TaNellie*, which was doing remarkably well on the *New York Times* best-sellers list. Frankie-boy was the finest man ever to enter her life. He encouraged her to unleash the power of words. She would be forever indebted to Frankie Flowers, and would always remember his cheerful greeting: "Hiya, toots!" It proved a fitting mantra when a little extra umph was needed to carry her over the top. On many a day she relied heavily upon those three little words, which never failed her.

The theater audience was not about to let Darla Carpenter leave without so much as a howdy-do. While standing on their feet clamoring for a speech, they continued applauding. The director obliged, gathering his actors and producers, leading them to the stage. After sharing comments concerning the making of the movie, he welcomed Darla Carpenter to center stage. Reluctantly she came forward, smiling at the faces of Sundance's cinematic aficionados. Darla walked up the stairs and onto center stage. She disregarded her prepared text.

Darla began speaking from the heart. "I thank you so much… for acknowledging the efforts of all those connected with this fine feature film. *TaNellie*, the book, is my fictional version of people who regularly survive by their wits. It depicts events occurring daily in our cities all around the world. I've worked hard for most of my life, in all sorts of dead-end jobs. At a very young age I was totally worn out and just plain old tired from living life. I started my writing career shortly after receiving a degree from SUNY in Westbury. My two children, Monica and Frankie-boy, were the primary impetus in writing the book. Suffice it to say, the opportunity to create a life of wealth and comfort as a result of my undertaking was the farthest thing from my mind. This book was never intended to glorify any of the lifestyles featured…only to inform and entertain. I had hoped the road I embarked upon would eventually help sustain us with a living wage. Since all of the hoopla lately...our circumstances have changed greatly. I want to thank each of you for spending time wallowing inside my novel and sharing this new and exciting experience with us.

"I've enjoyed everything about the Sundance Film Festival. My profound thanks go to Mr. Robert Redford for selecting our film for his opening night screening. I'd also like to thank my friend, husband and executive producer, Mr. Ted August, without whom I couldn't have completed this project, I love you. My family and I are off to Cannes...where we hope to see you all. Before leaving, however, I'd like to share a quote from the book *The Little Prince*, by Antoine de Saint Exupéry. 'It is only with the heart that one sees that which is essential is invisible to the eye.' I'd like to further add my own words...what is perceived through our senses and welcomed within our hearts is equally essential, and allows us to enjoy a thoroughly satisfying and creative experience...just as the author intended. In closing, I want to thank you and my family from the depths of my heart and the essence of my being!"

As a consequence of inspiration, persistence, determination and even luck, talents are enabled. Allowing for effort and timing, creativity ultimately manifests itself. My truth is revealed in the forms of artistic renderings...and the art of storytelling witnessed herein. Thank you for allowing me, in a personal way, to spend some time with you, RLH.

A novel from the imagination of Richmond Lafayette Holton
© 2013

CPSIA information can be obtained
at www.ICGtesting.com
Printed in the USA
FFOW04n2328070715
14936FF